NIGHT LIFE

S.J. Hartsfield

RIPTIDE
PUBLISHING

Riptide Publishing
PO Box 1537
Burnsville, NC 28714
www.riptidepublishing.com

Night Life

Cover art: L.C. Chase, lcchase.com
Editors: Stella Li, Carole-ann Galloway
Layout: L.C. Chase, lcchase.com

ISBN: 978-1-62649-889-1

First edition
September, 2020

Also available in ebook:
ISBN: 978-1-62649-888-4

NIGHT LIFE

S.J. Hartsfield

RIPTIDE
PUBLISHING

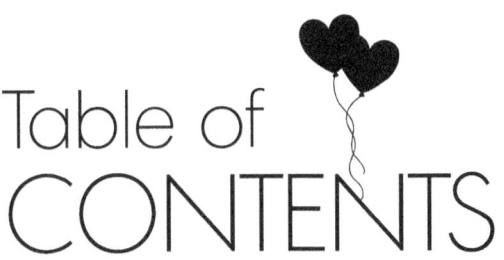

Table of CONTENTS

CHAPTER 1
Purely Therapeutic

Ronnie was standing in the produce section at Short's Grocery when her phone buzzed. She pulled it from her bra and checked the screen: *Night Life*. Must be a job. "This is Ronnie."

"Hey," a familiar voice said.

"Hey, Stacy." Ronnie palmed a cantaloupe and studied it. "You would not believe the melons I'm looking at right now."

"Gross."

For the scheduling manager of an escort service, Stacy sure didn't have much of a sense of humor.

"Wanna hear something weird?"

"Always," Ronnie said, replacing the cantaloupe and wandering toward the fresh herbs. They never seemed to have good basil here, but it was worth a shot.

"Okay, so you know how, usually, whoever schedules the meet has to be there in person?"

Ronnie frowned at the herbs as a fine mist of water began to spray on them. No basil. *Figures.* "Yeah . . . ?"

"Not so much with this job."

"Uh."

"I know, but hear me out. One of our regulars called—the bouncy one you've heard some of the boys talk about? She called and asked for our hottest blonde."

Ronnie laughed. "So of course you came to me."

"Of course."

She chose to ignore the note of irony in Stacy's voice.

"Anyway," Stacy continued, "she's got some friend who could apparently use your expertise. Karla talked to her personally, and I don't know what went down, but they agreed on it."

"Let me guess," Ronnie said, leaning on the handle of her cart. "Karla's getting extra money out of the deal."

"Oh for sure. More than you, even."

"That doesn't seem fair." It'd be great to know exactly how much she'd end up with, but Stacy couldn't get into that over the phone. Company policy was a pain in the ass sometimes.

"Yeah, well. If you feel like getting gift wrapped for a stressed-out rich girl, come in and look over the paperwork. If you think it's too sketch, you can always turn it down."

That was true. Sure, she'd never turned down a job before, but it was an option. Although, if this paycheck was as flush as Stacy made it sound, she suspected Karla would *strongly suggest* she take it.

And anyway, a couple of things about it appealed to her.

It wasn't just the money—that sure didn't hurt, and being considered Night Life's hottest blonde was a big plus too. But she also enjoyed being someone's first escort. It made her feel memorable, and she did like being memorable.

She'd also never been with a client who hadn't arranged the job themselves. The idea of being *given* to someone sent a pleasant shiver down her spine. "I'll be in around four," she decided. "See you then."

She ended the call, and swung her cart around. No basil meant no homemade pesto tonight. Time to see how disappointing the premade options looked.

The offer wound up being way more than Ronnie had ever pulled for a single night, even after Karla's considerable cut. Ronnie would never be able to live with herself if she said no: the pay was too good and the job too intriguing.

So, two nights later, she was standing outside the Hotel Öde, dressed to thrill and looking hot to death. Her short hair was artfully tousled and swept away from her angular face, and she'd paired smoky shadow with a nude lipstick to emphasize her eyes. She didn't wear this suit often, but maybe she should—it hugged her long-limbed frame enticingly beneath her gray pea coat, the white shirt left open at the collar to expose her throat.

Worth every penny.

As she was pulling out her phone to check the time, she caught movement from the corner of her eye and glanced down the sidewalk to see a woman in a dark blue overcoat approaching her. Ronnie checked the clock on her lock screen. Right on time.

The next thing she knew, the woman was at her elbow, breath visible in the February air. "Are you Ronnie?"

Ronnie slipped her phone back into her coat and turned. *Time to get to work.*

Her interest was captured instantly. The woman was stunning, with dark brown hair that framed her open face and brushed past her collar in soft curls. She was watching Ronnie with clear blue eyes, her expression a frank mixture of curiosity and caution. Ronnie couldn't remember ever finding a client so attractive.

But she'd been an escort for a long time. She knew better than to get flustered. So all she said was, "You must be Diana."

That was the name Stacy had given her, at least. As a precaution, clients and escorts started out on a first-name basis, and they never saw each other's legal names in print; contracts were kept completely separate from one another to preserve privacy on both ends of the exchange. Some escorts gave aliases—some clients did too—but others were honest. Ronnie wondered whether Diana's friend had bothered.

With a tentative smile of recognition, Diana said, "I'm sorry about all this." She had one hand in the pocket of her coat, the other clutching at the collar. "My friend Phoebe seemed to think I needed . . . Well, she said you'd been paid in advance and the room was already booked, and I'd hate for it all to go to waste."

"Sure." Ronnie nodded. *Easy does it.* She tilted her head toward the hotel's door. "You wanna go in?"

Diana's eyes flitted to the entrance, then back to Ronnie. She hesitated for a second, drawing a sharp breath before answering. "Yes." Then she turned and strode inside, her kitten heels clicking against the pavement. Ronnie followed.

The Hotel Öde was thoroughly modern, with concrete floors, white walls, and recessed lighting. Ronnie had been here on jobs in the past, and the whole place always had a distinctly Scandinavian feel, like IKEA in a tuxedo. As they passed the tall waterfall in the center of the lobby, Diana pulled a slim clutch from her coat and turned to Ronnie.

"I'll need to check in. Will you wait for me by the elevator?"

"I can do that."

Diana looked her up and down, quick enough that it might have been accidental. Maybe. "Would you like something to drink?"

"I never say no to a sweet red wine," Ronnie said with a grin. "But I'll take anything you wanna give me." She hadn't meant for that last part to sound like an innuendo, but there it was.

One of Diana's brows quirked, her eyes darkening. Then her lips parted, and for a hot second, Ronnie thought she might pick up the double entendre and run with it.

Instead, she closed her mouth and cast Ronnie a brief smile before clipping away.

Rats. Ronnie sighed and ambled toward the elevators. *This is weird*, she mused as she leaned against the brushed-silver doors, watching Diana chat with the front desk attendant. *First-timers usually can't wait to get their hands on me. I guess she did say she only showed up for her friend's sake, but . . .*

But nothing. There had definitely been heat in Diana's gaze, both outside and just now before she walked off. She looked at Ronnie like she wanted to swallow her whole, but seemed to be holding herself back.

Which is a shame, Ronnie thought, her eyes roaming the other woman's form. She wouldn't mind seeing what happened if Diana cut loose.

Still, she was a professional, and Diana was the client. They'd do whatever Diana wanted to.

Even if that meant Ronnie had worn her favorite lingerie for nothing.

She realized then that Diana was walking back across the lobby, bottle of wine in hand, eyes trained on her face. There was something intimate about the way she pinned Ronnie with her gaze, like they were the only two people in the room. Warmth spread through Ronnie's body, a tingle beginning at the tips of her fingers. She could have a pretty good time with just about anyone, but it had been a hot minute since she'd been this actively affected. She shouldered away from the wall, hands in her coat pockets, as Diana approached. "Going up?"

Diana brandished a white key card in response, expression a little exasperated. "Phoebe sprang for the top floor."

In the elevator, she offered the wine to Ronnie. "Is this all right?"

Ronnie took it. She'd never had this kind before. "It's great." She glanced back up, ready to turn on one of her more winning smiles, but Diana was watching the elevator's display as it counted floors. So Ronnie rolled the bottle between her hands, staring down at the label like she could actually read the Italian on it.

After a moment of silence, Diana said, "You know, I'm a bit surprised." Ronnie frowned at her and Diana continued: "That you haven't . . ." She seemed to search for the right word. "Pounced."

Ronnie grinned. "This is your first time, yeah?"

"Yes. Well, with a . . ."

"A professional."

"Yes," Diana said, softer this time.

Edging a touch closer to her, Ronnie said, "You're the client. That means you're in charge. We'll move at your pace, and we won't do anything you don't want to."

Diana's eyes searched her face. "Phoebe did say we could just talk."

Ronnie nodded. "Yep. We can." She dropped her voice slightly. "But if you *do* want me to pounce, all you gotta do is say the word."

Before Diana could respond, the elevator gave a low, soothing chime, and the doors slid open. They'd arrived at the thirtieth-floor penthouse.

As they stepped into the hallway, a loud jangle made Ronnie jump. Diana closed her eyes and sighed, then pulled a phone from her coat. She didn't even look at the screen before saying, "I have to take this." She passed the key card to Ronnie. "Leave the door on the latch for me?"

Ronnie nodded. As she unlocked the door and slipped inside, she heard Diana answer the phone. Her tone was surprisingly pleasant, considering the face she'd made when she got the call.

When Ronnie turned and got a good look at the penthouse, her eyebrows rose. *No wonder she didn't want this to go to waste.* The suite was spacious and, like the lobby, artfully minimalistic. In the main room, sleek, low-profile furniture sat around a marble fireplace, where a low fire simmered invitingly. To Ronnie's right was an open, brightly lit kitchen and, down the hall, a closed door. *Bedroom.* She felt a pleasant twinge of anticipation.

She sat the wine on the kitchen island, keeping one ear on the half conversation happening outside. "You know my schedule better than anyone," Diana was saying. "First thing tomorrow." Her tone was brisk, professional—whatever it was about must be pretty important.

So, Ronnie mused, *she's a busy lady who gets stressful phone calls.* She peeled off her coat and draped it over the back of the long, black sofa. *What does she need? More important, what does she want? Comfort. Relief. Me.*

An idea began to percolate in the back of her mind.

Moving quickly and fluidly, she opened the wine and poured two glasses, taking both with her down the hall, through the bedroom, and into the en suite. A large soaker tub stood against one gray-tiled wall. *Perfect.*

Water spilled into the tub in a white rush, and Ronnie snatched a bag of bath salts from the shelves under the sink, dumping them into the foamy froth. Steam spiraled into the air, sweet and a little spicy, and Ronnie hoped it wouldn't melt her makeup. She'd spent too much time on her face for it to get ruined so soon. She stripped, folding her clothes and laying them on the double vanity, along with one of the glasses.

When she stepped into the tub, the water was almost too warm, but not quite. Ronnie shut off the tap right before the fragrant foam reached the undersides of her breasts. There was enough room for Diana to get in, if she wanted, without the tub overflowing, and she'd get a tantalizing view if she didn't. Placing her wine on the floor and leaning her head back, Ronnie sighed. *This is why I'm the best.*

Soon the tap of Diana's heels sounded on the hardwood floor, slowing to a stop as she reached the bedroom. "Ronnie?"

"In here."

Diana appeared in the doorway, eyebrows rising as she took in the scene. "I thought we were just going to talk."

"We are. I'm just gonna talk from here." Ronnie grinned and nodded toward the vanity, indicating the second wineglass.

Diana glanced at it. "Oh, no, I don't drink." She looked almost apologetic. "My m— Well. I don't drink. Thank you, though."

Why bother with wine, then? But Ronnie wasn't about to pressure anyone, so she shrugged silently and reached for her own glass, taking a slow drink. It was delicious.

When she opened her eyes, she found Diana watching her the way she had in the lobby. Her attention seemed laser-focused, but her lips were slightly parted, gaze wandering ever so slightly below Ronnie's neck.

"You *can* do more than look," Ronnie offered quietly. Diana's eyes snapped back to hers, and she added, "Plenty of room for two."

Something in Diana's expression changed, going hard and hot, like she'd come to a decision.

Sure enough: "All right."

Ronnie sipped her wine and watched with interest as Diana stepped out of her shoes and unzipped her dress with measured care. Bit by bit, she revealed smooth, pale skin and matching underthings—dusty-pink silk, pretty but modest; after all, she probably hadn't planned on anyone seeing them. When she bent to remove her briefs, Ronnie's eye was drawn to the crease at the junction of her hip and thigh, and all she could think about was burying her face there.

Everything about this woman was eye candy, and Ronnie suddenly had one hell of a sweet tooth.

Funnily enough, Diana seemed less uncertain now that she was naked. She lowered herself into the bath easily, making the water lap against Ronnie's breasts. She hadn't clipped up her hair, and the tips were soon dark and slick, clinging enviably to her neck.

"So," Ronnie said on a sigh once Diana had settled, "why'd your buddy think you needed me?"

Diana rolled her eyes and scoffed, but a smile danced at the corners of her mouth. "Phoebe is my best friend, and I love her very much, but we . . . often focus on different things."

"And you focus on megahot blondes."

Diana's laugh rang off the walls, light and unguarded. "Oh, so does she, believe me." She visibly relaxed, sinking further into the water and lifting an eyebrow as she considered Ronnie. "And brunets, and gingers. Her escapades just involve a very different type of blond."

Watching her was distracting; Ronnie's gaze followed the subtle movements of her throat, couldn't help noticing the flash of pink tongue tip that darted across her lips to wet them. Diana's calf was smooth against her ankle beneath the water. "And what, she figured you needed some escapades of your own?"

"Apparently." Diana tucked a damp strand of hair behind one ear. "It's been a while since I've slept with anyone, and she seems to think that needs to change."

"And what do you think?"

"If I need an orgasm, I'm perfectly capable of giving myself one."

Now *that* was an interesting mental image. Ronnie took another steadying sip of wine. For somebody who didn't want to do more than talk, Diana sure had driven the conversation straight into Sexytown.

But maybe that hadn't been her intention. In an effort to steer things back, Ronnie cleared her throat and tried to change the subject. "So, what do you do?"

One of Diana's brows slowly lifted, something like a smirk unfurling across her face.

Ronnie realized how it sounded. "Oh, not . . ." She laughed. "Not for that. I mean, in general." She gestured vaguely toward the living room and the hallway beyond. "For work."

"I know what you meant." Diana's smile was wide and teasing, and the room suddenly seemed a few degrees warmer. "I'm an event planner for my parents' law firm." She paused and frowned. "Well, I *was*, anyway. I've been repurposed."

"'Repurposed'?"

A heavy sigh. "My mother's decided to run for city council next term. She'll hire an official campaign manager, but she wants me working alongside them."

"Wow." Ronnie swirled her glass idly. "That'll be interesting."

"Won't it, though."

"So I guess Phoebe had the right idea, booking me." At Diana's questioning look, Ronnie explained: "You're a busy lady, and you're about to get even busier. Sounds like it'd do you good to unwind a little."

Diana's expression, which had gone slightly flat, grew playful again. "Hence the bath?"

"Exactly." Ronnie cocked both elbows up to rest them on the edge of the tub, knowing full well what the movement would do. Her body slid far enough for her toes to make contact with Diana's thigh. "This is a purely therapeutic measure."

Diana's eyes narrowed and went back to wandering, an incredulous smile tugging at the corner of her lips. "Are . . . are you trying to seduce me?"

"Why, is it working?"

"You've already been paid. Why do you care what we do?"

"I don't," Ronnie lied. "I just wanna help you relax."

They watched each other for another handful of heartbeats. Then Diana nodded and said again, "All right."

More gracefully than Ronnie would have thought possible, Diana braced herself and shifted around before rising to her knees. Ronnie downed the rest of her wine in one swallow and set her glass aside, ready to follow her lead.

But Diana laid a hand on her shoulder, just firm enough to keep her in her place. Something below Ronnie's waist gave a distinct throb, both at the authority of the gesture and the smoky look in Diana's eyes as she placed her other hand on Ronnie's knee. Then she eased it aside, prompting Ronnie's legs to spread and her pulse to quicken. Diana turned and sank into the bath once more, settling between Ronnie's legs, her back to Ronnie's front. Ronnie felt every point of contact like a spark of electricity, amplified by anticipation and the heat of the water. It was nice and all, but she was also a little confused.

Diana gathered her hair into a twist, smoothing it down to one side. "I carry my tension in my shoulders."

For a moment, Ronnie did nothing but stare, strangely mesmerized by a small, dark birthmark on the nape of Diana's neck. *A massage*, she realized, probably a lot later than she should have. *She wants me to give her a massage.*

Well, it wasn't the kinkiest thing she'd ever been asked to do. She laid her hands on Diana, thumbs slotted against her shoulder blades, and tried to ignore the twinge of disappointment at the edges of her mind.

At the first bit of pressure, Diana hummed in contentment, and Ronnie's stomach clenched at the sound. She could feel the softness of Diana's hips against her inner thighs, smell the last breaths of perfume that the steam hadn't melted away.

"How long have you been an escort?"

It took a second for the question to make its way to Ronnie's brain. "Uh, about six years now."

"You must enjoy it."

"Oh yeah." Ronnie pressed a gentle knuckle into a knotted muscle. *She wasn't kidding about the tension.* "The pay is good, flexible hours, keeps me just social enough. When I first got to the city, I went through a string of gross temp jobs, but I wasn't really good at anything."

She ran her thumbs along either side of Diana's spine, eyes on that damn birthmark as she kept talking. "Then my boyfriend at the time got me into cam-girl stuff, and that's how Karla found me."

"Karla?"

"My boss. She's pretty okay. A stickler for the rules." She considered, then chuckled. "Usually, anyway."

Diana half turned, enough for Ronnie to see her brow knit. "What does that mean?"

Ronnie used the heel of her hand to rub slow circles into Diana's spine and tried to focus on the conversation, rather than on Diana's quiet sigh of pleasure. "Well *technically*, this kinda setup isn't supposed to happen. One person making the call for somebody else, I mean. When people schedule a meet, it's supposed to be for themselves only—that way they can sign the paperwork, get cleared, all that."

"Cleared?"

"Medically. Y'know, make sure they're not gonna pass anything on." When Diana turned fully, looking horrified, Ronnie blinked. "What?"

"How can you be sure that *I'm* clear?" Ronnie narrowed her eyes, and Diana rolled hers. "I am, but that's not the point. How could you know?"

Ronnie took her by the shoulders and turned her back around, smoothing her thumbs along either side of her neck, a little too softly to be anything but a caress. "Your buddy Phoebe is a frequent flyer," she explained. "She vouched for you. Signed on all the dotted lines and everything."

"So if anything *were* to happen . . ."

"It'd be her ass in court," Ronnie finished, nodding.

After a beat, Diana said, "You'd still be sick."

"Sure," Ronnie conceded slowly. "But at least we'd get compensated."

It occurred to her that she couldn't quite remember what her contract said about what she'd be compensated *with* if that ever happened. She knew the agency would get paid for damages—she just didn't know how much of it would go to her. She frowned to herself and made a mental note to check that out at some point.

A few silent moments passed. Diana's neck and shoulders went slightly red under Ronnie's hands, her posture loosening significantly. As Ronnie let up on the pressure, allowing her fingertips to wander at will, Diana spoke again. "Why would you take a job like this? Was the compensation that good?"

Ronnie ducked her head, trying to think of a way to tiptoe around financial specifics. "Well, it wasn't *only* the money."

Diana stayed quiet, obviously waiting for an explanation.

"I liked the idea of being a present," Ronnie said. "Being the best we had to offer, being . . ." She remembered the dominant edge in Diana's earlier expression and repressed a pleasant shiver. "I dunno, gift wrapped and given, I guess."

Her words hung in the air, joining the steam from the bath.

Diana slid away then, and every part of Ronnie's body that had been touching hers went cold. Diana didn't turn and her voice was soft when she said, "Why don't you get out and dry off?"

Shit. What happened? The night had seemed to be going pretty well. Had she put Diana off by talking too much shop? *Way to go.*

She rose carefully and stepped out onto the mat. She could feel Diana's pretty blue eyes on her body, and as she grabbed a plush white towel from the vanity, goose bumps broke out across her skin. *Probably just the cool air.*

Two terrycloth robes hung from silver hooks on the wall. After Ronnie dried off, she shrugged into one and tied it closed. *No reason to keep showing off, I guess.* Water licked against the sides of the tub as

Diana stood too, but Ronnie kept her gaze averted—the sight of that body would bum her out all over again.

Then Diana murmured, "Will you dry me?"

She was standing by the tub with her back turned, arms held to her chest to ward away the chill. Ronnie snatched up a second towel and snapped it open, pressing it to Diana's skin and taking a moment to enjoy the return of their closeness from before. *Maybe nothing went wrong after all*, she thought, hope glimmering at the edges of her mind. She ran the towel across Diana's shoulders before trailing it down the length of her spine.

She was on one knee, sliding the towel around Diana's thigh, when a light touch grazed her hair and she glanced up.

Diana was gazing down at her, eyes dark and half-lidded. "I think . . ."

Ronnie stood, staying close but not quite making contact. Their next few silent breaths mingled. Then Ronnie whispered, "Anything you want."

Diana's breath hitched. "I think I want you to pounce."

Ronnie didn't need to be told twice.

She instantly dropped the towel and gripped Diana by the waist, dipping her head to nuzzle in the crook of her neck. When she gently sank her teeth into the delicate flesh there, Diana breathed, "Oh God," before turning, twining her fingers in Ronnie's hair, and yanking her up to kiss her with scorching intensity.

The next thing Ronnie knew, Diana was scrabbling at her belt, wrenching the robe open and sliding her arms around Ronnie's waist. Her breasts and belly were still damp; she skated her teeth along Ronnie's bottom lip, making her groan.

They stumbled out of the bathroom, Diana finally managing to jerk the robe off Ronnie's shoulders and sling it behind them as they made their way to the bed. When Diana shoved her onto the duvet and straddled her, Ronnie's last clear thought was *Thank you, Phoebe*.

Later, they lay on the rumpled bed, bodies cooling, breath slowing. Ronnie was on her back, hand cast over her forehead. Diana had curled up at her side, one arm draped across her hips. For a while, the room was silent except for the distant hiss of the fire in the living room.

Then Diana sighed and pushed herself up onto one elbow, dark hair spilling over her shoulder as she looked down at Ronnie. "Well—" she sighed "—nothing against your skills as a masseuse, but I think I prefer this for stress relief." She smiled.

Ronnie's ego felt swollen enough to pop. "You're welcome."

Diana arched a brow, eyes skating across Ronnie's bare body. "All that and modesty too." With that, she slid off the bed and ran her hands through her hair, heading to the bathroom.

It hit Ronnie then that the evening was drawing to a close. She sat up and stretched, frowning. Weirdly enough, she was in no hurry for that to happen. It was a completely new feeling and, if she was being honest, she wasn't really sure where it was coming from. She had plenty of clients whose company she enjoyed, but she was never exactly disappointed when the job was over.

When Diana reappeared, fully dressed, Ronnie gave her what she hoped was a confident grin. "So, you had a good time?"

The first answer she got was a low, throaty chuckle that made her skin twitch pleasantly. "I did. Zip me?" Diana turned, and Ronnie leaped to her feet, stepping forward to do up the dress like some sort of naked valet. "Phoebe may be a bit too absorbed in my personal life," Diana added as Ronnie smoothed the fabric across her shoulders, "but I'll have to remember to thank her." She looked back at Ronnie, crystalline eyes flicking once more over her from top to bottom. "I'll leave you to it."

Ronnie was an old hand at getting dressed in a hurry. She was tying up her shoes in no time, turning the night over in her mind. She'd done a good job, earned every bit of her paycheck.

And she was glad Diana had had fun. She had too. Which wasn't as important, but still. Pretty nice.

In the living room, she found Diana was standing at the door, wrapped in her coat, tapping out a text message. When Ronnie entered, Diana smoothly locked the screen and smiled up at her. "Well. Thank you again for a lovely evening."

"No problem." Ronnie grabbed her own coat, draping it over one arm as she considered Diana. It wasn't exactly standard procedure to ask, but it wasn't against the rules, either. So she hedged, "Think you'll give Night Life a call yourself, one of these days?"

Diana quirked an eyebrow. "We'll see."

Ronnie grinned as another unfamiliar—but not unwelcome—feeling flooded her body at the possibility. *I sure hope so.*

CHAPTER 2
It's Not Nice

The morning after her bizarre, delightful rendezvous, Diana was getting ready to meet her mother—and her mother's new campaign manager—for lunch. Her mother hadn't revealed who she'd gotten for the job, but during her call that morning, she'd hovered somewhere between smug and cagey. She'd also told Diana to "dress nice," which was unpleasantly vague.

So Diana had spent the last half hour going through her closet, recalling comments each outfit had garnered in the past. A pair of tailored trousers had gotten, *"I've never seen that style on legs like yours, how creative."* For a top with a lower neckline: *"That would be darling with a camisole under it."* A blousy sundress: *"That looks comfortable,"* the adjective laden with subtext.

She was running out of things to wear.

As she considered a dress that her mother would almost certainly deride as too casual, her phone jangled. Glad for an excuse to step away for a moment, Diana sighed and went to her nightstand. The phone's screen read *PHOEBE!!!* followed by three sparkling heart emojis.

Phoebe had personalized her contact information the first chance she got.

"Hello?"

"Well?!"

Diana could practically hear the interrobang. "Well what?" she said, drifting back toward the closet.

"You *know* what." Phoebe huffed. "What happened?"

A few choice happenings replayed in Diana's mind and her face warmed. "We talked," she said slowly, pushing a few outfits aside. They were fine, but her mother would almost certainly deride them as too casual. "She was nice."

Phoebe's voice jumped a half octave. "Nice? She wasn't supposed to be nice, she was supposed to be sexy!"

"Oh, she was sexy too," Diana assured her. "She was . . ." She settled on a pantsuit in deep Prussian blue while trying to think of a suitable intensifier. "Very sexy."

An aggravated sigh hissed down the line. "So why was there no sex?"

Diana hesitated for only a moment, but it was enough.

Phoebe gasped. "There was! Oh, Dee, I'm so proud of you, how was it?"

The heat in Diana's cheeks sharpened, but she couldn't help smiling. Of the two of them, Phoebe's sex life was infinitely more noteworthy and a constant source of entertainment. Having a somewhat salacious story of her own was equal parts thrilling and embarrassing. "Hold on, I'm putting you on speaker."

"Don't change the—" Phoebe's voice was momentarily muffled as Diana lowered the phone from her ear and tapped the screen. "—wanna hear all the deets, I mean every single one."

Diana returned the phone to her nightstand and raised her voice a bit. "You'll have to hear them while I get dressed."

"Fine, fine." Phoebe was almost certainly flapping her hands, flashing some lurid nail color. "Just spill."

So Diana spilled. She wasn't accustomed to putting words to the things she did in bed, so it took a little while. But by the time she'd changed into her pantsuit, pinned back her hair, and finished her makeup, all the details had been conveyed.

Around the part where Diana got into the bathtub, Phoebe had fallen almost completely silent. When she didn't respond to the end of the story, Diana added, "That's all."

"Are you gonna see her again?"

Diana remembered Ronnie asking her something similar—and thought of her initial desire to say yes. "Probably not," she said slowly. "I doubt I'll have time with the campaign coming up."

"The what now?"

As if on cue, Diana's call waiting began to beep. She picked up the phone, her mouth twisting as she looked down at the screen. *Mother*.

"Dee?"

"Sorry." Diana sighed, swiping to ignore the call. "I didn't find out until last night. Mummy's decided to run for city council and she wants me to help."

"Gross."

Diana wouldn't have thought to put it that way, but she couldn't disagree.

"How's that even gonna work?" Phoebe went on. "I know you had to take, like, business classes back in school, but do you know anything about politics?"

"I do not. But she wants me 'side-by-side with her campaign manager,' so I assume I'll be booking venues and hiring caterers, same as always, only for speeches instead of case wrap parties."

"And that's worth giving up a great regular diddling?"

"Don't . . . don't say—" Diana shook her head. "Whether it's worth it is immaterial. I have to do it, and it'll take most of my time and energy. End of." As she spoke, she headed out of her room and down the hall.

"You're too nice," Phoebe informed her matter-of-factly.

"It's not *nice*," Diana said, locking the front door behind her. "It's just doing what's right." The insistent tone of another call waiting filled her ear; she needn't bother checking the screen to know that it was her mother, calling again.

Diana's car—or rather, the car her mother let her use—was idling by the curb just in front of the town house, its driver standing alongside like an ice sculpture. Her mother had presented her with her first chauffeur when she'd turned sixteen, in lieu of allowing her to get her license. Since then, Diana had seen a parade of stylish cars and drivers, the latest of which was an Aston Martin and a woman named Skylar.

Skylar waited by the open rear door today, straight-backed as ever. Diana had told her more than once that she was welcome to wait for her in the sitting room, but Skylar insisted on maintaining a certain level of professional detachment. It reminded Diana of her mother, who firmly believed in never getting too chummy with the help. True, in her case it was to avoid their inevitable dismissal becoming awkward, but the effect was precisely the same.

On the other end of the line, Phoebe made a noncommittal noise and grumbled, "I guess. But I still think you should see her again if you get a minute. You want the number for the office?"

Diana offered Skylar a nod as she slid into the car. The gesture was returned mutely (Diana could count on one hand the number of times Skylar had actually spoken to her) and the door closed behind her. "No, thank you. I'm sure that if I do find the time, I'll be too tired for that sort of . . . exertion." Phoebe tittered lewdly and Diana smiled.

The smile was wiped almost instantly from her face at the sound of yet another call waiting. "I have to go," she sighed. "I'm off to meet the campaign manager."

"Boo. Maybe *she'll* be sexy."

"Even if she is," Diana said, "I sincerely doubt my mother would appreciate me sleeping with the most important person on her staff." *Not to mention she would have to be utterly* astonishing *to come anywhere close to Ronnie.*

"Still," Phoebe chirped, "might be a nice bonus. Okay, go do grown-up things, have fun if you can, kiss kiss love you!"

"Love you too." Diana hung up and looked at her screen. Three missed calls, one number. She heaved another sigh and tapped.

She got an answer within one ring. "Where on earth have you been?"

From the corner of her eye, Diana saw Skylar glance at her through the rearview mirror. She must have been able to hear Diana's mother from the front of the car. Diana shifted in her seat, tiny talons of embarrassment pricking her skin. "I was on the phone."

"I tried calling you three times," her mother snapped. "I could have been hurt, dying in a horrible car accident."

Diana pressed her lips together, but couldn't quite manage to stop herself: "*Are* you dying?"

"Don't take that tone with me. Who were you talking to that was so important?"

"Phoebe."

Her mother gave an unimpressed hum. It was a noise she often made when Phoebe entered the conversation. "You'll need to rethink your priorities from now on. Are you on your way?"

"Yes. I should be there in ten minutes or so."

"Don't be late."

With that, the line went dead.

Diana's grip on her phone tightened as she lowered it from her ear, biting down hard on her tongue in frustration. She'd been late exactly three times in her entire adult life. If she arrived at La Reine when she expected to, she'd even be early.

The car paused at a stoplight, and Diana snuck a peek at the rearview mirror. Skylar's eyes were fixed on the road; any interest she might have held earlier had evidently faded. Diana released a long breath and leaned back against the headrest, closing her eyes. Ten minutes until she had to put on her professional face and be sociable. She could do it, and was quite good at it, but it was always tiring.

A memory, completely unbidden, bubbled into her mind: the flash of a confident smile, heat and steam, a low voice saying, *"I just wanna help you relax."*

She shook her head and opened her eyes. She'd enjoyed relating the evening to Phoebe, and her time with Ronnie had been fun—and far less awkward than expected—but she had to put it aside now. What she'd told Phoebe about a lack of leisure time was true, and her mother was right: she did need to make sure her priorities were in order. And if she was wrong about what this new responsibility would entail, if she was about to dive headlong into unfamiliar territory, the last thing she needed right now was to get hung up on someone.

Especially someone who'd only slept with her because she'd been paid to.

La Reine was a posh little bistro just a few streets away from Diana's parents' high-rise. Given its dim lighting and small, intimate tables, it seemed to Diana more like a place for a date than a business lunch. But she knew better than to question her mother's choice of venue.

When she gave her name at the front, the hostess informed her that she was the first of Silver, party of three, to arrive. Irritation prickled through Diana like an itch as she was led to their table, and as soon as she was seated and the hostess had gone, she surreptitiously checked her watch. Two till. *If she's late, I swear . . .*

She didn't bother to finish the thought. She knew she wouldn't do anything.

In the end, it didn't matter—not thirty seconds later, Maggie Silver swanned through the front door and announced herself to the hostess. "Silver, party of three. I'm probably the first one here." Diana could hear each word clearly, even from their table near the back. Her mother had a voice like the cry of a hawk: powerful, majestic, and more than a little piercing. She fought the urge to sink down slightly in the booth.

"Well, look at you!" her mother exclaimed in completely unwarranted surprise when she was shown to the table.

Diana stood, accepting the double-cheeked air kiss that had always been her mother's preferred method of greeting. She expected her mother to take the seat beside her, but she swept to the other side of the table instead.

To the hostess, her mother said, "A bottle of sparkling mineral water, room temperature, and a glass with half a lime slice, not too thin."

As the hostess went off—probably to convey the order to someone whose actual job it was to fulfill it—Diana's mother settled into the seat across from her with a satisfied sigh. "I can't wait for you to see who I've gotten."

Not even a perfunctory *How are you?* As per.

Diana made herself smile. "You seem very excited."

"Oh, I am." Her mother reached across the table to take the tip of Diana's jacket collar between her finger and thumb, rubbing an imaginary wrinkle out of it with a small frown. "Hm. But yes, it'll be a master stroke, we—" Her eyes leaped from Diana to something just past her shoulder and lit up. "There she is!"

She was on her feet almost instantly. Diana rose as well, albeit a bit more slowly, and turned.

Heading toward them was a woman about Diana's age, maybe a few years older, with long, straight hair pulled into a low ponytail. She wore well-fitted black trousers and a matching waistcoat over a delicate pink button-up, the sleeves cuffed to the elbows. Her face seemed shrewd but kind, like someone with a sharp mind but never a sharp word. She looked vaguely familiar, but Diana couldn't think where she might have seen her before.

"Evelyn," her mother cooed, giving the new arrival the same welcome she'd given Diana. "So good to see you again."

"You too, Maggie." The woman looked at Diana, dark eyes sweeping over her face, and smiled. "Hi," she said, holding out a hand. "Evelyn Richards."

The name rang a distant bell too; Diana couldn't put her finger on it, though. She shook Evelyn's hand, offering a smile of her own. "Diana Silver."

"Oh!" Evelyn glanced at Diana's mother, eyebrows raised. "Your daughter?"

She didn't even tell her I'd be here. Diana knew she had no reason to be mortified, but she was anyway.

"My eldest," her mother confirmed. She settled back into her seat and gestured to the other side of the table. "Diana, why don't you make some room over there?"

Only then did Diana realize that Evelyn was still holding her hand. She withdrew and sat down, scooting over enough to let Evelyn slide into the booth beside her. She'd thought her mother would want to sit next to her campaign manager, but maybe she was more interested in eye contact than proximity.

A server arrived with the requested mineral water and, after rattling through the day's specials and asking for Diana's and Evelyn's drink choices, disappeared again. Diana's mother picked the lime slice off the lip of her glass and examined its thickness.

Not having any interest in the current citrus scrutiny, Diana turned to Evelyn, a bit surprised to find the other woman already watching her. "I feel like I've seen you somewhere before," she said. "Or heard your name, or—"

"Now, Diana," her mother admonished. "I've told you all about Evelyn and her family's history, remember?" She cast an indulgent smile at Evelyn, as if to say *Don't mind my scatterbrained daughter; she's so forgetful.*

She had absolutely never told Diana about any of this. Diana bit her tongue.

Evelyn's light laughter was entirely devoid of cruelty. "That's okay. There's a lot to remember." To Diana, she said, "My family's been in local politics for . . . forever, it feels like. You've probably seen one of them in the news."

"Her mother was our first female governor," Diana's mother added, looking awfully smug for someone describing accomplishments that weren't hers. Apparently satisfied with the lime, she popped it into the glass and poured herself some water. "Her grandfather was mayor during the Second World War, and she has a cousin in the House."

At that moment, the server returned with Diana's ice water and Evelyn's lemon seltzer. While Diana's mother asked pointed questions about the menu, Diana turned to Evelyn and lowered her voice. "I'm sorry she didn't warn you I'd be here."

Evelyn smiled brightly. "Oh, that's okay. It's always a good idea to meet the candidate's family. Make sure nobody's a potential PR problem," she added, her tone teasing.

"Ladies?"

The server was watching them expectantly, pen poised over a notepad. Evelyn ordered first, giving Diana a chance to inspect the menu. As she did, she caught a glimpse of her mother, who was watching her with an alarmingly sly smile.

For the next hour or so, they discussed the campaign. Evelyn, it turned out, had been her own father's campaign manager for years, but he had recently retired due to illness, and no one else in her family needed her services. Diana's mother, through one grapevine or another, had heard the news and snatched Evelyn up immediately—much to her own pride.

Diana could certainly understand the logic behind it. Not only did Evelyn have hands-on experience, but having the scion of a prominent political family on the team would be a master stroke when it came to her mother's public image. *If someone like that trusts Maggie Silver*, people might think, *we can, too.*

When Evelyn excused herself to the restroom, Diana's mother barely waited until she was out of earshot before folding her arms on the table and leaning in. "Well? What do you think of her?"

Frankly, Diana was surprised that she was getting asked for her thoughts at all. "She's a smart choice," she said, reaching for her glass. "She seems very intelligent, she's spent plenty of time in the field—"

"No, I know all that," her mother cut in, waving Diana's opinion away like an irritating insect. "But what do you think of *her*?" She lifted her eyebrows, as though the repetition of the question gave it some sort of significance.

For a moment, Diana stared at her. Then understanding crashed in on her like a demolished building. "Mummy, are you trying to—"

"Just a thought," her mother said, straightening up and taking a dainty spoonful of her consommé. "You've been single for too long now, and she comes from a wonderful family."

A painful memory nudged at Diana's mind, like pressing on a fading bruise, and she fought valiantly to keep her expression neutral. "You do remember the last time you set me up with someone from a wonderful family?"

That got her another hand wave and an eye roll. "That could have worked out if you'd really wanted it to. But that's been ages now, and Evelyn would be good for you."

She'd be good for you, *you mean.* Diana didn't say it, partly because there was no point and partly because Evelyn herself chose that moment to slip back into the booth.

Her mother's smile from before made more sense now. Diana fought the urge to physically shake her head in an attempt to make this revelation settle in her brain. What was her mother thinking? Even if Diana was remotely interested in Evelyn—and frankly, she didn't think she was—a relationship with her mother's campaign manager would be an aggressively stupid idea.

The rest of the afternoon passed without incident. Evelyn ("Evie," she insisted) paid their bill, despite token protests from Diana's mother, and offered to drive them both home. Diana's mother accepted and, when Diana said she'd already texted Skylar, seemed surprisingly all right with the refusal. When she hugged Diana goodbye, which was a rarity, Diana expected her to whisper something about Evie. But she didn't. Evie shook Diana's hand again in parting, and the gesture earned them no suggestive looks.

But she hadn't been in the car ten minutes before her phone pinged with a message.

Mother: *I gave Evie your number and told her to feel free to use it anytime.*

For Skylar's sake, Diana didn't scream in frustration. It was a close call, though.

Traffic forced them to take a different route back to Diana's town house, and the next thing Diana knew, they were idling at a stoplight across from the Hotel Öde.

Diana gazed out the window at the entrance, remembering the way Ronnie had looked while she was waiting outside. Waiting for her.

She shook her head, turning away. *Priorities.* She turned her thoughts instead to everything that had been discussed at lunch. She had a lot to learn, and no mental power to spare on anything else.

Besides, Ronnie had probably already forgotten all about her.

CHAPTER 3
However She Likes

"So there I was, pants around my ankles, wondering exactly how long I had until the maid came back and found me!"

Ronnie laughed. She laughed because she'd been paid to laugh at this man's jokes, but it was a pretty funny story too. That helped.

She was having an early dinner at Vivant, one of the city's swankiest cafés. Technically it was supposed to be her night off, but another escort had had to cancel on the job last minute and it wasn't like Ronnie had anything else to do. She never really had anything else to do.

And the client was a good guy, it turned out. Ronnie wouldn't have picked him up at a bar or anything, but he had warm brown eyes and a good head of hair. She didn't mind that the name he'd given ("Call me Larry.") was probably an alias. He'd wanted someone in red, so she'd picked a knee-length dress that offered a glimpse of cleavage when she leaned forward. What cleavage she had, at least.

He didn't seem to mind.

Someone else's laughter cut through the murmur of the restaurant, and Ronnie turned reflexively toward the sound.

The hostess was showing two women to their table. One was a shrewd-faced woman, a slacks-and-cardigan type Ronnie had never seen before. The other, though . . . dark hair, broad smile, mesmerizing eyes that somehow found Ronnie's across the room.

Diana.

Ronnie's breath caught somewhere around her neckline. It had been less than two weeks since her job with Diana, but she'd found herself thinking about it almost every day since. Her thoughts were always pretty evenly divided: first she'd wonder how Diana was doing, whether she was stressing over her new job. Then she'd remember Diana's skin on hers, Diana's hands in her hair, Diana's thighs bracketing her hips. She crossed her legs under the table.

"You okay?"

Call-me-Larry was watching her intently, thick brows furrowed. Ronnie smiled at him. "I'm fine," she said, placing a hand on his. "Just trying to find our server. You're almost out of wine."

He made a deep-throated, noncommittal noise. "Well. Don't want to drink *too* much." He winked, then went pink, like he was surprised at himself. Ronnie laughed again, pretending not to notice where Diana was being seated.

She couldn't pretend for long. Her gaze seemed to slide across the room of its own free will, whenever there was a pause in the conversation or an apparent lapse in her client's attention.

Diana clearly didn't have the same problem; she was turned to her companion every time Ronnie snuck a peek, speaking animatedly or smiling, shaking her head in exasperation or maybe amusement. Whoever the other woman was, she was lucky. Diana looked incredible.

"How was it?"

"Amazing," Ronnie said. Then she came back to herself. Her client was gesturing to her half-eaten chocolate mousse. *Oh.* "I just can't eat another bite," she added, placing her fork by the delicate white plate and silently scolding herself. *Get it together. You're better than this.* "Don't want to fill up." She raised a suggestive eyebrow and his ears went red. He was surprisingly bashful for a man in his fifties. "Give me a minute to fix myself up," she went on, standing, "and we can get out of here." She squeezed his shoulder and walked to the ladies' room, determined not to glance in Diana's direction on the way.

In the restroom, she dug in her purse for a lipstick that matched her dress, but once she'd pulled it out, she didn't apply it. She stared at herself without really seeing anything, trying to shake all thoughts of Diana from her mind.

Which got a lot more difficult when the door edged open behind her.

Diana's eyes met Ronnie's through the mirror, and she smiled before dragging her gaze down Ronnie's body. Then the corner of her mouth quirked up. "I liked the suit better."

Ronnie grinned, turning. "What, you don't think I can pull this off?"

"I didn't say that." Diana let the door ease shut and stepped forward. "I saw your date. Business or pleasure?"

Ronnie's skin felt warm. She narrowed her eyes and leaned one hip against the double vanity. "Don't tell me you're jealous."

"I don't get jealous. Nice client?"

"He's all right. Better than sitting around at home." She could smell Diana's perfume, sweet and woody. She crossed her arms, because she couldn't think of anything decent to do with them. "Who's that I saw you with?" At Diana's arched eyebrow, she clarified, "I *definitely* don't get jealous. Just asking."

Something around the edges of Diana's eyes softened, and her shoulders sagged, like she was tired and trying not to show it. "That's Evelyn. My mother's campaign manager."

"She's cute."

A casual shrug. "She's not really my type."

But I am. Ronnie didn't say it. She also didn't say, *Are you ever going to hire me again?* There was a pleasant tension in the air, a pull toward Diana like a thread between them, tight enough to snap. She opened her mouth to say something stupid.

"I should go," Diana said. "Evelyn might worry. I just . . ." She looked Ronnie up and down again, her gaze leaving a wave of heat in its wake. "Wanted to say hello." The door swung open and a middle-aged woman entered, giving them a politely curious glance before heading into one of the stalls.

"Right. I better finish up too." Ronnie brandished her lipstick. "Gotta make the donuts."

Diana smiled. "Have fun." Without another word, she was gone. Ronnie turned, screwing open her lipstick and scowling at herself in the mirror.

"'Gotta make the donuts'? Seriously?"

Her reflection had nothing to say. She shook her head and began to freshen up.

A few days later, Ronnie was out running, her whole body shaking each time her sneakers hit the pavement. As a general rule, she hated exercise, but Karla could get bitchy if she thought an escort was "letting themselves go." Jogging seemed the least boring way to avoid that, even if it did mean getting up earlier than she'd like. She just had to be sure not to wake up the neighbors on her way out.

Spring hadn't sprung yet, and there was a lingering chill in the air. Ronnie's pace turned the light breeze into a gale that whipped her hair into a blonde frenzy and dried her lips. Slowing at an intersection, she checked her watch and pressed the crosswalk button. *Ten more minutes. Another lap around the block and then—*

"Ronnie?"

The voice made her freeze. After taking a moment to brace herself, she glanced over her shoulder.

She'd stopped in front of a corner café, one of those local coffee shops that stayed open on nothing but hope and some rich person's whim. Standing at the double doors, like an early-morning half-dream, was Diana. She wore her blue coat and the smile of someone who'd gotten an unexpected birthday present. Ronnie leaned on the streetlight, one hand pressed to her side as she willed away the stitch there. "Diana." She'd been running, she reasoned. A little breathlessness was to be expected.

Diana held a paper cup, its cardboard sleeve stamped with the café's logo. A faint curl of steam spiraled up through the hole in the lid, disappearing into the morning air. She made no attempt to disguise her evaluative gaze, and Ronnie was suddenly conscious of her appearance: hair wild, no makeup, soaked with sweat.

"I promise, I usually look much better than this."

Diana's smile widened. "Oh, I don't know," she said, voice colored with velvety amusement. "You don't look so bad right now."

The chill in the air seemed to disappear instantly. "You're up early."

"I usually am. Especially these days." Diana stepped forward, taking a slow sip of her coffee, eyes never leaving Ronnie's. It was like watching an eclipse. Ronnie glanced away. The *WALK* light had come and gone. Her attention was dragged back to Diana when she said, "Funny how we keep running into each other."

Ronnie grinned. "Pretty funny."

"You're not following me, are you?" Diana's tone was teasing, her eyes glittering, and the combination made slow heat uncoil like a snake in Ronnie's stomach.

"Hey, I was at Vivant first," she reasoned.

Diana nodded in silent concession, then turned toward the intersection. "Walk with me," she said, stepping past Ronnie and into the white-striped street.

Ronnie wasn't on a job. This woman hadn't hired her. She was under no obligation to do as she was told.

She followed Diana without a second thought.

They must have made quite a pair, strolling together down the increasingly crowded sidewalk. People kept glancing at them as they walked past. Ronnie ran a hand through her hair, trying to smooth it. *Not that it'll help much,* she thought, peeking sidelong at Diana. She wished they were out together under better circumstances. If they were, they'd get nothing but stares of envy.

When she swerved to avoid a man with a briefcase, her arm brushed Diana's and her pulse fluttered at the contact. "So, how've you been?" she asked. Part of her needed a distraction, but she'd also just realized she hadn't asked at Vivant. "Mom's campaign keeping you busy?"

Diana gave a rueful smile and nodded. "And it hasn't even properly started yet. You?"

It was small talk, but it didn't really feel like it. "Oh, you know me." Diana didn't, actually, but whatever. "The usual. Coming and going."

Diana laughed, the sound low and warm in the back of her throat, and idiotic pride danced through Ronnie's body.

They were close to the next intersection, where a small crowd waited at the crosswalk. When Ronnie and Diana stopped, others gathered behind them, jostling them together. Ronnie took the opportunity to study Diana properly and found the other woman watching her too, mouth hovering at the lid of her cup as she blew into the drink to cool it. Her bottom lip was slightly fuller than her top one. Ronnie wanted to bite it.

Instead, she asked, "Where are we going?"

The light changed and they pressed forward, separating as the crowd dispersed.

"You're walking me to my car," Diana replied. From the corner of her eye, Ronnie saw her glance over. "Unless you have somewhere to be?"

Ronnie almost laughed. "Nah." She dodged another pushy pedestrian and lightly added, "I don't do crack-of-dawn coffee dates. Unlike some people."

She cut her gaze toward Diana to find her rolling her eyes. "Hardly a date," she muttered. Before Ronnie could ask her to unpack that, she veered toward a sleek gray Aston Martin. A slim woman in a high-buttoned jacket and a black hat waited at the curb, her expression indifferent.

"Skylar," Diana said to the driver, "this is Ronnie." Skylar, still looking unimpressed with Ronnie's general existence, offered a curt nod. "I'll just be a minute," Diana told her, returning to Ronnie.

"Well," Ronnie said.

"Well," Diana agreed. "I hope you have a good day." She smiled and Ronnie's knees went a little weak.

Must be the run.

"You too. Are you gonna give me a ride?"

Diana's eyes drifted from Ronnie's face to her neck. She reached up and Ronnie froze, standing like a statue as Diana eased the zip of her jacket down to the hem of her sports bra, fingertips trailing lightly along her skin on the way. Ronnie's exposed chest tingled in the cool air. She felt dizzy.

"Not this time," Diana said, so quietly that Ronnie almost didn't hear her. Then, with another wide smile, she said, "See you later," and whisked away from Ronnie like air being punched from her lungs.

By the time Ronnie had recovered, Skylar had closed the door and tucked herself into the driver's seat. Ronnie could only watch, helpless, as the car pulled into the flow of morning traffic and disappeared.

A week later, Ronnie was hunched over her cart at Short's, earbuds wedged in her ears, browsing the spice aisle. She was pretty sure she was good on spices, but it never hurt to stock up on essentials. After grabbing white pepper and paprika, she rounded the corner and stalled at the meat cooler. Did she need chicken breasts? She should've made a list.

She wasn't sure what made her look up. But she did, and saw a dark-haired, blue-coated figure opening one of the dairy cases. "Oh, no way." She tossed the chicken into her cart and pushed it forward, taking her time. Diana hadn't seen her yet—or, if she had, she hadn't acknowledged her.

What's a girl like you doing in a place like this? For some reason, the ideas of *Diana* and *grocery shopping* seemed mutually exclusive; it was too mundane an activity for her. But here she was, at Ronnie's local supermarket like it was the most natural thing in the world. Had she come here before? *Surely I'd have noticed you . . .*

Diana plucked a carton of almond milk from the case and closed the door, turning toward the frozen aisle. Ronnie scampered after her, swerving around a woman and her baby at the last possible second. "Sorry!"

She reached the aisle Diana had gone down and stopped, pulling out her earbuds and peeking around the endcap. Diana was considering the freezers, a handbasket looped over one arm.

"Excuse me."

The voice almost made Ronnie jump into her own cart. A teenager stood behind her, indicating the snack cakes on the endcap with a pointed look.

"Oh," Ronnie said. "Sure, yeah, sorry about . . ." She glanced back down the aisle. Diana was putting a bag in her basket, and turning in Ronnie's direction. "Oh, shit." Ronnie whirled the cart around. "Sorry," she said again to the boy, flinging herself into the safety of the next aisle.

What am I even doing? If I'd seen any other client here, I'd walk right past them. She stood stock-still, hoping Diana might walk right past her. Diana wouldn't recognize her from behind, would she? *This is stupid; if you're gonna say something, say something. If you're not, go get dish soap.*

"Hello again."

Smiling in the face of the unexpected was one of the many things Ronnie had perfected during her time as an escort. When she turned to see Diana—who looked like she'd just heard a hilarious joke—Ronnie was almost positive that she didn't appear as guilty as she felt. "Hello." She was pleased to hear that the greeting sounded normal. Then she ruined it with, "What are you doing here?"

Diana's eyebrows rose. "I'm on my way to see my parents. My mother wants to make smoothies but didn't have anything she needed for them."

"Must be nice," Ronnie said. "Her own personal delivery service."

Diana laughed wryly and the sound nudged at Ronnie's groin. "Well of course, what are children for?"

Ronnie wanted to come back with a witty reply, something with the perfect amount of friendly barb to get a reaction. But when she opened her mouth, what fell out was, "When are you gonna hire me again?"

They did nothing but stare at each other for a moment, mirror images of surprise. Overhead, a distant voice scratched out a daily special on bottled water.

"Not that you have to," Ronnie said, far too late. "I know you're busy. Only, last time you kinda implied that you might, and it's been a while, and . . ." She shrugged and grinned. "You said you had fun."

Diana's gaze seemed headed toward a dangerously high temperature, but her tone was light. "I did." Ronnie could almost swear she saw her pupils dilate. She wondered about the legal ramifications of public indecency.

Then, before she knew what was happening, Diana had stepped in close, bringing her lips to Ronnie's ear. A pleasant shiver ran up her spine at the warm breath on her skin when Diana whispered, "I don't have the number."

It took longer than it should have for the words to grab hold of Ronnie's brain. When they did, she gave a bark of undignified laughter. Diana backed up, eyes glittering with amusement.

"Guess that'd help," Ronnie said, running a hand through her hair. "You want me to give it to you?"

"I would very much like you to give it to me."

Heat spread through Ronnie's limbs in a rush as Diana pulled her phone from her coat and unlocked it. Just as Ronnie was opening her mouth to give her the number, Diana passed the phone to her.

"Oh," she muttered, taking it. It was still warm from its place in her coat. Its proximity to Diana's body. Ronnie had never envied a phone before.

She punched in the main office line, highly aware of Diana's eyes on her. On a whim, she saved the contact information under her own name. *Not like she'll be calling for anybody else. I hope.*

As soon as she'd handed the phone back, Diana tapped the screen a few times before bringing it to her ear. Her eyes met Ronnie's like a targeted attack. Through the blood roaring in her ears, Ronnie heard Stacy's muffled voice through the phone's speaker.

"Hello," Diana said, never breaking eye contact. "This is Diana Silver. A few weeks ago, a friend of mine—"

Ronnie heard Stacy's voice, but couldn't make out specific words. Diana's brows jumped up, face brightening. "With Ronnie, yes. Thank you for remembering. When is she next available?"

A pause as Stacy spoke. A flicker of what might have been indecision crossed Diana's face, but it was gone so quickly Ronnie must have imagined it.

"That's perfect. Yes, please, the same as last time." She smiled and Ronnie swallowed. "No special requests. She can come however she likes." Ronnie could feel their held gaze like a physical presence in her body. "I look forward to it. Thank you very much." With that, Diana lowered the phone and quirked an eyebrow at Ronnie. "Better?"

"Better." Ronnie had apparently forgotten how to breathe, because the word was basically a gasp. Before she could ask when they'd be meeting, her phone jangled at her chest, startling them both into looking away.

"Your bra is ringing," Diana observed.

Ronnie managed a laugh. "Wonder who that is." She pulled the phone out and silenced it. "She can leave a message. I should go, though," she continued. "Got some more things to pick up, then . . ."

"Job tonight?"

"Always." The details of it escaped her at the moment, but still. "I guess I'll see you later."

"I guess so." With another smile, Diana turned and clipped up the aisle.

Ronnie watched her go, then leaned on her cart and released a long, silent breath. She thumbed her phone to life, ignoring the voice mail and flipping straight to her contacts.

"Hey, Stacy," she said, heading toward the dairy cases. "Sorry I missed you. What's up?"

CHAPTER 4
Nice to See You

"Before we get started," Diana said, "I feel I should remind you that I have no idea what I'm doing."

Evie grinned at her. They were sitting at a table in Diana's mother's office, a laptop between them, staring at a screen that promised intuitive, beginner-friendly web design. Evie had told Diana's mother that having her own site would go a long way toward engaging a younger voter base. Diana's mother thought that was a wonderful idea, and had immediately tasked Evie and Diana with the site's creation, content, and launch.

Diana's protests about her own lack of experience had fallen on deaf ears.

"It's okay," Evie said, swiftly navigating through the signup process. "I've seen plenty of campaign sites, so I know what works. And this seems pretty easy." As the payment for the domain name went through, she glanced sidelong at Diana. "Still not sure why she didn't hire a professional, though."

Diana sighed. "I have a sneaking suspicion that we'll wonder that more than once, before all is said and done." She rested her chin on her hand and stared down at the notebook in front of her. After a moment, she scrawled *Site Content* across the top of the page, just to write something down.

Her mother's campaign announcement was tonight. It was going to be a relatively small affair, but Evie had still drummed up an impressive number of attendees, considering that Maggie Silver was not a name yet known in the city's political circles. The whole thing was set to start at eight o'clock, and Diana was expected to be there by seven at the latest.

As it happened, Ronnie's next availability was tonight as well. When the girl from Night Life told Diana, she'd almost abandoned the whole venture. But Ronnie had been right there, standing in front of her, looking positively *eager*. Diana hadn't been able to turn her down—hadn't *wanted* to turn her down. She'd remembered Ronnie's lips on hers and her fingers inside her and had scheduled the meet-up. She'd even gone to the office and signed her part of the contract already. It was a done deal.

She'd just have to be pretty quick about things, that's all.

"Diana?"

Evie's voice jerked her back to the present, and she sat up straight in her chair. "Sorry, what?"

"I asked if you wanted to handle the personal bio." Evie tapped the notepad. "If you can do that, I can whip up general policy bullet points."

"Oh." Diana fought the urge to shake her head to clear it. Her appointment with Ronnie wasn't for another four hours. She needed to focus. "Yes, I can do that. What information do you need?"

Eyes on her laptop screen, Evie gave a light shrug. "Oh, you know, her involvement in your school while you were growing up, extracurriculars, stuff like that. People love a family-oriented candidate." She tilted her head thoughtfully, then glanced over. "You have siblings, right?"

"One," Diana said. "A younger sister. Esther." Why hadn't her mother introduced Evie to the rest of the family? Although, considering what she'd said at lunch, it shouldn't be surprising. Esther had zero interest in relationships of any kind. *No sense in shoving the two of them into a bistro booth together.*

As soon as she thought it, she was ashamed of her cynicism. Maybe there simply hadn't been a good opportunity for introductions yet.

"Great," Evie was saying. "Anything she did for Esther too. Whatever you can remember, slap it all down and we'll refine it later."

Diana placed the tip of her pen to the notepad and delved into her memories, trying to recall any sort of academic involvement on her mother's part. Hesitantly, she wrote *Came to parent/teacher conferences* on one line. Report cards only said so much; her mother had always liked to make sure, in person, that Diana and Esther were both behaving and excelling in school.

When it got too hard to think of something else to add to the list, Diana's concentration slithered toward tonight's schedule. The Hotel Öde wasn't exactly far from the union hall where her mother's announcement would take place, but it wasn't exactly close to it, either. If Diana allowed herself a half hour to get across town, plus ten minutes or so to get touched up after . . . well, after Ronnie, then that would give them about twenty minutes together . . .

"You okay?"

Diana looked over to see Evie watching her, brow furrowed slightly, fingers hovering above her laptop keys. "I'm fine," she assured her. "Just running through the plan for tonight."

That was true, at least.

Evie smiled encouragingly. "It'll be fine." She glanced at the screen and adjusted a few options on the site-builder. "You want to have dinner somewhere, five thirty or sixish? Maybe that'd take your mind off it." Before Diana could even wonder whether Evie was asking her out, she added, "I'd like to meet the rest of the family too, if that's okay with Maggie."

A group dinner. Relief flooded through Diana's body. "I would, but I actually have an errand to run beforehand." It wasn't really a lie; her errand just involved nipping out for a quick orgasm. "You might still ask Mummy, though."

Evie nodded and went back to tapping away at the keyboard. Diana turned her attention to her notebook, frowning at the single item she'd written. She gripped her pen tightly, resolving not to let her mind wander any more that afternoon. *Priorities.*

"And how will I recognize your friend?"

Diana stared at the night manager of the Hotel Öde. She'd finished giving him instructions for when Ronnie arrived, and they were simple enough: greet her, give her a key to the penthouse, and tell her that Diana was waiting. It hadn't occurred to her that he wouldn't know who Ronnie was.

"She's . . . extremely good-looking," Diana began, feeling as though she was making the world's most impressive understatement. The manager raised his eyebrows, as if to point out the subjectivity of that description. Diana tried again. "She's blonde. Short blonde hair, and she'll probably be wearing a suit. She'll be . . ." *How to put it?* "Sure of herself."

That must have been enough, because he smiled and inclined his head. "Very good, Ms. Silver. Let us know if there's anything else you need." Diana thanked him and strode across the lobby, ignoring the manager's knowing gaze as it burned into her skull. He could think what he liked.

In the elevator, she took long, deep breaths: in through her nose, out through her mouth. She had a precise timetable, and in order to stick to it, everything needed to be ready as soon as Ronnie got there. Including Diana.

In the suite, she dropped her tote off in the bathroom. She'd brought everything she needed to fix her hair and face before leaving. And she rather hoped she'd need plenty of fixing.

In the sitting room, she considered the layout. The first thing Ronnie would see when she came in was the sofa. It seemed as good a place as any, so Diana unzipped her dress and shuffled out of it, arranging it over the backrest. She sat her shoes side-by-side beneath it, then peeled off her hose and cast around for a place to put them.

Finally she decided on the floor, halfway between the sofa and the hallway. Her bra joined the hose a few paces down. At the end of the hall, she pulled off her underwear, dropping it at the threshold with a sigh of satisfaction, then surveyed the path she'd laid. Just a hint at first, a suggestion, the implications becoming clearer the closer Ronnie got to the bedroom. It was a nice effect.

And probably something Ronnie had seen a thousand times before.

Diana puffed out her cheeks in a frustrated huff. "Oh damn it all," she muttered, whipping inside the bedroom and easing the door half-closed behind her.

After she'd checked herself in the mirror once more, she stood stark naked in the middle of the room, frowning thoughtfully at the bed.

Under the sheets? On top of them? She wanted to look alluring, not like a panting amateur. Then again, any time spent dealing with covers might well be time wasted. She lay across the duvet, trying a few positions before settling on one that was likeliest to present the best picture.

The clock on the nightstand read 6:03. Any minute now. Diana wished her heart would stop pounding. If Ronnie got anywhere near her chest—and Diana rather hoped she would—Diana didn't want her thinking she was anything but composed.

Before long, a distant beep drifted down the hall, followed by Ronnie's voice: "Diana?"

The sound of her name did nothing to slow Diana's pulse, but it did change the rhythm. She was slowly edging away from nervousness, away from worrying about the time, away from anything but anticipation. She was hot all over, blood thundering somewhere around her hips as she waited for Ronnie.

The door eased open, and Ronnie slipped inside. When she caught sight of Diana, her eyebrows shot up.

It was only fair to warn her. "I don't have much time."

Ronnie released a puff of laughter. "Nice to see you too."

With a steely authority that she didn't really feel at the moment, Diana replied, "Why are you still dressed?"

Ronnie's eyes darkened. "Right."

As Ronnie thumbed open the button of her jacket and stripped it off, Diana remembered what she'd said that first night, about her desire to be given to someone. Did Ronnie have a submissive streak?

That would be interesting.

Ronnie tossed her jacket aside and was about to unbutton her shirt when Diana said, "Slowly."

Ronnie's eyes darted to the clock. "I thought—"

"I have time for this."

Ronnie smirked, making Diana's groin twinge with desire, and murmured, "Yes, miss." Diana couldn't stop her eyes from widening.

Ronnie returned to her buttons, taking her time, her eyes wandering Diana's body. Diana realized her own hand was following the gaze, fingers dancing listlessly just above her groin. Once Ronnie was in nothing but her underthings, she put her hands on her hips, chin raised almost arrogantly. Her swagger was deeply appealing; it ignited an impulse that Diana hadn't indulged in quite some time. Her last girlfriend hadn't been interested at all in being dominated, and Diana would never even think of insisting. But if Ronnie liked the idea, it would be delicious to try taking her down a peg or two.

Ronnie's bra hit the floor, and she slipped her hands into the waistband of her scant red tanga, but Diana shook her head. "Leave them," she said, surprised to find that her voice was steady. She straightened, pulling her knees up before moving to the edge of the mattress. "Come here."

Ronnie obeyed, her pace measured. When she reached the bed, Diana took her by the hips, running her hands up to hold her by the waist. Ronnie's skin against hers made her tingle all over, like a muscle that had been asleep and was beginning to wake up. "Exactly like I remember you." She pressed her lips to the space below Ronnie's navel, reveling in the soft skin there. Then she took the band of the tanga in her teeth, pulled back, and released. The elastic snapped quietly, and Ronnie gasped, her hands flying up to grip at Diana's hair.

At the scratch of fingertips against her scalp, Diana sank onto the duvet, bringing Ronnie with her. "Come on," she rasped, taking Ronnie's wrist and guiding the hand to the ache between her legs.

If her grip was painful, Ronnie didn't say so. In fact, her breath quickened and she plunged two fingers into Diana with a low groan.

"Yes," Diana hissed as her eyes fluttered shut. "Yes, harder, oh perfect." She was barely aware of what she was saying; all she could focus on was Ronnie inside her, the weight of Ronnie's body on hers, the steady red beat at the edges of her mind—

Then pressure on her thigh, warm and wet and with a slight scratch. Lace. Ronnie was straddling her leg, grinding against her and panting. Diana planted her heel on the edge of the bed frame, hoping to give her better purchase.

"Come on," Diana urged her again. Ronnie's breath was hot against her lips. "That's it, come on, yes, I—"

Her voice failed her and she only managed to gasp. When Ronnie lowered her face and pressed their foreheads together, Diana lifted her chin to capture Ronnie's lips with her own.

The kiss was electric. Diana released a strangled cry into Ronnie's mouth as her orgasm ripped from her body like thunder. A few more thrusts, then Ronnie's body stiffened and she broke away with a long, low moan. Diana clung to her as she came, blunt nails biting into her shoulders, letting go only when Ronnie slumped bonelessly to her side.

In the stillness, the sounds they'd made seemed to echo against the bedroom walls. She was suddenly very glad that the penthouse had its own floor.

Ronnie grumbled contentedly and the mattress dipped. Diana opened her eyes to see Ronnie rolling onto her side, propping her head up on one hand to gaze down at her. "Pretty sure my underwear's ruined."

Diana couldn't help feeling a little pleased with herself. She shifted slightly, snaking a hand down to test Ronnie's assumption. At the contact, Ronnie sucked in a sharp breath and her eyelids fluttered.

"Don't start that," she rasped as Diana fingered the wet lace. "Not unless you have time for another round."

Diana glanced over her shoulder at the clock: 6:17. She couldn't remember the last time she'd had an honest-to-God quickie. She sighed and pulled back her hand. "I do have to go."

"Hot date?" Ronnie guessed.

"Yes." Diana turned to her, lifting a brow. "I'm having a torrid affair with the abstract concept of political ambition."

Ronnie laughed. "Kinky." She stood, shaking out her hair and offering Diana a hand. Diana took it and Ronnie helped her to her feet, adding, "Campaign stuff?"

"My mother's announcement." It didn't escape Diana's notice that neither of them had released the other's hand yet.

Ronnie gave a low hum, eyes glittering. "Well, now you've got something to think about, if you get bored." She tugged Diana gently toward her for a kiss that made Diana's head spin.

Then she pulled away, still grinning, and let go. "I'll grab your stuff," she said, striding out of the bedroom without bothering to get dressed.

Diana released a quiet breath and went into the en suite, digging in her tote for her brush and trying to calm herself down. She could *easily* go another round, but she didn't want to arrive at the hall all keyed up. In fact, she very much wanted to give no sign of where she'd been or what she'd been doing. She tugged the brush through her hair and tried to think of boring things.

Then Ronnie appeared at the bathroom door, still naked but for her underwear, and Diana's mind filled with decidedly unboring things.

"Here you go." Ronnie presented her previously scattered outfit.

Diana thanked her and took the clothes, unable to stop her gaze from skating over Ronnie's body. She thought she'd been fairly brief about it, but when her eyes met Ronnie's, the escort was smiling knowingly at her. "I'll get dressed," Ronnie said. "Don't wanna distract you."

It was a little late for that, but Diana didn't say so. She rolled her eyes without conviction, and Ronnie disappeared into the bedroom.

As she dressed and refreshed her makeup, Diana's mind seemed split directly down the middle. Half was hurrying her along, reminding her that she had a schedule to keep, that there'd be hell to pay if she wasn't at the union hall on time.

The other half was picturing Ronnie with her wrists lashed together. Thinking of blindfolding her, ordering her to her knees, twining fingers in her hair and pulling. Having Ronnie at her mercy.

Her phone buzzed and she nearly jumped into the tub. It was a message from Skylar, letting her know she had the car outside. Six thirty on the dot. She really did need to go.

She tapped out a reply and came out into the bedroom, relieved to see that Ronnie was fully clothed again. Ronnie put her hands into her pockets and considered Diana, eyes wandering over her plum sheath dress and low d'Orsay pumps. "You look great. Very constitutional."

Diana snorted, even as her face went warm at the compliment. "Thank goodness for that." She headed for the corridor, tilting her head in an indication for Ronnie to follow.

As they made their way toward the living room, Diana added, "You can stay, if you want. I've got the room until tomorrow. Feel free to get something to eat or order a movie, whatever you want. They'll put it on my bill."

"Thanks."

"Of course."

If Ronnie stayed, maybe Diana could come back after the announcement do was over. Would that be against some rule? She'd only paid for an hour, but if Ronnie happened to stay once she was off the clock, and Diana happened to return to her room . . .

She was getting ahead of herself.

When they stopped at the door, she let herself run a thumb along Ronnie's jaw. Ronnie let her do it. "It was good to see you again," Diana murmured.

"You too." Ronnie still had her hands in her pockets, but was watching Diana with a soft expression that set off all sorts of sparks in Diana's mind.

"Do you have a safeword?"

She'd asked before she even realized she was going to. Ronnie blinked, like her mind was trying to shift gears. "I use the traffic light. It's pretty standard. Why?"

"I'm going to hire you again." Diana didn't know when, or how she'd find the time. She just knew it was going to happen. "You said you liked being a present. And I sometimes . . . I like to be in control." She searched Ronnie's face. "Is that something you're interested in?"

For a moment, Ronnie did nothing but look at her. She looked at her for long enough that Diana began to wonder if she'd completely misunderstood the things she'd seen, if her intuition was so utterly broken that she'd gotten it all wrong.

Then Ronnie swallowed, as if she was thirsty. "Yeah," she said. "I can do that."

Can do was very different from *want to do*. But Diana didn't have time to get into that discussion right now. So she nodded and said, "I'll see you later," leaving the suite before she had the chance to be tempted into further dawdling.

Diana got to the union hall with five minutes to spare, and mercifully everything seemed to be in order. The caterers had arrived when they'd said they would, the center manager was on-hand should they need anything else, and the small cadre of security guards was discreet enough that no one ought to feel unduly intimidated. Diana had been skeptical about the need for security, but Evie had recommended it, her only grounds a cryptic, "You'd be surprised."

So everyone and everything was in its place, including the incipient candidate. Diana wasn't surprised; when it came down to it, her mother excelled at being where she should, when she should. This had obviously come as something of a relief to Evie, who was evidently used to wrangling her candidates.

The whole evening went smoothly, all told. Her mother's announcement was met with enthusiasm, so much so that Diana wondered if she might actually have a chance of winning the election. She didn't exactly doubt her mother's abilities, but Evie had warned her that first-time candidates often didn't face good odds.

After the announcement, while everyone sampled canapés and mingled in the foyer, Diana found Evie standing apart from the crowd, sipping a small bottle of elderflower tonic water. Her dark eyes were scanning the throng—not suspicious, just evaluative. "I'll give her this," she said as Diana approached, "she knows how to work a room."

Diana glanced over to where her mother was flitting around the foyer, shaking hands, accepting congratulations, likely sowing the seeds of support. "She certainly does," Diana agreed. "What's the time?"

Evie shook back the cuff of her checked blazer and looked at her watch. "Ten till nine." She glanced out at the room. "People are already thinning out a little." Then she turned to Diana. "Do you need to be somewhere?"

She seemed genuine, the question posed utterly without guile. Diana shook her head. "No, it's not that. . ." She indicated the room at large. "I can only take so much at a time."

That was completely true. Anyone who'd spent a lifetime with Maggie and Theo Silver for parents knew how to be sociable, and Diana was fairly good at it. But it was mentally exhausting.

Besides, even if there was nowhere she *needed* to be, she could think of one place she'd very much *like* to be.

Evie was nodding. "I get that. You squared away everything with the caterers and the manager, yeah?" When Diana confirmed, she jerked her chin toward a side door. "Get out of here, then. I'll let your mom know—I'm sure she'll understand."

Diana was almost certain that she would not understand, but maybe she'd be high enough on the success of the evening that she wouldn't worry too much about it. "Thank you," she said, laying a hand briefly on Evie's arm. Evie smiled and lifted her bottle in lazy acknowledgment.

One text to Skylar and ten minutes later, Diana was on her way back to the Hotel Öde. Her mind might have been spent, but her body was far from tired.

If Ronnie had taken her up on her offer to stay at the penthouse, Diana could . . . She chewed her lip as she imagined Ronnie, asleep on the bed they'd so recently employed. She imagined sliding her slow way up Ronnie's body, waking her with barely there kisses and teeth on her collarbone. The thought made her slightly light-headed.

When they eased to a stop, Diana didn't wait for Skylar to open the door for her. "Stay close," she said as she climbed out. "I'll let you know." Skylar gave a quick nod and the car rumbled away.

Diana was just in time to catch the elevator, along with a young man holding a massive bunch of flowers. As the floors dinged by, Diana gave the bouquet a sidelong glance and offered him a smile. He grinned nervously. "Think she'll like them?"

"They're lovely," Diana said. "Big date?"

"I hope so. How about you?"

"Something like that." The elevator slowed and the young man got off on ten. Diana raised a hand. "Good luck."

"You too!"

The doors slid shut and Diana sighed. When they opened again on the thirtieth floor, she stepped into the hallway and drew the key card from her clutch.

The penthouse was dark when she slipped inside. She'd half expected to find Ronnie lounging on the sofa, watching television. But all was quiet and someone had turned down the flames in the fireplace. The vision of Ronnie sleeping returned and Diana shivered. She crept toward the bedroom.

The bedroom, as it turned out, was as dim and deserted as the sitting room. Diana blinked into the blue emptiness for a moment. Then, though there was nobody to hear, she said, "Oh."

It was fine. After all, she hadn't given Ronnie explicit instructions to stay. She hadn't even mentioned that she might be back later. Maybe if she had . . .

But probably not.

So she tapped out a text to Skylar—*Coming down*—and marched out the door, tossing her key card onto the coffee table on the way out. In the elevator, she watched the tenth floor slide past and remembered the young man with the flowers. Hopefully his night was going well, at least.

It had started to drizzle while Diana was inside. Skylar stood at the curb, holding an umbrella over Diana as she folded into the car. "Home, please," she muttered. Skylar nodded, silent as ever, and shut the door gently.

There's always next time. Ronnie had seemed amenable to the idea of being hired again and, as Diana had suspected, to the idea of a bit of power play.

The problem was, she had no idea when *next time* might be. Her schedule would be densely packed in the months leading up to the election, as she'd told Phoebe. And she knew that the campaign ought to be her top priority. But surely she'd have *some* free time? Even if it was only an hour or two, here and there, whenever she could get away.

She'd just have to be ready to jump at her first opportunity. *And I intend to be.*

CHAPTER 5
Completely Neutral

Ronnie considered herself pretty tight when it came to money. Sometimes she'd splurge if she came across a great pair of earrings or a set of extra-sexy lingerie, and she had a tendency to make up for leaving her hometown by sending a ton of presents back to her family for birthdays and Christmas. But she squirreled away most of it, especially since starting at Night Life—there was nothing and nobody else to spend it on, and she didn't maintain a six-digit savings account by throwing her money around.

That sort of moderation meant, among other things, only getting clothes when she really needed them. And she didn't really need them.

And yet here she was, at an upscale midtown boutique called Ashworth's, a place she'd probably never have found on her own. But she wouldn't be on her own for long; Diana would be meeting her here soon, per the contract she'd signed a few days ago.

As she waited outside the shop, she eyed the tall golden letters on the sign and the outfits on display in the window. They were great suits, all in wool and linen and blends. Ronnie would never get something quite so ritzy for herself.

And if Diana was planning on buying something for her . . .

The idea made something in her gut tighten, not unpleasantly. Even so, she'd have to politely refuse. Rules were rules.

The Aston Martin rolled up to the curb and Ronnie grinned as Diana's chauffeur got out and circled around front. "Hey, Skylar." Skylar didn't even offer her customary mute nod—she ignored Ronnie completely, reaching for the rear passenger door. *Welp.*

Diana stepped out of the car looking delicious. She wore a champagne-colored button-down, sleeves cuffed to the elbows, and a black pencil skirt that clung to her hips in a way that made Ronnie a little envious. She'd put her hair up, but a few dark tendrils had sprung free and brushed against her neck when she turned to smile at Ronnie.

She was a picture of refinement. Ronnie wanted to *devastate* her.

As Skylar drove away and Diana approached, her eyes flicked over Ronnie's body, and her smile widened. Ronnie hadn't been sure about her own outfit—a pair of dark blue slacks and a gray wrap blouse— but Diana must have liked what she saw.

"Hello."

"Hi."

Diana stepped in close, as though to kiss her, but hesitated. Ronnie didn't mind initiating, though—hands in her pockets, she brushed her lips against Diana's. When she drew away, Diana's eyes were all but glowing.

"So," Ronnie said, "you in the market for a suit? Need my expert opinion?"

"I don't think I could pull one off quite the way you can."

"Oh, I dunno." Ronnie's gaze was slow and deliberate as it dragged along Diana's body. "I can imagine you pulling off just about anything."

Diana pursed her lips, clearly trying not to smile. "Classy."

Ronnie had always been a natural flirt, and she'd gotten pretty good at sweet-talking clients over the years. But Diana's easy reaction warmed her all over in a way she hadn't expected.

"To answer your question, no," Diana continued, "we're not here for me. I've been tasked with picking out some things for my mother. She wants a brand-new wardrobe for the campaign trail." Ronnie glanced dubiously at the window displays, and Diana laughed. "Not from here. There's a Nygaard West around the corner; this is just a fun detour." With that, she slipped her arm into the crook of Ronnie's elbow and led them inside.

As soon as they stepped through the doors, they were immediately set upon by an attendant. He was a small man, wiry, with slick black hair and a leathery tan. "Good afternoon, ladies!" His voice dripped with customer service. "How may I be of assistance today?"

Diana pulled her arm from Ronnie's and reached into her clutch. "I'm Diana Silver," she said as she presented the man with a small card. "I have a two o'clock with Petra."

"Of course!" He actually clicked his heels. Ronnie stifled a laugh. "You'll be in room seven. If you'll follow me?"

He ushered them through a red curtain and past a short pedestal surrounded by full-length mirrors. Beyond that lay a long hallway lined with doors, each numbered with a small golden plaque. They definitely didn't need the little man to guide them all the way down to the end of the hall, but he seemed to think it was vital. "Petra will be with you momentarily," he said, opening room seven for them. "Can I get you ladies a drink?"

Diana looked at Ronnie as though passing the question to her, and Ronnie shook her head. "Oh, no, thanks, I'm good." Diana shook her head too, and the man clicked his heels again, then offered them something that was either a shallow bow or a deep nod.

"Excellent, ladies, excellent," he said. "My name is Marcel. Do please let me know if there's anything else I can help you with."

They waited until the sound of his clipped footsteps grew faint, then glanced at each other.

Diana gave an unladylike snort before clapping a hand over her mouth, shoulders quaking. Ronnie shook her head and blinked, unable to suppress her widening grin. "What a weird little dude."

"Very weird. Very little."

"Very dude?"

That made Diana break into a fresh fit of giggles. They held each other's gaze for a moment, warm amusement rippling between them. Then Ronnie turned her attention to the deep red walls and gold accents of the fitting room. "This is pretty swanky."

When she glanced over her shoulder, Diana was watching her with a smile. "I'm used to the best."

Ronnie had a feeling she wasn't just talking about boutiques. Her face went warm, but before she could respond, someone whipped into the room.

She was tall and pointed, with white-blonde hair buzzed close to her skull and a strip of neon green measuring tape slung over the back of her neck. "I am Petra," she announced in an indeterminately

European accent. Her pale eyes swept over them, and she seemed to make a decision, extending one long hand toward Diana. "Ms. Silver?"

"That's me," Diana said, accepting Petra's handshake. "This is Ms. . . ." She blinked, then looked at Ronnie helplessly.

For a second, Ronnie didn't understand her hesitation. Then she realized that Diana still only knew her first name. She rarely had reason to give her surname to clients; most weren't interested.

She held out a hand to Petra. "Ronnie."

"Ronnie," Diana echoed faintly. Then, with more confidence, "You'll be dressing her."

I was afraid of that. Ronnie grimaced mentally but kept her expression neutral as Petra turned a shrewd gaze on her.

"Charmed." She took Ronnie's fingers in something that was almost a handshake, then glanced at Diana. "Yours, is she?"

Diana's eyes flitted to Ronnie, then back to Petra. "For the moment." Her tone and expression were perfectly indifferent, but Ronnie couldn't shake the feeling that she'd somehow disappointed her.

The reedy woman hummed knowingly. "Very, very, *very*," she muttered, looking Ronnie over. "I think I have the size of you."

Yeeeah, she's not talking about measurements.

Ignoring Ronnie's wry expression, Petra added, "But we'll get you under the tape, just to be sure." She stepped out of the room and gestured up the corridor. "Go."

For the next few minutes, Ronnie stood in front of the mirrors and did her best to hold still. Petra circled her and measured her and made notes on a pad she'd apparently pulled from nowhere. All the while Diana stood by and watched, her eyes trailing over Ronnie's body like a caress when Petra was scribbling numbers.

Finally, Petra straightened and turned to Diana. "You want her in anything special?"

Heat seeped into Ronnie's skin as Diana considered her for a moment that was probably a little longer than necessary. "I like her in gray." She spoke to Petra but kept her eyes on Ronnie. "Something a bit darker than the top she's got on, maybe."

Petra nodded. "Splash of color with the shirt?"

"Perfect."

"Yes." Petra tossed the measuring tape around her neck. "I'll bring a few selections to your room." Then she was gone, the red curtain swaying in the wake of her departure.

As they made their way back to the end of the hall, Ronnie said, "She might as well put me in pink polka dots." Diana glanced at her questioningly. "This is nice and all, but I'm not actually gonna *buy* anything."

"I was planning on doing the buying."

Ronnie sighed as they reached room seven. "I was afraid of that." Diana blinked and, latching the door behind them, Ronnie clarified: "I'm not allowed to accept gifts." She gave an apologetic shrug. "Flowers are usually okay, since they die, and dinner and drinks are allowed. But nothing major."

Diana stared at her, brow furrowed. "Why?"

"Karla says she's afraid we'll get accused of playing favorites," Ronnie said. "You know, somebody gives an escort a diamond necklace or whatever, another client finds out, thinks they're being one-upped." She crossed her arms and leaned against the full-length mirror with a sour chuckle. "Doesn't stop *Karla* from accepting all kinds of gifts, but . . ."

Diana narrowed her eyes. "Isn't bribing the boss a bigger risk than bribing the escorts?"

"You'd think. But she definitely didn't have a problem letting us know when some CFO sent her a bracelet."

Diana gave a dark, thoughtful hum. Then her face cleared a little. "So I can't give you anything."

It was the perfect setup for a dirty joke, but Ronnie resisted. "Flowers," she reiterated. "Or a tip, if I do a really good job."

"I see. Do you like flowers?"

"Nah. They make me sneeze." Diana smiled and Ronnie added, "So, should I go tell Petra not to bother with the suits?"

"Absolutely not." Diana stepped toward her, expression playfully haughty. "I paid for my time, and if I want to spend it watching you try on suits, that's how I'll spend it." The firmness of her tone made Ronnie's skin tingle. "Besides, these places are used to people who just want to play dress-up. That's why they charge a consultation fee."

"God, that'd drive me crazy," Ronnie said, shaking her head. She slipped her fingertips just past the waistband of Diana's skirt and tugged her forward. As Diana ran the tips of her fingers along the wrap line of her blouse, she added, "Glad I've got an exciting job."

"I'm glad you do too."

When Diana sank her teeth into Ronnie's bottom lip, any thoughts about rules and gifts and hypocrisy left her mind in a puff of smoke.

After a moment, she straightened, grinning. "So is this one of your kinks?" she asked, toying with the buttons of Diana's shirt. "Watching women get manhandled by snotty retail workers?"

Diana gently swatted her hands away. "*I* need to keep my clothes on." She grazed her lips against Ronnie's and reached down to undo her pants. "*You* do not."

She pushed the waistband down past Ronnie's hips and Ronnie chuckled. "Don't get too carried away." She nipped at Diana's earlobe and put on a vaguely European accent. "Any minute, Petra will return."

Diana gave an irritated hum. It was almost as good as an admission that Ronnie was right. So Ronnie stepped back to undress herself, leaving Diana to take a seat on a pillowtop bench in the corner. She crossed her legs, lips pursed peevishly, and Ronnie laughed.

"Come on," she said, smoothing her pants over her arm. "It's not like we could get very far in a public dressing room anyway."

The smoldering look Diana turned on her plainly disagreed. Then the whole stall rattled with a knock. "Ms. Silver?" Petra called.

Diana smiled and stood to slip outside, allowing Ronnie to lay her pants on the bench. Stripping off her blouse, she couldn't quite hear the low conversation outside. When Diana ducked back into the room, she held a pair of hangers, each sporting a sleek gray suit. In her other hand she had an assortment of colorful button-ups. "I told her I'll deal with you for now," she said, eyes glittering. "She'll wait up front."

Ronnie, in nothing but her bra and briefs, folded her arms beneath her breasts. "You'll *deal with* me?" The phrase sent a wave of excitement straight to her groin. Hopefully she didn't look as weak-kneed as she felt.

"Mm-hmm." Diana hung the suits on one of the gold hooks and considered the shirts. "The yellow is good with the gray," she muttered, "but not with your hair." She tossed the offending top onto the bench. Ronnie watched her, fascinated. "Ugh." A purple top joined the yellow. "Hmm."

She glanced from Ronnie to the bubblegum-pink button-up in her hand and back again. "Try this one," she instructed, handing it to her. "With the lighter suit." She shuffled the items on the bench, moving the discarded options to the floor before pulling Ronnie's clothes to her lap as she sat.

Ronnie unfolded the shirt and started on the buttons. "So you really do just wanna watch me try on suits."

Diana nodded.

Ronnie shrugged. "You're the boss."

"Yes, I am."

So Ronnie got dressed. She had to admit that when Diana said she liked being in control, this wasn't quite what she'd imagined. She focused on hooking and zipping and smoothing, only a little bit disappointed.

The suit was nice. It didn't fit perfectly, of course—she had subtle curves that menswear didn't expect—but Petra had done a pretty good job of matching Ronnie's measurements to what she could pull off the rack. Finally Ronnie buttoned the jacket, smoothed her hair, and turned back to the bench.

Diana's expression was weird. She seemed to be both genuinely appraising the suit and taking it off again with her eyes. Ronnie was used to hungry stares from clients, often reveled in them. But nobody had ever looked at her quite the way Diana was right now. She was glad for her long sleeves: they hid the sudden goose bumps that prickled at her arms. "Well?"

Diana lifted her chin. "Come here." Ronnie stepped closer. "Turn around."

Ronnie turned, and Diana ran a hand down her spine, then up under the hem of the jacket. When Ronnie felt Diana squeeze her backside, she smirked. "Is that strictly necessary?"

"Have to make sure the trousers fit." Diana's voice was low. She slid her hand between Ronnie's legs, blunt nails scraping along her inner thigh. Ronnie widened her stance, breath quickening, but the warmth of Diana's touch disappeared. Ronnie frowned and glanced over her shoulder.

Diana had leaned away, hands folded demurely in her lap. Her expression might have been almost clinical if not for her dilated pupils and a specific tension in the lines of her lips. Ronnie didn't move, waiting to see what she'd do.

What Diana did was turn aside, indicating the darker suit with a jerk of her head. "Try the other one," she said. "With the teal shirt." She stood and unlocked the door with an almost dismissive, "I'll be right back," then disappeared.

A silent moment passed. Then Ronnie blew out a frustrated puff of air and stripped off the jacket, forcing herself to take more care than she really wanted to.

She was straightening her collar when the door opened again, and when she turned, Diana's gaze was raking down her body. "Oh, I like that one," she murmured, stepping in and locking the door behind her.

At Diana's heated expression, Ronnie's body fired up almost of its own accord. Her eyes dropped to the necktie Diana held, a few shades darker than the shirt Ronnie had changed into. "The whole nine yards, huh?" she asked, reaching for it.

But Diana yanked the tie out of her grasp, her lips curling into a wicked smile. "Turn around."

"Ah, right." Ronnie turned. "Gotta check out those trousers."

She didn't hear Diana step forward, just felt the close, sudden heat of her and heard her roughly order, "Hands." Ronnie raised an eyebrow but obeyed. Then she felt silk at her wrists, a single knot tied swift and tight. Diana tugged on it. "Give me a color." The demand was hot at Ronnie's ear. "Quick."

This was what Ronnie had imagined.

Night Life escorts were generally expected to follow the rules of common decency and common sense, which meant getting busy in public spaces was discouraged. Still, Ronnie's body was screaming at her: *Do it, who cares? If you get caught, Diana can pay Petra to keep quiet.*

Unless she can't be bought, her mind hissed. *If she complains, Karla will be humiliated. She'll skin you alive.*

She flexed her hands, the knot at her wrists tightening with silken temptation. Diana was pressed against the length of her back, desperation obvious in her labored breath. She wanted control. And Ronnie was dizzy with desire to give it to her. "Green."

Diana shoved them forward and they smacked against the mirror. She laid a forearm across Ronnie's shoulders, pinning her in place. Ronnie's breath fogged her own frenzied reflection as Diana fumbled with the front of the slacks. She yanked them down, taking Ronnie's briefs with them, and grated, "Spread your legs." Ronnie did and the fabric caught at her knees. When Diana's hand slid between her legs, she fought against a groan, but lost the battle as nimble fingers slipped inside.

She was already wet and only grew wetter as Diana worked, twisting and pressing and curving her wrist. "Incredible," Diana sighed, voice quiet but shaking. She crushed her face against the nape of Ronnie's neck, breath dampening the fine hair there, and sank her teeth into sensitive skin.

Ronnie was nearly blind with arousal, eyes rolling in her skull as she drove her hips back to meet Diana's movements. She was a little taller, and Diana's arm wasn't really enough to keep her where she was. But she let Diana do it, let Diana hold her down and press into her with an aching, steady rhythm. Let herself be controlled.

It wasn't long before her pelvis tensed and she grew tight around Diana's fingers. The pressure against her shoulder let up, and Diana's arm circled her front, palm clamping over her mouth as she whispered, "Not a sound."

Ronnie fell apart, pleasure coursing through her in warm, powerful pulses, rendering her almost light-headed. Her breath hissed hard through her nose as Diana worked her through her orgasm, but otherwise she did as she was told.

It felt like forever before she finished, and when she did, she sagged against the mirror, choking on a gasp as Diana pulled out. She could feel Diana watching her and was suddenly very aware of how she must look: pants caught on her knees, makeup smudged, hands still bound. The word *wanton* sprang to mind.

She started to shoulder away from the mirror, but a hand on her spine made her go still.

The knot at her wrists loosened and Diana purred, "Will you hold this for me?"

Ronnie's brain was still a little sluggish—she couldn't figure out why Diana was asking, but in that moment, she was pretty sure she'd do anything for her. So she clutched the tie in both hands, bound no longer by silk but by Diana's request.

When Diana stepped away and Ronnie looked back, she was staring at Ronnie with a smile that seemed born from sheer delight at the power she held. It made Ronnie's blood run hot, hot enough that she almost wanted to go again.

But it wasn't her turn.

Diana moved calmly to the bench and pulled a handkerchief from her clutch. She wiped her fingers on it, took a deep breath, and unzipped her skirt.

Ronnie's eyebrows rose. Diana must have wanted to avoid a line. She wasn't wearing any underwear.

She stepped out of the circle of black fabric and settled onto the bench, crooking a finger at Ronnie. The motion made Ronnie stagger forward as though pulled by a string, and she sank to the floor between Diana's knees.

Diana threaded the fingers of one hand through Ronnie's hair, nails scratching at her scalp. The sensation made Ronnie's eyes flutter shut, but a gentle tug snapped them open again. Diana was watching her intently, pupils blown wide. "You'll tap me if it's too much?"

Of course. Diana had freed her hands because her mouth was about to be occupied. Forced to be.

Ronnie nodded eagerly and Diana hooked a leg over her shoulder, the heel of her flat digging into Ronnie's spine. Then Diana wrenched her forward, and she was helpless, unable to do anything but open her mouth and hang on.

It was exquisite. She knelt there and let Diana ride her face until her jaw ached—it was almost harder to beat back her moans now than it had been with Diana's fingers inside her. Soon, Diana's body went stiff and wet warmth spread down Ronnie's chin; the grip on her hair loosened, and she looked up to see Diana easing back onto the bench. She'd thrust the heel of her hand into her mouth, teeth sinking into the skin to keep herself quiet. Ronnie grinned.

"I think I underestimated your suit kink."

Diana lowered her hand and opened her eyes, arching a sardonic brow. "I am completely neutral on the subject of suits." She sat up, gazing down at Ronnie with a soft, almost sleepy expression. When she reached out to smooth Ronnie's disheveled hair, she added, "Depending on who's wearing them."

The qualification made Ronnie's ego swell more than a little. Then she remembered the tie, which she still held in a death grip. She relaxed, rolling her shoulders with a quiet grunt.

"Are you all right?" Diana asked. Ronnie nodded and Diana took her by the elbow, helping her to her feet. "Good." As she straightened, their eyes met. Diana scrubbed her thumb against Ronnie's chin. Then she let her fingertips rest on Ronnie's cheek, pulling her in for a kiss so fierce that, for a moment, Ronnie had trouble breathing.

When they parted, Ronnie blinked and looked down at the two of them. "Guess we need to get dressed."

"Guess so," Diana said, sounding amused. She stooped to gather up her skirt, wrinkled from where Ronnie had knelt on it. Ronnie yanked up her underwear, then started to slip out of the gray slacks.

"No, leave them on."

Ronnie glanced up. Diana was tucking her blouse in, smoothing the creases in her sleeves. "Petra will need to pin it, for tailoring."

Ronnie frowned. "No, she won't." Even as she argued, she pulled up the pants and fixed her own shirt. "You're not buying it, remember?"

Diana studied her, then stepped forward and took her by the shoulders, turning her toward the mirror. There was a smear of makeup on the glass where Ronnie's face had been pressed against it, but Ronnie ignored that and concentrated on her reflection. The suit was a little more rumpled than it had been when Ronnie first put it on, but the gray and teal complemented each other and both sat well against Ronnie's skin. Diana peered over Ronnie's shoulder at her, eyes sparkling. "You look good," she hummed. "Don't you think so?"

As a matter of fact, Ronnie did think so. She ran a hand through her mussed hair. "Well, yeah."

Diana gave a quiet laugh, a warm puff of air that tickled Ronnie's neck. "Yeah." She ran her hands down Ronnie's arms, squeezing them. "Do you trust me?"

Considering what had just happened, Ronnie would have thought that was obvious. But she nodded anyway and Diana echoed the gesture.

Once they were as presentable as they could get, they made their way up the hall to the circle of mirrors. If Petra had any idea why they'd been shut away for so long, she didn't say. *Maybe she's discreet*, Ronnie thought. *Or jaded. Or stupid.*

Petra pinned and measured, following Diana's directions as to the way the suit should sit on Ronnie's body. Diana had wrapped the tie around her hand, idly stroking it as she watched. Petra must have noticed too, because she nodded toward it. "You didn't like the tie?"

"Not with this," Diana said. "But I'll take it. Bill it to my account."

Now why in the world do you have an account here? Diana had said she'd never been here before, and suits weren't her style anyway—for wearing, at least. Ronnie's blood ran a little hot at the idea that she might have opened an account specifically for today.

Petra nodded and stuck a final pin in the cuff of the shirt before stepping away. She surveyed Ronnie with a satisfied expression, then waved a hand at her. "All right, take it all off. Mind the pins."

As Ronnie stepped off the dais, she glanced at Diana. She was going to drop the act and tell Petra the truth, wasn't she? But Diana just smiled and stayed quiet, running her thumb over the tie. So Ronnie sighed and traipsed back to the dressing room.

She removed the suit, gingerly returning it to its hanger and changing into her own clothes. As fun as this had been, she couldn't help the slight knot of tension in her gut. She hated to admit it, but they'd gotten incredibly lucky, not getting caught during their little tryst. And now Diana showed every sign of going through with this purchase. Ronnie technically couldn't stop her from buying anything, but that wasn't the point. If Diana was willing to ignore this rule, what others might she break?

What rules might Ronnie break right alongside her?

She thought of the way she'd submitted to Diana, the way her judgment had clouded for the sake of the thrill. She shivered and wasn't sure how much of it was from worry.

When she came out of room seven, she found Diana leaning against the wall opposite the door, scowling at her phone. She was surprised to feel her own misgivings melt into concern and heard herself asking, "You okay?"

Diana looked up and the scowl dissolved, a bright smile taking its place. "I'm fine. Are you ready? They're waiting up at the counter." She turned to go.

Enough was enough.

Ronnie took her by the arm. "Hey." Diana turned, brows up, eyes on Ronnie's hand. She didn't seem angry, but Ronnie let go anyway. "Come on, you said you wouldn't buy this."

"Oh, I'm not. You are."

She strode up the hall. Ronnie stared after her, then forced her body into motion, tripping along behind her. As they passed through the curtain, she hissed, "Listen, I like the suit, but I don't like it *that* much. I can't *afford* this." That wasn't strictly true, but it was easier than getting into her full philosophy on unnecessary spending.

"Don't worry, you don't pay until you pick it up."

They passed racks lined with suits, overcoats, even an entire wall dedicated to nothing but hats. As they approached the counter, Diana took the suit from Ronnie and looked up at her, expression unexpectedly earnest. "Trust me," she whispered again.

Before Ronnie knew what was happening, she was filling out the paperwork to set up an Ashworth's account of her own. Her whole world felt a little fuzzy. *What are you doing?* a voice at the edges of her mind chided. *This is* not *how things are supposed to work!* She silenced it with her signature, crossing the *t* of her surname with finality.

They finished up and made their way to the front of the shop, where Ronnie opened the door for Diana on instinct. She barely heard Diana's quiet thanks, and as soon as they were out on the sidewalk, Ronnie frowned at her. "Diana—"

Before she got any further, Diana pulled a slip of paper from her purse and handed it to Ronnie.

It was a personal check. "What—"

"You said I could give you a tip."

Ronnie was hardly modest, but even *she* wasn't sure she'd earned the amount she held in her hand right now. It was a lot of money— exactly enough, probably, for a nicely tailored suit from a midtown boutique.

When she glanced back up, Diana was watching her with a smile. "Now," she said, gaze wandering Ronnie's face, "have I broken any rules?"

Despite herself, Ronnie felt an answering grin sneaking onto her face. "No," she admitted. "I guess not." Diana stepped in close, face upturned invitingly, and Ronnie added, "You sure do know how to bend them, though."

Diana paused, something that looked a lot like doubt flashing across her features. "Do you mind?"

Ronnie thought about it. She thought about Diana's hot breath on her skin, about her eyes and that smile of hers, the one that made Ronnie's legs feel like fettuccine. She thought about how badly she'd wanted Diana to hire her again, how she'd never wanted that from any other client, ever. And she thought about Diana's mouth at her ear, whispering, *"Trust me."*

"No," she decided. "I don't mind."

A broad, relieved smile spread over Diana's face, and Ronnie nodded to her other hand, which held the boxed-up teal tie. "What are you gonna do with that?"

The Aston Martin pulled up to the curb and Diana quirked an eyebrow. "I'll hold on to it," she said as Skylar emerged. "Just in case." She and Ronnie held each other's gaze for another moment. Then she said, voice low, "See you next time."

Ronnie offered a little wave as Diana settled into the back seat, then watched the car disappear around the corner. As it did, she quietly echoed, "Next time."

CHAPTER 6
Taking Care of Yourself

The interview with *The Bayside Crier* was going well. The reporter, a young man with a patchy beard and a nose ring, had been nothing but respectful. Diana's mother had given answers that were clear and concise, sometimes even funny without sounding silly. She and the reporter spoke easily over the iced macchiatos Diana had bought for them.

Diana had set up the voice recorder on her phone and let them have at it. She was on her own this time; the appointment with the reporter had happened to coincide with a previously scheduled meeting with the graphic designer who was doing all the branding for the campaign. When they'd been trying to sort out who would go to what, Diana's mother had chimed in. *"No real decisions will need to be made at the interview. Evie should go deal with the graphics."*

It had been hard to take that comment as anything other than an insult. But Evie had seemed to readily agree, and Diana had told herself she was probably overreacting.

So now she was sitting in a quiet little coffee shop, at the other end of the table from her mother and the reporter, half listening to the interview. The other half of her brain was . . . otherwise occupied. It had been a couple of weeks since she'd met up with Ronnie at Ashworth's, but the details of the encounter were as sharp as if it had just happened. She couldn't help remembering the way Ronnie had surrendered to her, how she'd dropped to her knees without even being told, buried her face between Diana's legs like she was starved for it—

At the sound of her mother's laughter, her full attention snapped back to the moment. "That's true! That is so true!" Her mother laid a hand on the reporter's forearm. "You are a delight to talk to, Brandon. I really mean that."

Either it was Diana's imagination, or the reporter looked a bit unnerved at the physical contact. She didn't blame him. Her mother removed her hand, but Diana suspected it wasn't because she'd noticed his discomfort.

Brandon cleared his throat. "I wanted to touch a little bit on your views on education."

Diana's mother folded her hands around her half-empty cup. "Oh, education is so important," she said, voice appropriately serious. "Too many of our schools are understaffed and underfunded, and it breaks my heart. All those bright kids, and they don't have access to the resources they should." She took a sip of macchiato. "My daughter is in college right now, about to get a degree in marine biology, and she never would have gotten there if she hadn't been fortunate enough to get a good primary education. We have to invest in our schools if we want to invest in the future."

It took everything Diana had to govern her expression. She was as proud of Esther as anyone, but her mother spoke as if Esther was the only daughter she had.

After that, she had a hard time tuning in to the rest of the interview, now unable to even reminisce about Ronnie. All her energy was focused on not being visibly upset.

Fortunately, it didn't go on for much longer. Soon, Brandon thanked them for their time and told them the article ought to be up on the *Crier*'s site within a couple of days. He never said a word to Diana.

Skylar was waiting outside to drive the two of them back to the office. As soon as the door closed behind them, Diana's mother said, "Well! I think that went wonderfully, don't you?" She pulled her phone from her purse and started to check her email, apparently ignoring Diana's noncommittal hum. As she tapped and swiped, she added, "Did you record it like I told you to?"

Diana stared out the window, watching the city roll past. "Yes."

"The whole thing?"

"Yes."

"Good. I'll want Evie to hear it, see what she thinks. And this way we'll have insurance if they try to pull any libel stunts."

There was nothing Diana could say to that, so she kept quiet.

Her mother tweaked her knee. "What's the matter with you?"

She probably shouldn't get into this. It didn't really matter, in the grand scheme of things. But it nibbled at her mind, sharp little snakebites of indignation that wouldn't go away.

So she said, quietly, "You know, I went to college too, Mummy."

There was a pause. Then her mother laughed. "*That's* your grump?" She sounded amazed. "Your degree is in party planning."

Diana was very aware of a vein throbbing near her temple. "Hospitality management."

"It's the same thing, boo-boo," her mother said, her tone infuriatingly patient. "You wouldn't have wanted me to tell them that—it would have looked embarrassing next to Esther."

Finally, Diana turned to her. "If you think so little of my degree, why have I been the family's event manager for so long?"

Her mother sighed. "It's not that I don't think you're good at what you do," she explained. "You are. You're a wonderful little party planner. I wouldn't have hired you if you weren't." She reached into her purse, pulled out a compact, and touched up her powder as she spoke. "I'd like to hire Esther too, but she went into a field I can't use."

She snapped the compact shut and fixed Diana with a frank gaze. "I love my family. I want to keep them near me." Which was a nice sentiment, but she was still using her politician voice. "I like being able to keep an eye on you."

Diana's pulse skyrocketed, her eyebrows twitching upward before she could stop them, but her mother just gave a slippery sort of laugh. "You know what I mean. And I don't have to worry about you working for someone who'll underpay you or mistreat you or fire you. You don't have to worry, either." She smiled and patted Diana's knee. "Most parents send their children out into the world once they turn eighteen. I've never wanted to be that kind of parent."

She shrugged. "If your sister had to pick a career so unrelated to ours, I'm glad she picked something respectable. It's her own bad luck that she'll have to be self-sufficient."

Then she went back to her phone.

Diana turned to the window again, willing her heartbeat back into normalcy. *She didn't mean she was actually keeping an eye on you*, she told herself. As for the rest of it, there was a lot of truth to what her mother was saying, and it was at least nice to know that she thought Diana was good at her job.

She just couldn't help feeling that maybe Esther had had the right idea, and that maybe "self-sufficient" was her mother's nasty way of saying "free."

It was two weeks later, and Diana was running late.

It wasn't really her fault, but she hated it anyway. The streets between her mother's office and the Öde were clogged with traffic, and Skylar's phone informed her that, despite the standstill, they were on the fastest route to their destination. So she strode into the lobby twenty minutes past the agreed time, hoping the staff had let Ronnie into the penthouse.

A pleasant young woman at the front desk informed her that yes, they had given her guest a key, and that she had gone straight up. Then she cheerfully checked Diana in, gave her a key of her own, and told her not to hesitate to ask, should she need anything else.

Diana thanked her, but there was only one thing she needed right now.

She hadn't really had a moment of her own for almost a month. It was about time she had a night for herself, a night to unwind and forget about everything, if only for a little while.

And she knew just how she wanted to spend it.

When she opened the door to the penthouse, she thought that Ronnie wasn't there after all. Then she saw her, leaning against the far wall, gazing out the wide expanse of windows at the city skyline.

She wore a sky-blue button-up with the sleeves rolled to her elbows, hands in the pockets of her navy slacks. When Diana entered, she turned, a smile spreading across her face.

Diana's breath caught.

"There you are." Ronnie shouldered away from the window.

Diana returned the smile, trying to steady herself. "Afraid I wasn't coming?"

A smirk tugged at the corner of Ronnie's lips, and Diana got the distinct impression that she was beating back a lewd comment. But all she said was, "Never been stood up yet." She circled the sofa, eyes trained on Diana's face. Diana didn't move. Maybe if she let Ronnie come to her, she wouldn't look too desperate.

Then Ronnie was right there, all loose collar and cocksure grin, and Diana let herself fold into her arms.

She had never really thought of kissing as a *skill*, something that could be perfected and performed with intent or precision. But Ronnie was excellent at it. She tilted her head at just the right angle, applied and released pressure in even turns, and—yes, there, the barest hint of teeth on Diana's bottom lip. *This must be what comes of dealing with a professional.*

As Diana was trying to decide what sort of mint Ronnie's mouth tasted like, Ronnie's fingertips brushed her jaw, moving almost carefully up her neck and into her hair. The movement sent a pleasant shiver up Diana's spine; she tightened her grip on Ronnie's shirt and arched into the touch, surprised at the quiet groan that escaped Ronnie's throat when she did. Was that something else she'd honed over the years, that reaction, that eagerness? Was each draw of erratic breath carefully calculated to give the best impression of desire? Ronnie's attentions wandered slowly, her lips trailing down Diana's throat, eyelashes fluttering against her cheek.

Did she kiss *all* her clients like this?

Probably.

Diana was wrenched from that disheartening train of thought by Ronnie's voice close to her ear. "So, what are you in the mood for tonight?"

She honestly hadn't thought that far ahead, and Ronnie was making it increasingly hard to concentrate—the hand not wound in Diana's hair was smoothing down the curve of her hip, the heat beneath that palm muddling Diana's thoughts.

Which might have been why she said, "Let's start by getting naked."

Ronnie laughed and Diana felt like a fool, but then she pulled back, a gleam in her eye. "Well, all right, then."

She leaned in again, both hands now at the zipper of Diana's dress, pulling it down with slow deliberation. Diana responded in kind, fingers flying to the buttons of Ronnie's shirt. She'd gotten three undone before she noticed Ronnie had paused. She looked up to see Ronnie gazing at her with a strangely thoughtful expression. "What is it?"

Ronnie shook her head. "I just realized that this is the first time I've actually gotten to undress you."

Gotten to, like she was unwrapping a present. Diana's cheeks went warm and she replied, a bit breathlessly, "Then what are you waiting for?"

With a wicked smile, Ronnie stopped waiting.

They shed clothes on their way to the bedroom, pausing only to rid themselves of whatever piece came next. Beneath Ronnie's shirt, Diana found a sheer black bandeau that left very little to the imagination. When Diana dipped her head to ruin it with lips and tongue and teeth, Ronnie hissed and grabbed her by the hips, pulling the pair of them against the hallway wall. Her fingers slipped past the band of Diana's underwear, grabbing two handfuls of her backside and giving it an emphatic squeeze. Diana laughed faintly and sank her teeth into wet lace, making Ronnie whimper.

By the time they made it to the bed, Ronnie was entirely undressed and Diana wore only her briefs. When Ronnie reached for them, Diana pushed her hands away and took her by the chin, lifting her face until her bewildered eyes met Diana's steady gaze.

Diana didn't get many opportunities to make her own decisions these days. But she could take charge here.

"I don't think so," she said, pleased at the command in her voice. "Not yet."

Ronnie's nostrils flared. Then she smiled, lifted her hands, and stepped away. Pleasure-tinged relief surged through Diana all the way to her core. *She understands.*

Diana cast around the room, looking for ideas, and saw an armchair near the vanity. "Lie down on the bed," she told Ronnie, crossing to the chair. She turned it to face the bed, so that Ronnie was visible but still a respectable distance away, and sat. Ronnie lay on her side, propped up on her elbow, watching Diana curiously. "If you want me," Diana continued, hoping this wasn't an idiotic thing to say to an escort, "you'll need to earn me."

One of Ronnie's eyebrows twitched. "Yes, miss."

Oh God. Diana took a deep, measured breath and crossed her legs. Had someone taught Ronnie to respond that way, or did it come naturally? In the end, it didn't really matter; all that mattered was the effect it had on Diana's body, the drumming heat it stoked low in her belly. She laid her hands on the slope of the chair's armrests and raised her chin, feeling like a queen on her throne.

With Ronnie to rule. Her groin throbbed.

"I want to see you come."

Ronnie narrowed her eyes, but was still grinning.

"I want you to prove that you know what you're doing," Diana explained. "Touch yourself the way you'd touch me."

It was complete nonsense, of course. They were both well aware that Ronnie knew what she was doing. But Ronnie's gaze dragged down Diana's body, and she lay back obediently, offering Diana a tantalizing side view of her naked form, and closed her eyes.

She started slowly, running her hands up and down her torso, back arching ever so slightly. Pausing to flick her thumbs over her nipples with a quiet hiss, she then gave both of them a sharp pinch and groaned. Diana's breasts ached in sympathy.

Ronnie's splayed hands moved again, dipping down to massage her inner thighs. She still hadn't properly touched herself yet, but her hips surged up off the bed as if of their own accord, as though seeking out the pressure currently being denied. Just as Diana was about to say something—to insist, maybe, that she give herself some relief for God's sake—Ronnie's fingers disappeared between her legs and she gave a rough, deep-throated moan. Diana's chest tightened and she gripped the arms of the chair.

"Yes," Ronnie whispered, more a sigh than a word. She shifted, half rolling back onto her side toward Diana and pulling one knee up to spread her legs wider. Diana felt a rush of warmth between her own legs at the sight and squirmed, trying to relieve some of the ache without being too obvious. Ronnie's new position gave her a much better view of the proceedings, and she suspected that was exactly the intent. She could also see Ronnie's face fully now: brows drawn tight over her closed eyes, cheeks flushed, lips parted. One cheek was pressed against the duvet, her hair falling across her forehead. She growled out a word that was almost certainly profane.

Then the melodic trill of Diana's cell phone drifted in from the living room.

Ronnie kept moving, two fingers deep, the steady press of a palm, other hand busy at her breast. She was panting quietly now, and when she drew her hand away before pushing her fingers back inside, the extent of her arousal was obvious.

Diana tried to block out the sound as well, but had a harder time of it. She set her jaw.

You don't have *to answer,* she told herself. She was thirty-four years old; she was allowed to ignore a call if she so chose. There was no one she wanted to talk to right now anyway. She breathed evenly, in through her nose, out through her mouth, and eventually the ringing ended. Ronnie was writhing, her jaw slack, the pace of her hand picking up speed.

When her eyes fluttered open to meet Diana's, Diana barely kept herself from making an embarrassing noise. Ronnie's pupils were huge, her gaze simmering as she watched Diana watching her. For an instant, she looked nothing but sure of herself, triumphant at the obvious effect she was having. Then the insolence was replaced by something else, something almost like desperation, and Diana realized she was about to come.

"Stop."

Ronnie gave a strangled groan but obeyed. Her hand went still even as her chest heaved; her jaw was taut, teeth gritted behind her lips, eyes sparking with frustration. She was magnificent like this, teetering on the brink, dependent on Diana's word.

Diana felt dizzy. "Beautiful," she breathed. Then: "Do you want to come?"

"Yes." Ronnie's voice creaked like a rope pulled taut.

Diana rose, slowly circling around to the foot of the bed. When she reached it, she stood there, considering the sight before her. Ronnie was on her back again, spread open and waiting. Diana let her gaze wander, then wet her lips, forming her next word very deliberately. "Beg."

With a rough exhale, Ronnie's neck went slack, her head falling against the pillow beneath it as she whispered, "Please."

"Please what?"

"Oh God." Her spine arched, but her hand remained dutifully still. "Please." When she raised her head, her eyes locked with Diana's. "Please let me come."

Diana smiled. For another moment she stood in silence, then gave a minute nod.

Ronnie began to move again, moaning with relief. It didn't take long—a few more frenzied thrusts, a blur of wrist and fingers, and a cry tore from her throat as she pitched over the edge. Diana stared, hands planted on her hips to keep herself from doing anything else. Her breath was uneven, the desire pulsing between her thighs almost painful, and once Ronnie touched her, she wouldn't last long. But she made herself stay there, because her own discipline was just as important as Ronnie's, if not more so.

Still, it wasn't easy.

Once the seizing waves subsided, Ronnie sank back onto the duvet, heaving an almost comically loud sigh. She pulled her hand away and lay there, slick and sated and possibly one of the most enthralling things Diana had ever seen.

Then Ronnie took a slightly steadier breath and lifted her head with a smirk. "Think that'll do?"

Diana was tempted to end things there, teach her a lesson about overconfidence in a submissive. But Ronnie had had her fun, so the only person who'd go unsatisfied would be Diana. And Diana was positively panting for it.

So she made a perfunctory show of considering, then said, "I suppose."

Ronnie's face lit up. Diana slithered out of her briefs, then gave in to temptation and ran her lips up Ronnie's body to her face. The moment their mouths met, she found herself locked in Ronnie's arms and melted into the sensation, reveling in Ronnie's apparent attempt to envelop her completely. As she was running her fingers through

Ronnie's hair and sucking on her lower lip, she could swear she heard music.

Wait. Not music. Not exactly.

A ringtone.

Son of a bitch. Diana pulled away, scowling.

Beneath her, Ronnie squirmed and grinned, brow furrowing. "Is that important?"

Diana might have been wrong, but she thought she heard, behind that question, another: *Is that more important than me?*

Because it was safer, Diana answered the one she'd actually heard. "It . . . might be," she admitted, grimacing and rolling off of Ronnie. Ronnie grunted quietly, out of either discomfort or annoyance. So when Diana glanced back at her, she added, "I'm sorry," apologizing for both.

But Ronnie shook her head, offering an amiable shrug. "You're fine."

With no regard for clothing, Diana padded down the hall to the sitting room and rummaged through her discarded clothes for her phone. By the time she found it, it had mercifully stopped screaming at her.

Her father answered after one ring, "Hi, baby, we were starting to get worried."

A string of lies flashed through Diana's mind: *I'm at the movies, my phone was on silent, the call didn't come through.* She closed her eyes, silently puffing out her cheeks, and said only, "Sorry, Daddy. What's wrong?"

"Oh, nothing." Theo Silver had a basso profundo voice that he'd never bothered learning to bridle; speaking with him on the phone was something of a trial. "You busy?"

Diana peered down the hallway. What she thought was, *I'd like to be.* What she said was, "Not really."

"Need a favor." Of course. "Stephanie Maurer is doing a recital tonight—you remember her, plays violin?"

"Viola, I think."

"Whatever. And she invited us last minute, said to bring the family. Might be a good opportunity for your mom to shake hands."

Honestly, was there anything these days that her parents *didn't* consider an opportunity to shake hands?

"It's at the Monte Blanco." He had this way of saying things with finality, as though answering a question that hadn't been asked about an agreement that hadn't been reached. "Doesn't start until eight, so you've got a little while to get ready."

Very generous. Diana bit back a sigh. "All right."

"Just a second." Her mother's voice pierced the distance behind her father, a wheedling tone with no recognizable words. When her father returned to the phone, he added, "Mom says to let you know that Evie'll be there."

Oh for God's sake. "All right," she said again, hoping she didn't sound as irritated as she felt. "I'll be there." She didn't really have a choice.

"Knew you would. Love you."

"Love you too."

She ended the call and checked her phone. Ten to seven. Just enough time to get home, get dressed, and get across town to the Monte Blanco. Diana let out a long breath, tapping the phone against her forehead.

"Everything okay?"

Diana turned to see Ronnie standing at the mouth of the hallway. She was still naked and a little mussed, wearing a guarded expression. Even through her annoyance, Diana felt a mild rush at the sight of all that skin. "Everything's fine," she said. Ronnie's eyes stayed fixed on her face, but Diana was aware of her own nudity in a way she hadn't been before. She looked down at her phone. "I have to go."

All Ronnie said at first was "Oh." Diana thought she sounded disappointed, but when she glanced back up, the escort was only nodding considerately. "I'll call the office," she went on, gaze wandering the trail of their clothes on the floor. "I may be able to swing you a refund."

"A refund?"

"Well, sure." Ronnie crossed her arms over her bare chest with a shrug. "I mean, you paid for a service you won't be getting."

Don't I know it. "I paid for a hotel room that I won't be using too," Diana pointed out. "I don't mind."

Ronnie drifted toward her. "I guess you've got a lot going on," she said, showing a talent for understatement. Diana inclined her head in acknowledgment and Ronnie went on: "Are you doing okay? I mean . . ." She drew up her shoulders in an inquisitive gesture. "Are you taking care of yourself?"

The idea of Ronnie thinking about her well-being made heat rise both in Diana's face and farther down. "When I can," she answered. It was a diplomatic response.

Ronnie nodded but didn't look terribly convinced. She drew in close and brushed Diana's throat with her fingertips, her other hand sliding around her waist. "Don't let 'em run you too ragged."

Diana didn't want to be pulled back in but couldn't help it; suddenly her free hand was tangled in Ronnie's messy hair and she was kissing her hard, barely fighting the urge to wrap a leg around her. It wasn't exactly dignified.

"Do you have to go right now?" Ronnie asked, hand sliding down Diana's hip and between her legs. Diana gasped and bit at her jaw and Ronnie added, a little smugly, "I don't think it'd take long."

God, it was tempting.

But Diana's phone was heavy in her other hand: a cold, hard reminder of obligation. "I can't," she groaned. Ronnie paused, then drew away, clearing her throat. "Next time I'll make sure we aren't interrupted," Diana promised. Then she felt like an idiot—as long as Ronnie got paid, why would she care what Diana did?

But Ronnie grinned and nodded. "Good." Her eyes flicked down to Diana's lips and for a moment Diana thought she might start kissing her again, almost hoped she would. Instead, Ronnie released her and bent down to retrieve Diana's dress from the floor. "Here," she said, offering it to her. "I'll grab the rest." Then she ambled down the hallway.

Diana stared after her, then sighed and looked at her phone, pulling up her messages to text Skylar. She loved her parents, she really did.

But, just at that moment, she didn't like them very much.

Once Ronnie had rounded up all their things, they dressed together in the sitting room. As Diana was smoothing her dress down over her hips, she glanced at Ronnie, who was doing up the last button of her shirt. "You can stay if you want," she said. "*Someone* ought to take advantage of the room."

Ronnie cut her eyes toward her and somehow Diana already knew she was going to reject her offer. "I don't think I'm classy enough to stay here by myself." She flipped down her collar. "Thanks, though."

"Of course." Diana stepped toward her and raised a hand, smoothing Ronnie's wayward hair as best she could.

"Thanks," Ronnie said again, softer this time.

Diana nodded mutely, biting back a sudden urge to kiss her goodbye. If she did, she might not be able to talk herself out of staying.

So she said, "I'll see you later," and walked away on legs made of lead. She wouldn't turn around, couldn't stand seeing Ronnie all tousled and tempting. She didn't want to think about the dull, distant ache in her groin, the promise of release never fulfilled. It would die before long.

CHAPTER 7
The Triangle

Nobody was opening their door. Diana wasn't surprised. She'd seen more than one security camera, and her current outfit—jeans, a clipboard, and a T-shirt emblazoned with *SILVER FOR THE CITY*—screamed *soliciting*. She probably wouldn't open the door for her either. On the other side of the street, Evie didn't seem to be having much better luck.

They were going from house to house, using something Diana's mother called "the triangle." Diana and Evie were supposed to speak with anyone who answered, giving out literature and letting them know that Maggie Silver was on-hand right now to address any questions or concerns they might have.

Which meant her mother was strolling down the middle of the road like she owned it. She looked good, wearing one of the more business-casual ensembles Diana had found during her shopping trip. Her posture hadn't lost any of the confidence she'd had when they started, but Diana could tell she was getting peevish.

"Are you sure you're knocking loudly enough?" she asked when she approached Diana and gestured briskly for her water bottle. After taking a sip, she added, "Maybe they can't hear you. Don't be afraid to make some noise!"

Before Diana could suggest that going out of her way to disturb constituents at home might not be a great tactic, Evie called: "Maggie!"

They turned to see her waving at them from an open door, where an elderly woman stood peering across the lawn at them. "This lady's got a couple of questions!" Evie added.

Diana's mother thrust the water bottle at her, muttering, "Finally," before heading in that direction. Diana didn't even have to see her face to know that she'd already plastered on a smile.

Sighing, Diana returned the bottle to her bag, which was heavy with flyers, buttons, yard signs, spare pens and pads, and makeup so her mother could retouch if needed. Evie had offered to carry the bag, but Diana's mother had insisted that Diana didn't mind.

While Diana's mother chatted with the old lady, Evie shaded her brow and threw Diana a little wave. Diana waved back. Evie tilted her head and offered a thumbs-up, as though asking how she was doing.

Diana's feet hurt. She was hot and she was tired and they had at least six more blocks to walk before they could head back to Evie's car. She felt like a child, allowing her petulant complaints to bully their way to the front of her brain, but she couldn't help it.

That was a bit much to convey with hand gestures, though. So Diana just returned the thumbs-up.

At the end of the street, they found a pocket park, and the three of them settled onto a bench, Evie in the middle. When Diana let the strap of her bag flop unceremoniously to the ground, Evie leaned over and asked quietly, "Doing all right?"

"Nobody answers the door anymore!" Diana's mother groused before Diana could answer. "What happened to neighborliness?"

Evie chuckled and lifted her ponytail, fanning the back of her neck with a flyer. "Maybe that could be a talking point during your next speech. A return to a sense of community."

"Hmph." Diana's mother leaned forward, frowning past Evie at her. "Where's the water, boo-boo?"

Evie glanced at Diana from the corner of her eye, grinning. Diana could have died—she hated that nickname, she always had. She'd been fourteen when she'd finally asked her mother to retire it. Her mother had laughed, pinched her cheek, and replied, *"But you* are *my little boo-boo!"*

She'd been seventeen before she'd finally realized it was a saccharine way of saying she hadn't been planned.

She reached into her bag and silently passed her mother the water bottle, trying not to fume.

"Oh, don't be mad," her mother teased. "Evie had to hear it sometime!"

"I won't use it," Evie added. She was still grinning.

Thankfully, Diana's phone chose that moment to start ringing. She pulled it from the bag as well, and relief washed over her when she caught sight of three exclamation points on the screen. Hauling herself off the bench, she headed for the small nearby playground, hoping for at least a little privacy.

The last thing she heard her mother say was, "She can be such a grump. She needs someone to help her lighten up."

Diana sank onto one of the swings and swiped the screen. "Hello."

"Hey, chickadee! Whatcha doing?"

How could Phoebe have so much energy when Diana was so tired?

"We're trying to reach the voters in Broadhurst." Diana sighed. "The voters in Broadhurst do not want to be reached."

Phoebe gave a sympathetic coo. "That blows a big one. I was gonna see if you wanted to grab lunch and a mani-pedi, but I guess not."

"Oh, I'd *like* to." Diana rocked on her heels, lightly pushing the swing back and forth. "But we'll be out here for most of the afternoon, and then Mummy wants to try Laurel Ridge."

"Wow, you're hitting all the fancy burbs."

Diana hummed. "I *have* noticed that we've been avoiding anything south of Fifty-seventh."

"Well, good luck," Phoebe said. In the background there was a rumbling baritone, and Phoebe's voice grew slightly distant. "Shoosh, I'm on the phone." Full volume again. "Sorry, he just woke up."

"Quite all right," Diana said, smiling for the first time that day. "Go take care of whoever he is and send me pictures of your nails once you're done."

"Obvy. Call me if you ever get a break. Love you!"

"Love you too." Diana lowered the phone and sighed again. A pedicure sounded like heaven right about now.

She looked up to see Evie walking toward her, bag slung over one shoulder. Her mother was nowhere in sight. "Where's Mummy?" she asked, standing and brushing swing dirt off the seat of her jeans.

Evie tilted her head in the general direction of the street. "Getting my car. She's going to start driving instead of walking."

Diana's hackles raised. She forced them back down, but couldn't keep from muttering, "That must be nice."

"No kidding, right?" Evie chuckled and offered the bag to her. Diana considered asking if she'd mind carrying it for a while after all, but could already hear her mother chastising her for "making Evie do all the work." So she took it. "It makes sense, though," Evie added as the two of them started toward the next block. "If she does need to talk to somebody, this way she won't be all sweaty and gross."

"Like us," Diana pointed out.

"Well, like me. You look fine." Evie glanced at her. "Who was that on the phone? If you don't mind saying."

Diana shrugged. Why would she mind? "My friend Phoebe. She wanted to do lunch."

"Friend?"

Something about the way Evie said it prompted Diana to turn. Evie's gaze was aimed stalwartly straightforward, her expression neutral, but it was almost as if she was consciously trying to keep it that way.

Surely she didn't think . . .?

"Friend," Diana reiterated, hoping her tone made it clear that that was all there was to her relationship with Phoebe. The idea of anything else was laughably bizarre. And why did it even matter?

"Sorry you're not going to be able to meet up with her," Evie said. They'd reached the top of the block, but hadn't yet separated to their respective sides of the street. "Maybe we can grab a bite once we're done in Laurel Ridge."

With a low rumble, the BMW rounded the corner. Diana's mother seemed perfectly collected behind the wheel—which was impressive, since her mother's driving license was almost a formality. The car pulled up next to them. Evie's back was to the street, so she didn't see the way Diana's mother watched them with undisguised intrigue.

"Mummy's already got me doing up another message for the mailing list," Diana said. "We've gotten a few more subscribers."

Evie nodded, then frowned. "You are going to eat at some point, right?"

"Surely we'll have something while we're working on the email," Diana said. There was nothing sure about it—both of her parents had a history of working through lunch—but she'd eat eventually.

Evie didn't look convinced. "Listen," she said with a tentative step forward. Diana fought the urge to step back. "You've been working hard lately. Maybe you should take a break."

An acidic chuckle escaped from the cracks in Diana's throat. "Believe me, I don't think Mummy will be keen on that."

"I'll talk to her." Evie's voice was firm. "I always appreciate your help, really, but I'm sure we could do without you for a couple of days."

"What about you?" Diana asked.

Evie smiled. "I'm much more used to this kind of thing." Her gaze leaped briefly aside, indicating the car. "Maybe not quite *this* much legwork, but still." When Diana opened her mouth to apologize on her mother's behalf, Evie waved her off. "It's fine; I promise I don't mind. She pays well, and I actually think she may do a good job on the council. But she could loosen up on you a little."

Diana almost felt guilty for agreeing, however privately.

"I'll talk to her," Evie said again. "Now come on, let's knock on some doors." With that, she jogged across the street, starting up the sidewalk to the first house.

Diana looked toward the car. Through the driver's-side window, her mother shot her an exaggerated wink and an OK sign. Diana didn't return the gesture; its meaning was obvious enough in this context, and she didn't want to do anything that might imply that her mother's plan was working.

So she just turned, rearranged the bag's strap on her shoulder, and headed up the drive. This was a tiring, tedious task, but she might be better able to bear it if it came with the possibility of having a weekend off.

Especially since she knew exactly who she wanted to spend it with.

CHAPTER 8
What I Want

When Ronnie breezed into the Night Life office, the papers on the front desk rustled, and Stacy turned with a heavy sigh. Ignoring that, Ronnie whipped around her desk to grab one of the butterscotch candies Stacy kept in a bowl near her monitor. (*"You're like a grandma,"* Ronnie had once told her, *"but cuter."*)

"Checking in," Ronnie chirped. Before she could comment on her own outfit—tonight's client wanted her in black, and the dress's hemline was barely decent—she noticed that Stacy had turned back to her screen and was glowering at it. "You okay?"

Stacy blinked up at her, expression clearing. "Oh yeah, my bad. Just . . ." She glanced toward the door that led to the inner offices. "I was trying to finish up my essay and Karla bitched me out."

Ronnie frowned. "Why?"

"I don't—!" Stacy seemed to realize she'd raised her voice and dropped it midsentence. "—know. There was nobody in the lobby, the phone wasn't ringing, I'm done with the week's schedule. I don't know." She propped her elbows up on the desk and rubbed her temples. "This paper's due tonight, and I don't get off till ten."

"I'm sorry," Ronnie said, leaning one-hipped against the desk. "That sucks."

"Yeah," Stacy sighed. "It does." She shook her head again, clearing the cobwebs of irritation, and straightened in her chair. "*Anyway*," she said, yanking a red folder from a stack by the candy bowl, "Princess Charming called."

Everything else fled from Ronnie's mind and she perked up. "Diana?" It had been almost a month since the job at Ashworth's, and she'd be lying if she said Diana hadn't crossed her mind once or twice.

A day.

She tilted toward Stacy, peering at the folder. "What'd she say?"

Stacy rolled her dark eyes in good-natured ridicule. "You're a puppy dog. It's sad."

"I am in no way like a puppy dog. Unless I happen to be wearing a collar." *Maybe Diana wants me to wear a collar. I am one hundred percent okay with that.* She reached for the folder. "Gimme, gimme."

Stacy held the folder to her chest and leaned away with a mischievous smirk. "And you do tricks," she pointed out. "My God, you've got it bad!"

"Look," Ronnie huffed, "Diana is two things: gorgeous and loaded. That's literally the best possible scenario for me." Diana was also sweet and soft and elegant, but Stacy didn't need to know all that. Ronnie unwrapped the butterscotch and popped it into her mouth, speaking around it. "Not that I have to explain myself to you."

"Uh-huh." Stacy studied her for another second, then flipped open the folder and pulled out a few sheets of paper. "I'm glad you like her," she said airily, examining the contract. "She requested our weekend package."

Ronnie sucked thoughtfully on the candy. "We don't have a weekend package."

"We do now." Stacy nudged Ronnie off the desk and spread the contract out. "Karla had the terms drawn up just before lunch. Check out the last page."

"Holy shit, that's a lot of money."

"Don't get excited, Karla gets half of it."

Ronnie's gaze jerked away from the bottom line. "What!?"

Stacy shrugged. "That's what it says. She had legal add a clause or something." She scanned the text upside-down and tapped a paragraph with one black polished nail. "There."

A frown crept across Ronnie's face as she read. It wasn't really the loss of money that annoyed her. She always made way more than she spent. It was the principle of the thing that niggled at her.

Karla had gotten a little something extra for that first unconventional arrangement with Phoebe. At the time, Ronnie hadn't thought much about it. But now there was this, an entirely new kind of contract, one that included (if Ronnie was reading the legalese right) going to somebody's *house*. Rules were getting bent all over the place here, all for a few extra zeros in Karla's pocket.

How often did this happen?

"So?" Stacy said, shaking Ronnie out of her thoughts as she offered her a pen. "What do you think?"

Ronnie took it. "If this was anybody but Diana," she said, jabbing it at Stacy for emphasis, "I'd say no."

Stacy considered her with a lopsided grin. "I believe it." She watched Ronnie scrawl her signature across the contract, then swept the papers into a stack, tapping their edges against the desk. "Now get out of here. You've got a stupidly short dress to flaunt."

Ronnie gently chucked the pen at her and swept away. "And great legs to show off. Good luck on your paper."

The last thing she heard before the door closed behind her was Stacy's skeptical laugh. And, just maybe, a muttered, "Thanks, puppy dog."

A week later, Ronnie headed up to the thirtieth floor of the Hotel Öde as usual, with a couple of notable differences. It was her earliest job ever—not quite ten in the morning—and her outfit was casual, just a lightweight pink sweater over leggings. Nice, but simple. She also had a duffel bag slung over one shoulder. She'd packed pretty light—it was only two days, after all, and clothing probably wouldn't be very high on Diana's list of priorities.

Why they were meeting here for a housebound job, Ronnie had no idea. But oh well.

When she'd checked in at Night Life earlier, Karla had marched her back into her office and shut the door behind them. "Listen," she'd said, her clipped tone making the words sound like the snap of a rubber band, "obviously I don't want you getting hurt or whatever. If you feel unsafe, you can walk out. I've handled bigger names than Little Miss Fancypants; if she throws a fit, we can give her a refund."

Then she'd taken Ronnie by the shoulder, her eyes drilling into Ronnie's. "But this is a big deal. It's the most I've ever made on a single escort. So try not to be a chickenshit about it."

Ronnie wasn't a chickenshit, and she didn't plan on walking out. Still, the nebulous worry she'd felt upon signing the contract hadn't gone away. Ronnie couldn't imagine feeling unsafe with Diana, but what if, someday, someone else offered Karla a similar deal? Someone a little less friendly? Never in all her time with Night Life had Ronnie thought about the possibility of walking out, but if Karla tried to pull something...

Stepping off the elevator, she shook her head and sniffed. This was not the time to think about what might happen later on down the road. Right now, she was on a job. She needed to focus on the client. She knocked on the penthouse door and adjusted her grip on the duffel's strap.

The door opened, and focusing on the client got a whole lot easier.

Diana was as dressed down as Ronnie had ever seen her: dark jeans, a button-up that matched her eyes, hair swept back in a low ponytail. She looked incredible, and the smile that lit up her face when she saw Ronnie only made her look better.

Ronnie grinned. "Two days?"

"Trust me," Diana said, rolling her eyes, "I need the time off."

Dropping her bag by the door, Ronnie slid past Diana. "That bad, huh?" she asked, leaning against the sofa.

If Diana's heavy sigh was anything to go by, it was that bad and worse. "If I hand out one more button, I may scream. My mother didn't even really want me gone for the weekend." She crossed her arms over her chest and stared hard at the floor. "The only reason I'm here at all is because her campaign manager talked her into it."

"Y'know," Ronnie mused with a frown, drumming her fingers on the sofa's back, "the more I hear about your mom, the less I like her."

Diana glanced up, eyes wide, then averted her gaze as her cheeks darkened slightly. "I make her sound much worse than she is. Not many people get to work for their parents and actually use their degree, especially earning what I do. I shouldn't be ungrateful."

Before Ronnie could reply, Diana's sour expression disappeared, replaced with a bright smile. "But I do need a break. So here you are."

"Here I am," Ronnie agreed. She moved forward to slip her arms around Diana's waist. "For the next two days, you answer to nobody," she murmured, ghosting her lips over Diana's. "And I answer to you."

Diana kissed her, and Ronnie found herself tightening her grip as if by instinct. A strange feeling boiled in her stomach, something she couldn't quite name. It seemed vaguely familiar, like something she'd felt before but in a different context. She got a hold on it for a second, but then Diana nipped at her bottom lip and the thought scampered away.

Ronnie had gotten Diana's shirt half-unbuttoned before the other woman pulled away with a quiet, breathless laugh. "Wait, wait," she said, taking Ronnie's hands in hers. When she opened her eyes, they were dark with desire and a little glazed, but quickly cleared. "We can't do this right now, we have to go."

"Oh yeah." Ronnie's mouth screwed into a twist of disappointment. "I saw something in the contract about a private residence."

"Mm, my parents' lake house." Diana drifted away to do up her shirt. "Is that all right?"

Ronnie ran a hand through her hair. "I wouldn't be here if it wasn't. I mean, it's new, sure. But if it's gonna happen, I'm glad it's with you."

"What do you mean?"

"Just, usually it's not allowed. House calls." As she spoke, Ronnie gathered up her bag and looked around for Diana's. "It's a liability nightmare. Karla only agreed to it because the money was so good." She found a rolling carry-on leaning against the front of the sofa and pulled up its handle.

Turning back, she was surprised to see Diana's penetrative gaze fixed on her face, lips pursed. "Does that happen a lot?"

Ronnie opened her mouth to say *No, of course it doesn't*. Then she remembered her own worries and shrugged. "I don't know."

"Do you *want* to go? We can stay here if you don't. That's why I booked the room, just in case." Diana's voice was small, uncertain, her brow drawn tight.

The look on her face made Ronnie's gut twist. "Sure," she said softly, abandoning the luggage for the moment. She stepped in close, tucking back a lock of Diana's hair that had sprung free from its ponytail. "Like I said, I wouldn't be here otherwise."

On an impulse, she brushed her lips against Diana's forehead. When she pulled back, Diana's worried expression had been replaced by one of genuine wonder.

Ronnie cleared her throat and grabbed the bags again. Her gut was still twisted, less like a knot now and more like a pretzel: soft, warm. She had no idea what to do with the feeling. "Guess we better go."

"Yes." Diana blinked, like she was trying to wake up, and turned to the door.

Back in the elevator, Diana glanced at her. "I should have asked earlier, can you drive?"

Her tone was lighter, closer to normal. Ronnie was glad. "Sure. Why?"

"I had Skylar leave the car with the valet."

"She's not coming with us?"

Diana gave her a playful, sidelong smile. "Did you want her to?"

Ronnie thought of the chauffeur's perpetually deadpan face and bad attitude. "Nah."

"I thought not." Diana's eyes dragged down her body. "I'd rather have you all to myself." Her eyes lingered somewhere below the hem of Ronnie's sweater. "I like the leggings."

Grinning, Ronnie popped one hip toward her. "I bet."

Just then, the elevator eased to a stop, the door sliding open to admit a veritable gaggle of hotel guests. They all had luggage and they were all loud-mouthed and pushy. *Tourists*, Ronnie despaired as she and Diana were shunted aside unceremoniously to make room.

She opened her mouth to protest, but whatever she was going to say fizzled out in her throat at the feeling of warm hands at her waist. She glanced over her shoulder.

In the fracas, Diana had gotten pressed into a corner. Ronnie had been pushed in the same direction, and now found herself with her back to Diana's front, the pair of them nearly crushed together. Ronnie could feel the gentle pressure of Diana's breasts below her shoulder blades and the heat of one hand as it slid to her hip.

She snapped around to face the front. The vague arousal from earlier flared up again in full force, growing as the hand finally crept between them to knead at Ronnie's backside. Diana's quiet breath tickled the hairs at the nape of Ronnie's neck as she explored, making Ronnie's skin tingle. Ronnie was dimly aware of a suitcase digging into her knee, but that feeling was eclipsed somewhere around the third floor, when Diana's fingers dipped dangerously low.

The elevator stopped again, the display finally reading *G*, and the tourists spilled out as soon as the doors opened, still chattering among themselves.

Ronnie moved more slowly, in no hurry to give up their current position. She edged away from Diana and stuck an arm across the elevator's threshold, keeping the door open for her. She could see the faintest outline of Diana's nipples through her shirt and, as Diana passed, murmured, "You sure we don't have time to run back up to the room for a while?"

Diana looked as close to smug as Ronnie had ever seen her. "I did tell Lena we'd be there before noon."

Something sparked in the corner of Ronnie's brain. She ignored it and followed Diana toward the front desk. "Who's Lena?"

"The housekeeper," Diana said, glancing over her shoulder. She was still smiling, eyes glittering, but if she suspected Ronnie of being jealous, she didn't say so.

Which was good, since Ronnie wasn't.

Diana was talking again. "Wait for me outside," she said. "I'll check out and have them bring the car around."

The Aston Martin was pulling up to the curb before Diana even made it out. Ronnie loaded their bags and, once she stepped out of the revolving doors, Diana met the valet and slipped a bill into his hand. From the look on his face, Ronnie figured it'd be the biggest tip he'd get all day.

Diana's car was one of the nicest Ronnie had ever been in, and definitely the nicest she'd ever driven. She adjusted the leather seat and the mirrors as Diana buckled up beside her. "Can you get to I-5 from here?" When Ronnie nodded, she said, "It's easy from there. Just head south."

"I usually do." Ronnie smirked at her own joke, and Diana cast her a look that fell a little short of disparaging. Then Ronnie revved the engine—probably harder than necessary—and pulled into traffic.

They made the short trip to the highway in silence. Ronnie was glad; she had a car but didn't drive often, and this gave her a chance to concentrate. As she eased onto the on-ramp, she asked, "So, how far away is this place?"

Diana shrugged. "Forty miles, give or take." Her voice gained a smoky edge. "We could play a game to pass the time."

"It's not that long a drive."

"We could play a game anyway."

Ronnie grinned. "Don't tell me you wanna play Punch Bug."

"No," Diana said primly, "I don't want to play Punch Bug." A soft whir drew Ronnie's attention, and she glanced over to see Diana easing her chair back. She frowned in confusion but turned away. "This game is called . . ." The unmistakable *zwip* of a zipper. "Keep Your Eyes on the Road."

". . . What!?"

"Both hands on the wheel," Diana instructed. "Both eyes on the road. If you want to look or touch, you pull over. Yes?"

The white strips of highway blurred into each other as Ronnie forced out a reply. "Yes."

"Good." The leather creaked as Diana settled into her seat. Then there was a long inhale and, finally, a dark, quiet "Oh."

Ronnie tightened her grip on the wheel and set her jaw. She could do this. This wasn't so hard. It wasn't like she'd never listened to a client getting off before. She counted vehicles as they passed. *Five. Six. Punch Bug white.* Diana gasped softly, and Ronnie bit her tongue so hard it hurt. She knew it was a bad idea, but she heard herself ask: "What are you thinking about?"

Diana gave a low, dreamy hum. "I'm thinking about what happened in the elevator."

Ronnie took a few careful breaths through her nose.

"I wonder what I could have gotten away with," Diana mused, "if we'd had time. Maybe I would've slipped my hand into your leggings. You'd have spread your legs for me and you'd already have been wet." She laughed weakly. "You're probably wet right now."

She wasn't wrong.

From the corner of her eye, Ronnie could see Diana's hips moving in a steady rhythm. She concentrated on the road. *Twelve cars. Thirteen.*

"You'd have to keep quiet and stay still," Diana went on. "If you didn't, everyone would know. Would you be able to? Or would you grind back on my hand and whimper when my fingers slid inside you?"

Ronnie's hips felt tight, everything between her legs hot and swollen. She looked down at the speedometer to see the needle quivering at 85. "Geez," she muttered, easing her foot off the gas. If she pulled over, she didn't want it to be because a cop forced her to.

She didn't want to pull over at all, really—this felt like a challenge, and at this point it was a matter of pride.

"I'm close," Diana panted. "I want you, God, I *need*—"

The rest was lost in a rise of desperate gasps that peaked with a muffled cry, followed by the quiet complaint of leather as Diana sank back against the seat.

Somehow, Ronnie kept her gaze aimed straight-ahead, her breath measured. After a moment, Diana said, "I guess you win." Her voice was heavy with a strange combination of amusement, pride, maybe even a little disappointment.

Ronnie swallowed. "You did tell Lena we'd be there before noon." She loosened her white-knuckled grip on the wheel, fingers stinging as blood rushed back into them. "But as soon as we do get there," she continued, voice low, "I am going to *fuck you*."

The words came out in a growl.

When Diana laughed this time, the sound was coated in velvety satisfaction. "Well," she sighed, "if you insist."

Later, Diana pointed out their exit, but she didn't really need to—their destination was plainly visible from the highway. A cluster of swanky houses, all white walls and broad windows, huddled on top of a hill like popular girls at a middle school dance. "The lake's down there," Diana said as Ronnie followed her gesture, making a right turn. "We have a private dock. Do you know your way around a boat?"

Ronnie shook her head, foot easing onto the brake at the next light. "My dad took us fishing once when we were kids, but that's it. I'm a lot of things, but a sailor isn't one of them."

"Shame," Diana reflected. "You'd look cute in the little hat."

As they pulled into the circle drive at the front of the house, they were met by a stout woman, probably in her late sixties, with a soft, friendly face and tangles of graying brown hair. Ronnie killed the engine and hopped out of the car, and the woman cast her a dimpled smile. "You must be Ronnie."

"And you must be Lena," Ronnie replied, opening the door for Diana.

Diana eased out of her seat, and the housekeeper beamed at her. Ronnie couldn't remember having ever seen someone so pleased to see their employer. "Hello, baby doll," she said, gathering Diana into her arms for a hug, which Diana returned without hesitation. "I have about six different options for every meal," Lena added as she pulled away. "You wanna come into the kitchen and pick a menu?"

"Absolutely." Diana turned to Ronnie. "Will you take our bags inside? Second floor, last room on the right." Her gaze darted over Ronnie's body. "I'll be up in a minute."

"Sure," Ronnie said, heat creeping up her neck. Diana and Lena started inside, and Ronnie moved to grab their things from the car.

Her excitement from the first part of the drive had cooled. Now that her head was clear, she was actually a little ashamed of herself. She tried to shake herself out of it, slamming the trunk shut and hoisting her duffel onto her shoulder before starting for the front door. No luck—the scene in the car kept replaying in her mind. It wasn't like her to lose herself like that, to speak from a place of aching, unfiltered need.

When she'd started at the agency, one of the first things Karla had taught her was that a client's control was nothing but illusion. A Night Life escort could spend hours satisfying a client's every need, but once their time was up, they could—and *should*—walk away. *"You make them want you,"* she'd said, jabbing a finger at Ronnie's chest, *"and you keep them coming back for more. But you never, ever need them."*

Ronnie had needed. She'd been intentionally riled, and the desire was fleeting. But she had hungrily, desperately *needed*.

She stepped into a bright foyer, where a high-shined wooden staircase led up to the second floor. Ronnie headed straight up. *You're a professional,* she scolded herself as she climbed the stairs. *Start acting like one.*

The last room on the right turned out to be the master suite. It was about what she would have expected, if she'd thought to expect: pale gray walls, a pair of velvet armchairs, a modern four-poster king bed. A long bench sat beneath a stretch of windows overlooking the hill that sloped down to the lake. Through the door to the attached bathroom, she caught a glimpse of white tile and gold finishing.

As Ronnie laid their bags on the bench, the door *click*ed shut behind her, and she turned.

Diana was leaning with her back against the door, smiling crookedly. "That's that sorted." She pushed away and stalked toward Ronnie. "Now, I seem to remember something about you fucking me."

Her cultured voice somehow made the word sound extra filthy.

It was *so* tempting. And Diana's arms were winding around Ronnie's shoulders and all the places where their bodies met seemed to radiate heat and—

But Ronnie couldn't let herself boil over like that again. She balled her hands into fists and grinned as Diana's fingers crept into her hair. "Yeah . . . sorry about that."

Diana froze. "What."

"This weekend is supposed to be about you," Ronnie said, thinking of their earlier conversation "What *you* want. You didn't pay for me to tell you what's gonna happen."

Something shimmered in Diana's eyes, and she plucked at the neck of Ronnie's sweater for a thoughtful moment. Finally, she stepped away, taking Ronnie's hands in hers. "Okay." She backed toward the bed. "You're right, this is about me." When she bumped the mattress, she sank down and patted the space next to her. Ronnie sat obediently and Diana said, "So I'll tell you what I want."

It took Ronnie a few seconds to realize that her heart was racing. *What the hell is my deal?*

"What I want," Diana went on, "is for you to be honest with me."

Ronnie squinted. "Honest."

"Whatever we do together, I want you to enjoy it. Don't tolerate it because you're being paid or because it's what I want. If what I suggest doesn't interest you, tell me so. All right?"

Ronnie nodded, surprised to feel a lump in her throat.

"But, if it *does* interest you, I want to know that too." Sly amusement had returned to Diana's expression. "I may like being in charge, but I'm hardly going to complain if you get enthusiastic. Even if it means you get a little . . ." Her voice dropped. "*Forceful.*"

"Oh." Ronnie's whole body was beginning to feel heavy and hot, but another worry scratched at the back of her mind. "I just . . ." She turned her gaze to the floor, frowning at the low-pile carpet. "I dunno, I feel like you get told what to do all the time, and I didn't wanna—"

"Somehow—" Diana chuckled "—I suspect you won't give me the same sort of orders my mother does."

Ronnie released a puff of laughter. "No, I sure hope not." She glanced up and smiled. "So does that mean . . .?"

"Mm-hmm." Diana leaned in close. "I'm giving you full permission to have your way with me." Her whisper was warm as she feathered her lips over the space behind Ronnie's ear.

If she kept doing that, Ronnie was going to dissolve into a puddle. Time to reassert control over the situation. She turned, her mouth a breath away from Diana's. "You asked for it."

Then she grabbed Diana by the shoulders and thrust her back onto the duvet.

"*Look* at you," Diana gasped, clearly delighted, as Ronnie stood and stripped off her sweater. She sounded dazzled. It went straight to Ronnie's head.

And farther south.

"All right, tiger," Diana said, laughter at the edge of her voice, "if you're going to do this, do it right." Ronnie's hands paused at the waistband of her leggings and she cocked her head. Diana gestured to her suitcase, which lay on the bed above her head. "Open that up."

Ronnie did. Her eyebrows hit her hairline, and Diana gave a throaty chuckle.

She'd come prepared. The suitcase held a few clothes, but was mostly filled with a variety of brightly colored . . . *accessories*. Diana waved a lazy hand at them. "Pick one."

"You expect me to believe you don't have a favorite?"

Diana gave a catlike smile, then pushed off of the bed and came to stand beside her. As they surveyed their options, a hand slid into Ronnie's leggings, blunt nails idly scraping her backside. Her brain stalled, then stuttered and reset as Diana retrieved a bright-pink strapless strap-on.

"Those are fun," Ronnie conceded, trying to keep her voice light even as she felt a low, excited throb. She reached for the toy, but Diana jerked it away, pulling her hand from Ronnie's pants and dropping to her knees. The next thing Ronnie knew, her leggings were around her ankles. "Oh, okay—"

She choked at the first press of Diana's tongue.

For the next few minutes, the room was quiet but for Ronnie's hushed whimpers, entwined with the occasional satisfied hum from Diana. At one point, Ronnie glanced down to see that Diana had somehow managed to shrug off her shirt. Then she tossed her bra aside and the sight of her, on her knees in nothing but jeans, made Ronnie's skin burn. Soon she was panting. "Diana," she bit out through gritted teeth.

The heat of Diana's mouth disappeared, and Ronnie almost cried out. Then there was something else, the insistent press of the dildo's shorter end. It slipped inside—an embarrassing whine escaped Ronnie's throat.

Diana rose, wiping her chin demurely, then took Ronnie's face in both hands and gave her a searing kiss. "Tell me how you want me," she said, jerking down her jeans.

"On the bed," Ronnie grated as she kicked off her leggings. "And turn over."

Diana nodded, lips quirked up at one corner, and stretched out across the bed on her stomach, next to their bags. *Oh, that is nice,* Ronnie thought, taking in the sight before her. She bit her lip and gripped the dildo, making sure it was secure. It was. With a quiet sigh, she knelt on the duvet between Diana's knees and edged her legs apart, dipping one hand between them. Her fingers came away wet and she smirked.

She entered Diana slowly, letting her get accustomed to the stretch and drawing the moment out. This needed to last, especially if Diana was going to keep making noises like that. Her high gasps were easily audible, even muffled by the bed, and the tendons in her hands flexed as she clutched the duvet. She was obviously desperate and Ronnie loved it.

For a while Ronnie kept her pace almost sluggish. It was driving her a little crazy, not bearing down and taking Diana with all the urgency screaming through her bones. But as bad as it was for her, it must be ten times worse for Diana. And she'd been told to have her way.

With that in mind, she raised one hand and brought it down hard, the room ringing with the sound of her palm against Diana's backside. Diana gave an undignified shriek and twisted, eyes wild. She didn't look mad—just surprised.

"That," Ronnie growled, "is for forcing me to sit there and *listen* while you made yourself come." Diana bit her lip but apparently couldn't suppress the pleased little laugh bubbling low in her throat as she turned back around.

Ronnie rubbed the spot she'd slapped, knowing all too well how the reddening skin would sting. She rolled her hips, keeping a steady rhythm, and continued. "Making you come is *my* job." She pressed on the base of Diana's spine, pushing her into the mattress, and breathed through her nose. Slow. Restrained. She would not lose control again. Beneath her, Diana mewled and squirmed, trying to meet each drive of her hips, which did absolutely nothing to help with the whole control thing. Ronnie was pretty sure her mouth was watering.

When she laid fully across Diana's body, she placed her hands on Diana's above their heads and laced their fingers together. Then she bore down with more force but maintained the languid pulse of her hips.

"And if you want honesty," she panted into Diana's ear, "here it is. I want to do my job. I want to make you come." Diana moaned, forehead buried in the duvet. Ronnie could feel her own climax closing in, but ignored it: "I want to make you come so hard that you *scream*. And I want to do it again—and again—and again—"

Diana was keening, her grip on Ronnie's hands so tight it almost hurt.

Ronnie maintained her pace, knowing exactly how the slow, powerful presses would feel. She crushed her lips against Diana's temple, ready to keep talking. Then she realized what she was going to say.

That the truth, the honest truth, was this: she wanted Diana.

She'd never said it to a client before. She couldn't say it now. Instead, she moved away from Diana's ear and down to the crook of her neck, where she sank her teeth into the flushed skin there.

Diana did scream then, the duvet swallowing the sound. Ronnie's hips kept moving, her jaw clamping down as her breath seethed through her nose and her own orgasm washed over her. She rode it out with a handful of jerking thrusts, then relaxed against Diana's body as her heartbeat began to slow.

Eventually, Diana let go of her hands. Ronnie's fingers were stiff. She flexed them and was about to push herself off when she realized Diana was shivering.

"Oh my God." Ronnie eased out and pulled the dildo from herself, biting her lip against the aftershocks. She tossed it to the floor and settled back down at Diana's side, wrapping an arm around her. Diana still trembled. "Are you okay?" Ronnie brushed her lips across the red half-moon on her shoulder. "Did I hurt you?"

The laugh she got was shaky, but reassuring. "I'm fine," Diana breathed, turning to her. Her face was red, blue eyes brilliant. She laid a hand on Ronnie's cheek. "You're *incredible*."

She kissed her, then sighed and stretched lazily. Ronnie actually heard her spine pop and felt a twinge of guilt. But then Diana curled up against her, tucking her face into Ronnie's neck, so she figured there were no hard feelings. "I'll need a nap before that happens again," Diana murmured.

Ronnie chuckled and gathered her into her arms. "If you insist."

"I do."

The words were warm against Ronnie's skin and made her chest clench. She thought back to her earlier desperation and frowned as Diana's breath slowed and deepened. So she wanted Diana, big deal. *Want* was different than *need*. It was fine.

She nodded resolutely, which pulled a tiny huff from Diana. "Sorry," she whispered, stroking her hair. The stroking didn't last long though—before she knew it, she had dozed off too.

She was jarred awake by a rap on the bedroom door, her body significantly cooler than it had been when she fell asleep.

Peering over her shoulder, she saw Diana raising her head with a grimace, eye shadow slightly smudged. The wrinkles in the duvet had left lines on her cheek. It was kind of adorable.

"Yes?" Diana called as Ronnie looked toward the windows. Judging from the light, they hadn't been asleep very long.

Lena's voice drifted through the door. "It's me, baby doll. Lunch is about ready if you and Ms. Ronnie wanna come down and eat."

As if on cue, Ronnie's stomach grumbled.

"Thank you, Lena," Diana said. "We'll be down in a minute." She slid from the bed, stooping to gather her discarded outfit.

Ronnie lay back, arms behind her head, and watched. She rolled Lena's words over in her mind and made a decision.

"Kent."

Diana glanced up, tucking her underwear into the crumpled bundle in her arms. "Sorry?"

"My last name. It's Kent." Ronnie pushed herself up onto her elbows. When Diana did nothing but blink at her, she shrugged. "*Ms. Ronnie* makes me sound like a kindergarten teacher."

"You're definitely not that." Diana approached her, eyes half-lidded, and ran the pad of her thumb over Ronnie's lower lip. Ronnie kissed her fingers and her breath hitched. "Well, Ms. Kent," she said, voice husky, "you should probably get dressed."

Ronnie grinned and glanced down at herself, still in nothing but her bra. "What, you don't like this look?"

"Oh, I like it very much," Diana said, a smile creeping onto her lips. "But Lena's too well-paid for that kind of perk." Ronnie laughed as Diana stepped away, rummaged through her suitcase, and produced a makeup bag. "There's another en suite next door," she offered as she headed for the bathroom. "Get ready and go on downstairs. I'll be right behind you." Once inside, she didn't quite close the door.

For a second, Ronnie considered following her. She could breeze in casually, fix her makeup right alongside Diana. There was something appealing about the idea.

Something about the appeal scared her. She stood, scrambled for her things, then left the bedroom and her weird thoughts behind.

It didn't take long for her to reapply, clean up a little, and throw her clothes back on. In no time at all, she was coming down the stairs into the foyer, frowning at her reflection in the glass doors. Her sweater was all rumpled. She looked good, obviously—it'd take more than a few wrinkles to change that—but still.

She almost collided with Lena as the housekeeper rounded the corner out of the sitting room. "Whoop! Sorry lovin', you okay?"

"I'm fine," Ronnie said, smiling. Lena must be from the Southwest; she sounded like every homeroom mother Ronnie had ever had growing up. "Thanks for looking after us this weekend."

Lena waved her off. "That's my job, and I'm happy to do it. And you seem a lot nicer than the last gal she brought down here, so."

Ronnie's brow furrowed. "What do you mean?"

Lena opened her mouth, then glanced up the stairs and seemed to think better of it. "Nothing. I mean, it's not really my story to tell. Forget I said anything." She patted Ronnie's arm and started toward the dining room.

Well, *that* didn't sound good.

Ronnie was about to follow her and try, as politely as possible, to pump her for information. Then a creak from the stairs drew her attention and she turned.

Diana was barefoot and back in her jeans, but she'd swapped the button-up for a simple boat-neck blouse. Her hair was loose and when Diana brushed it away from her face, Ronnie caught a glimpse of the mark she'd left on her shoulder. Had Diana worn a top that would show it off on purpose? Ronnie's skin heated at the thought.

As Diana reached her, Ronnie finally managed to say, "You look amazing."

She told herself that it was hunger, and not Diana's smile, that made her stomach clench.

The table in the formal dining room was made of dark, well-polished wood, candles in tall silver sticks filling the space between the settings at each end. Diana rounded to one chair and Ronnie followed to pull it out for her.

Lena brought out a bottle of wine, the same red Diana had gotten for Ronnie on the first night they met. As Lena filled Ronnie's glass, Ronnie grinned across the table at Diana. "None for you again? "

Diana's lips pressed together thinly. "I'm afraid not. Mummy's always been an avid teetotaler."

To Ronnie's surprise, Lena pitched in. "Your mama's not here, baby doll." She cast Diana a look that implied peering over glasses, even though she wasn't wearing any. "You want some wine, you have some wine. I won't tell."

Ronnie beamed at the housekeeper, then turned to see Diana's gaze jumping between them.

"I have always been curious . . ." she admitted slowly. To Ronnie, she added, "Especially about that one, since you like it so much."

Apparently, that was all Lena needed to hear. She half filled another glass and set it by Diana's plate without a word, then disappeared back into the kitchen.

Ronnie watched, tickled, as Diana gingerly lifted the glass and sniffed the wine and said, "It smells good."

She took a sip and her eyes lit up. "It *is* good," she said, sounding genuinely surprised.

Ronnie couldn't help chuckling. "I'm glad you like it." She always liked introducing her clients to new experiences—especially if they wound up enjoying them. It made her feel memorable, and she did like being memorable.

If she was being honest, she also got a kick out of Diana doing something she knew her mother wouldn't like.

The first course was cantaloupe wedges wrapped in prosciutto. Ronnie wasn't easily impressed by home cooking, but she had to admit that it was delicious. Between the quality of the food and the sheer force of hunger, the two of them ate for a while in amiable silence.

They were finishing the main course—linguine in a spicy red sauce—before Ronnie felt like making conversation. She took a long sip of wine and sighed. "Lena's good. I'll have to get her recipe."

Diana looked amused. "You cook?"

"Girl's gotta have a hobby. You know."

"I do know."

The look in Diana's eyes sent a pleasant tingle down Ronnie's spine. When Lena bustled in to take their plates, she shot Ronnie a friendly wink. Ronnie grinned at her, and she was gone again.

Then Ronnie remembered what Lena had said before dinner. Between the temptation of wine and the excellent food, she'd almost forgotten all about it. Now she frowned before she could stop herself.

"What's wrong?"

Crap. Diana was watching her, brow knit.

She could brush it off, say nothing was wrong, change the subject. But that would feel wrong, especially so soon after being asked for honesty.

So she dove into the deep end. "What happened with the last woman you brought here?"

The concern melted from Diana's face, cold caution settling into its place. She straightened, sitting stiff-backed, then opened her mouth to reply.

"I'm not trying to be nosy," Ronnie hurriedly added, "and it's fine if you don't wanna talk about it, it's just . . . Lena mentioned it in passing, and I was . . ." She dragged her eyes away from Diana's and turned her wineglass by its stem. "Curious. Worried."

"Those are two different things."

Ronnie glanced back up to see Diana staring at her with a strange, guarded expression. "Yeah, well." Her laugh sounded off-key. "I guess I'm both."

Lena chose that moment to bustle in with dessert. Diana thanked her softly, and Ronnie kept quiet until she left. Once the housekeeper's footsteps faded into the kitchen, Diana took a deep breath.

"The woman Lena mentioned was my ex-girlfriend. Well, not ex at the time." Diana idly stirred her panna cotta. "We came here for a weekend with my family, last summer. There were a few groups in the other houses, mostly renters. A sorority had taken over the nearest house for a reunion or something."

Ronnie didn't like where this was going. But she kept her mouth shut—this was her idea, and it was too late to back out now.

"On the second night, I woke up and couldn't find Vivienne. I looked all over the house, and was about to wake my family when

I happened to see a light down the hill. Someone was in the boat. I went down to see if it was Vivienne, and . . . it was." She sighed. "She was with one of the women from the reunion." She shrugged. "That was the last time, but not the first. I told my family, and my mother asked me what I did."

Ronnie frowned. "What *you* did?"

"To make her cheat."

The feeling that had tugged at Ronnie's gut at the hotel came back in full force. She was surprised—but not very—to realize that she was angry. And she wasn't sure who she was angrier with: this jerk who'd cheated on Diana, or Diana's mother for implying it was *her fault*.

It must have shown on her face, because when Diana met her gaze again, her expression eased. "It's all right. I'm far better off without her."

"Yeah, but . . ." Ronnie gripped her spoon, shook her head. "What an asshole."

Diana gave a light, surprised laugh. "That's what Phoebe said. Well, not in those words, but." She cocked her head to one side, considering Ronnie. "Please don't be upset. Vivienne already spoiled one weekend; I don't want her to spoil another one."

Ronnie stabbed her panna cotta. "Okay." She glanced up, trying a grin. "I guess I'll just have to make this one extra good."

"You already have." Diana's smile was slightly suggestive at first; then it softened. "Are you always so protective of your clients?"

Protective. *That* was the word for it.

The realization was a little staggering. Ronnie wiggled her eyebrows in an attempt to mask her disorientation. "Why, you got a damsel in distress fantasy? Wanna see me on a horse?"

It made Diana laugh and the atmosphere lightened, and after that they didn't say any more about it. They ate the rest of their panna cotta and talked about meaningless things and it felt, for the most part, like it had before.

But something had changed. Ronnie could feel it, drifting in the air between them like smoke.

Later, Ronnie and her bag retreated into the master bathroom for a shower. Diana had left her makeup pouch on the counter, and when Ronnie placed her own next to it, she remembered her earlier impulse and smiled. For some reason, doing their makeup together didn't seem like such a crazy idea now.

Once she was clean, she stepped out onto the mat and shook her head. Drops of water dotted the mirror above the vanity and she wiped at them, cutting a swath of clarity through the fog. *Speaking of makeup . . .* Hers was ruined. She stared at herself for a moment, weighing the pros and cons of walking out there barefaced.

That would be a lot for Diana to take in. She pulled a small pouch from her duffel. She'd just touch up a little. A couple of nights wouldn't ruin her skin.

Face fixed, she bundled herself into a robe that had been hanging on the back of the door, and stepped into the bedroom. Diana was already in bed, propped up against the huge, fluffy pillows, eyes on a paperback. She was wearing a white silk negligee. Ronnie's mouth went dry.

She didn't know why it hadn't occurred to her sooner. A weekend job. An overnight stay. They'd be sleeping together. Really sleeping.

She wasn't sure what her expression looked like in that moment, but when Diana glanced up, she said, "Are you all right?"

Ronnie cleared her throat. "I, uh." She cleared her throat and tried again. "It's just . . . I guess I hadn't considered . . ." She laughed, because there was nothing else to do, and gestured to the bed.

Understanding settled on Diana's features. "You've never slept with a client?" Ronnie shook her head. Diana laid her book aside, expression wary as she pushed back the covers and stood. "I'll go find Lena and have her get one of the other rooms ready." She pulled a pair of jeans from her suitcase and started slipping into them. "Do you want the one next door? It's got the next biggest bed, but—"

"Stop that." Ronnie finally forced herself into motion, crossing to Diana and laying a hand on her arm. Diana paused and watched her carefully.

Ronnie knelt, easing the jeans down. Diana wasn't wearing anything under her negligee, but Ronnie focused on sliding a palm up her calf, urging her out of the rumpled circle of denim before tossing the jeans aside. Then she stood. "Can I tell you a story?"

Diana nodded hesitantly, and Ronnie took her hand, leading her back to the bed.

"A while back, when I first got to the city, I was dating this girl. Brianna." She ran her thumb along each of Diana's fingers in turn as she spoke. "We hadn't been together long. I was over at hers one night, and she said she wanted to try something new." She turned Diana's palm up, lightly stroking her wrist. "She wanted to try tying me up."

Diana took a slight, sharp breath, but Ronnie didn't know if it was in response to what she'd said or the movement of her hands. She kept her eyes down. "I hadn't started at Night Life yet and hadn't dated much, so I'd never done that before." *Funny to think there was ever a time like that,* she thought with a grin. "I had no idea if I'd like it, but . . ." A shrug. "I knew there was only one way to find out."

She looked up. Diana's worried expression had already loosened, but Ronnie figured she should finish the story, just to be sure. "Turns out I did like it. A lot," Ronnie said, finally drawing a smile from her. "So, I dunno. Maybe I'll like sharing a bed with you. As long as you don't drool on me or anything."

Diana snorted. "No promises."

The tension between them dissolved as Ronnie laughed and stood. "I should warn you," she said, tugging at the belt of her robe, "I didn't pack any pajamas."

A glimmer returned to Diana's eyes. "Oh, I don't think that'll be a problem."

Much later, when Ronnie blinked into consciousness, it took her a second to remember where she was. The room was dark, the only light the dim glow of the moon through the window. It was either very late or very early.

Her arm was asleep. It didn't take her long to realize why.

She and Diana were tangled up like a branch and a vine, legs entwined beneath the sheets, Diana's arm draped over her hip, her face tucked once again into the crook of Ronnie's neck. Weirdly enough, apart from the numbness in her arm, she was really comfortable. Diana breathed deeply, each puff warm on her skin, the measured press of her breasts against Ronnie's soft and steady.

It had been a long time since Ronnie had cuddled. She didn't remember it feeling so nice.

Turning down Diana's offer of another room had been a good choice. Still, it was sweet of her to have made it, to have been ready to rearrange everything for the sake of Ronnie's comfort.

Ronnie shifted a little, tightening her hold on Diana's waist. Diana murmured quietly but didn't wake.

Maybe Ronnie wasn't the only one feeling protective.

Stacy was on the phone when Ronnie staggered back into the office on Sunday evening. Ronnie shoved her hands into her pockets and waited, watching herself in the wall of one-way windows.

She looked happy. She also looked exhausted.

She turned away when she heard Stacy replace the receiver.

"So," Stacy said, drawing out the vowel, "how did it go?"

A full answer to that question was probably way more complicated than Stacy thought. "It was good," she said, putting it mildly. "But I definitely need some time to recharge."

"No kidding." Stacy pulled up the master schedule and examined it. Ronnie stared at the wall behind her head. "Calendar's open until Thursday. That enough time?"

"That's fine."

Stacy's fingers flew across the keyboard. "Ronnie Kent, off till Thursday. No calls." She stopped typing, pinkie hovering over the Enter key, and studied Ronnie with a sly grin. "What if she calls again before then?"

Something in Ronnie's chest clunked, and she chuckled. "She won't. She'll be too busy with other stuff."

"If you say so." Stacy didn't move. "Still, what if she does?"

Ronnie glanced back toward the windows.

She looked exhausted. She also looked happy.

"If she does . . . you have my number."

CHAPTER 9
Bribery

"You're in a good mood today."

Diana glanced up. She and Evie were sitting across a table from each other in her mother's office, sticking address labels to mailers. Evie had gently suggested that college students would be perfect for things like this, but Diana's mother didn't believe in unpaid internships.

She also didn't believe in spending any more money on the campaign than she had to, so the job had fallen to Evie and Diana.

"Why do you say that?" Diana looked back down at her pile of blank flyers. It was shorter than the stack of ones she'd finished, but still as thick as her wrist. She peeled another label from its page and reached for the stack.

She could feel Evie's eyes on her. "You were smiling just now. So you're either in a good mood or you really love addressing stuff."

Diana hesitated, then chuckled in a way that hopefully didn't sound nervous. "You've caught me," she said. "This is my secret passion. I could label mailers forever."

Evie laughed but made no other reply, and from her peripheral vision Diana could see her go back to her own stack. *Maybe that's the end of it,* Diana thought, resolving to be a little more conscious of her facial expressions from now on.

It was Tuesday, and Diana's mind kept wandering to the previous weekend. She couldn't remember the last time she'd been so relaxed for so long. Of course she had fun on the rare occasions when she saw Phoebe, but that was only for an hour or so at a time.

And she certainly didn't have the same *kind* of fun.

After the first night, Ronnie's trepidation about sharing a bed had apparently evaporated. In fact, she'd almost been enthusiastic.

She'd seemed that way about everything, lavishing Diana with attention and something that looked an awful lot like affection.

Diana had tried to tell herself that it wasn't real affection, that it was purchased, negotiable, available to anyone who could afford it. But at night, when Ronnie had held her tightly and kissed her neck and told her she was beautiful, it had certainly felt like the real thing.

"You have a good break?"

Oh, right, she was still in her mother's office with Evie. Diana tried to focus. "I did. I appreciate you insisting on that, by the way. I went to the lake house."

"That sounds chill." Evie started on a new sheet of labels as she spoke. "I like the beach better though. The real beach. My parents have a summer house too, out on Sunrise. Have you been there?"

"No, is it nice?"

Evie's face brightened with an enthusiasm Diana had rarely seen in her outside of conversations involving the word *constituents*. "It's great. My room has a balcony on the east side, and every time we stay there I run out first thing in the morning to watch the sun come up and throw bread to the gulls. And our place has a private beach, which is, you know." She cleared her throat. "Nice. Secluded."

The pocket of Evie's moto jacket bleeped, interrupting wherever that thought was going. When she pulled out her phone and checked the screen, she grimaced. "Hell, I still need to call AlphaGraph about those sign reprints."

"I already did," Diana said, fixing her attention on the corner of a stubborn label. She caught a glimpse of movement: Evie turning back to her.

"You did?"

"Mm-hmm. I'm picking them up on Thursday."

"Oh. Great, thanks."

Diana shot her a brief smile, then finally managed to free the label from its backing.

"I have to say," Evie hedged, "I've worked a lot of campaigns, but I think this is the first one I've actually enjoyed."

Diana snorted and glanced back up. "With my mother? You're joking, surely."

"No, not because of your mother. I mean, she's fine, I've had worse candidates, but . . ." Evie shrugged. She didn't meet Diana's eye as she spoke, focusing instead on the repetitive motions of her hands. "It's just been nice to know I'm working with somebody I can kind of . . . I don't know, trust and rely on, I guess."

It was unlike Evie to be anything but forthright. Diana couldn't, for the life of her, fathom why she was acting this way about a simple compliment. "Well, thank you." She paused in her labeling. "I hope you know that my distaste for the whole thing has nothing to do with you."

Evie grinned. "I figured. Nice to know for sure, though."

There was a lull then, as Diana finished and set aside her stack of flyers, then took some from the top of Evie's. The comfortable silence was broken when Evie said, "Once this is all over, you should come out to the beach house for a few days. We could celebrate."

"Only if my mother wins," Diana said dryly. "She won't celebrate if it's not a victory, trust me."

There was a quiet puff of laughter, then the sound of Evie drawing in breath for a reply. But before she could voice it, the door opened and Diana's mother swept inside.

"Hello, girls! How's it coming along?" She leaned down to plant a kiss on the crown of Diana's head, peering over her shoulder as she did so. "Make sure the labels aren't crooked, boo-boo. We don't want the voters thinking we're sloppy."

None of Diana's labels were crooked. She bit her tongue.

"I've got some bad news," her mother continued, not waiting for an answer to her question or a retort to her criticism. She was already flipping through her appointment book. "Your father needs help on the Spinecki case, so I won't be able to make it to dinner tonight."

It took all of Diana's self-control not to sigh openly. The reservations at Red Moon had been her mother's idea, of course. She'd claimed it would be good PR, to be seen at the opening of an exclusive restaurant. Evie had agreed, and before Diana knew it, the three of them had been booked. It would have looked very good, yet here her mother was, skipping out in order to help with a case that, to hear Diana's father talk, wasn't actually that complicated. So it would just be Diana and Evie, another table for two. Again.

Her mother wasn't terribly subtle.

Any response Diana could have made would have fallen on deaf ears anyway—her mother was already on the phone, talking to God knows who—so she turned back to her work instead.

While trying to think of a way to gracefully bow out of dinner herself, inspiration struck. As casually as possible, she said, "Maybe I should see if Phoebe wants to come with us. I haven't seen her lately, and she wanted a full report on Red Moon anyway. She'd be thrilled."

She'd labeled three more flyers before she realized Evie hadn't replied. She glanced up.

Evie's gaze was still on her own stack, but her brows were knit ever so slightly, dark eyes intent. When she spoke, her voice was quiet and level. "I wouldn't mind if it was just us."

Oh. *Oh.*

Oh no.

Her mother's matchmaking attempts had been so wasted on Diana that she hadn't even considered if they'd been working on Evie. Diana winced internally. She really ought to nip this in the bud.

Then again, how would Evie take the rejection? She certainly *seemed* levelheaded enough, but people usually did when things were going their way. If Diana made it clear that she wasn't interested, would they still be able to work together? Would things get awkward? Or, the worst possible scenario, would Evie leave the campaign entirely, leaving her mother furious and Diana to pick up the slack?

She didn't seem the type. *But you never know.*

Her mother was still on the phone. "Of course, it's no problem. I'll send the dream team over to get it tomorrow."

The dream team.

Ignoring the stone in her stomach, she smiled at Evie. "Well. Just us, then."

"So she *forced* you to go on a date with Evie?"

It was two days later, and Diana had barely managed to carve out enough time to meet Phoebe at Anchor, one of their favorite brunch spots.

Her oldest friend stared across the table at her, dramatic disbelief painting her round, animated face. Her lime-green nail polish clashed splendidly with the momentarily forgotten avocado toast in her hand.

Diana dragged the tines of her fork through the salad she'd barely touched. "Not technically." She twirled the fork into a rogue piece of arugula. "She didn't come with us, so it just sort of . . . happened."

Phoebe crunched into her toast and spoke around the mouthful. "That's totally what she was doing, though."

"I'm aware. But even if I'd confronted her about it, she could have easily claimed innocence." Diana sighed. "I don't know how to tell her that I don't have any interest."

"Evie or your mom?"

"Both." Diana took a sip of coffee and rested her chin on her hand, gazing around the restaurant. The dining area was kitted out in wood paneling, making the whole place look like a boat cabin. Maybe it was the mood she was in, but right now something about the myriad driftwood chandeliers made her think of bones. "The worst part is, I think Evie might actually like me."

Phoebe brushed crumbs from her hands and reached for her mimosa. It was her second. "That sucks, since you don't like Evie."

"I don't *dislike* her."

"No, I mean . . ." Phoebe held up a finger—*one second*—as she took a long drink. "You don't *like* like her."

"No. I don't." Diana's gaze continued to wander. Ever since the evening when she'd run into Ronnie at Vivant, she had an unfortunate tendency to keep an eye out for her when in public. "I almost wish I *did*," she added, turning back to Phoebe. "That would make this so much simpler."

Phoebe ran the tip of her index finger around the rim of her champagne glass thoughtfully. "I guess you could try sleeping with her. Maybe that'd change your mind."

Diana snorted, taking another stab at her salad. "That's your solution to everything."

"Hey, it usually works," Phoebe shot back with a wolfish grin. "And it's not like you have anything else going on." When Diana said nothing, Phoebe's eyes narrowed. "Or *do* you?"

Diana became suddenly engrossed in spearing a cherry tomato.

The clatter of a glass against the table made her jump, but she didn't look up. She could feel Phoebe's sharp brown eyes sparkling at her, could almost feel the lascivious interest radiating from her in waves. "You saw her again!" The whole table shifted slightly as Phoebe leaned forward, elbows flanking her half-empty plate. "Oh my gosh, you— Ooo, you little sneaky-butt, I can't *believe* you didn't tell me!"

Diana's neck went warm. "There was never a good time to bring it up."

"You are so full of it—You *know* I don't need a segue into sexy talk." She cackled. "No wonder I've barely seen you lately!"

At that, mild shame slithered down Diana's back. She peeked up to see Phoebe smiling with her entire face, despite her admonishing words. Even so, she felt the need to explain herself. "I promise, most of my time really has been taken up by the campaign."

But Phoebe flapped a hand at her. "Oh whatever, I love that you're using your free time to get fingerblasted." Diana slumped slightly into the booth, glancing around to see if anyone had heard that. Phoebe didn't seem to care. "You know you're gonna need to tell me all about it, right?" she went on. When Diana didn't immediately answer, she added, "I'm about to start flinging butter at you if you don't talk."

She'd do it too. Diana laughed. "All right, all right." She glanced up, caught their server's eye, and signaled him over. "Get yourself another drink and I'll tell you everything. Quietly."

It ended up taking two more mimosas to get Phoebe updated to her satisfaction. By the time Diana had finished reporting their weekend at the lake, Phoebe was staring at her, slack-jawed. Diana took a delicate swallow of coffee—she was on her third cup by now— and shrugged. "That's it."

"That's it?" Phoebe repeated. "That's *it*? You're like, president of the monogamy club and you tell me you've been seeing an escort for what, four months? And you say *that's it*?"

Diana lifted an eyebrow. "I'm still monogamous. Some of us don't have a Night Life punch card."

Phoebe grimaced playfully. "They don't even *have* punch cards. Trust me, I asked." She shook her head, still grinning in disbelief.

"This is crazy. No wonder you're not into Evie. It sounds like this Ronnie girl's got you spoiled rotten."

"She has, a bit," Diana admitted. "I don't know, she . . ." She smiled down at her mug as she remembered Ronnie's arms around her. "There's just something about her." A stretch of silence made her peek up. Phoebe was leering at her. "What?"

"You actually *like* her."

Diana blanched. "No, I don't!"

"Yes-huh!"

She'd never seen Phoebe so delighted. "I absolutely don't," she said. "I mean, I do *like* her—she's nice and we get along and we have great sex—but it's . . ." What had Ronnie called it? She scoured through her memory. "Purely therapeutic. It's stress relief."

"Some therapy," Phoebe tittered. "If my masseur went down on me, I'd probably marry him." She laced her fingers under her chin. "I wanna meet her."

"No."

"Aw c'mon! Bring her to my birthday party!" Her eyes popped. "You can still come to that, right?"

Oh thank God, a safer topic. "I can, but you won't want me there. I've been given instructions to *campaign*."

Phoebe's forehead crinkled. "So? You don't have to."

"I know, and I could technically tell Mummy I did, no matter what, but . . ." She hesitated.

"You'd feel bad if you lied."

"Yes."

Of course Phoebe knew the reason for her trepidation. They'd been friends since high school, and this was hardly the first time Diana's pathological honesty had been a problem.

"Well," Phoebe said, heaving an exaggerated sigh, "it's up to you. I don't care if you talk politics. It's not gonna hurt anybody, and I know you gotta stay on your mom's good side. But I think you'll for sure have a better time if you bring Ronnie."

That was true. But still . . . Diana's face twisted in a moue of consternation. "Doesn't that seem a bit . . . girlfriendy?"

Phoebe twinkled at her. "That's probably up to you too." She pulled out her wallet and tucked a few twenties under Diana's empty mug. Before Diana could protest, she held up a finger. "Nope, stop that, I'm buying lunch and you're bringing Ronnie to my thing."

"That's bribery."

"That's friendship, baby." She shot a finger-gun in Diana's general direction.

"Are you getting an Uber?" Diana asked, eyeing her. Phoebe didn't have a car and shouldn't drive right now even if she did, but it never hurt to pin down her plans. "Or do you want Skylar to take you home?"

Phoebe shook her head as she scooted out of their booth. "There's a new shoe place a couple of streets over: Zenith? I'm gonna check it out." Diana slid out as well, ready to help balance her, but she was surprisingly steady. "Once I'm done there, I'll see how I feel."

Outside, the Aston Martin idled by the curb. When Skylar stepped out and circled around to open the back door, Phoebe waggled her fingers at her. Skylar nodded.

"Please text me when you get home," Diana said, gently taking Phoebe's arm to get her attention.

"Of course!" Phoebe flashed her a dazzling smile and pecked her on the cheek. "See you Saturday. Love you!"

"Love you too."

As she watched her friend toddle away to Zenith, Diana sighed.

How would Ronnie feel about coming to the party, about meeting Diana's friends? Ronnie occupied an entirely separate portion of Diana's social space; the idea of that portion properly overlapping with Phoebe's had never occurred to her, despite Phoebe being the reason they'd met in the first place. Would Ronnie think it was weird, being with Diana in such a simultaneously public and intimate setting?

She remembered waking up in Ronnie's arms, the way Ronnie had kissed her good morning, Ronnie's anger on her behalf when she'd learned about Vivienne. Maybe she wouldn't find a party that weird after all.

Once Phoebe had turned the corner, Diana whirled around and strode to the car, thanking Skylar as she shut her inside. She pulled her phone from her clutch and thumbed idly through her contacts, mentally running through her upcoming schedule. If she didn't see Ronnie on Saturday, she wouldn't have time for nearly two weeks.

That settled it. She tapped Call.

CHAPTER 10
Mushy Friend Time

The scene that Ronnie walked into when she entered the Night Life office was not a good one.

Karla stood at Stacy's desk, fists planted knuckle-down on the glass top, glowering at her. When she heard Ronnie enter she glanced over, obviously realized it wasn't a client, and turned back to Stacy, whose eyes were rimmed in telltale red.

"I told you about my midterm weeks ago," she said through gritted teeth. "I *can't* stay all day on Wednesday."

"And what am I supposed to do?" Karla snapped. "Just let the phones ring?"

"We have voice mail."

"And who are my escorts going to check in with?" Karla went on, as though Stacy hadn't spoken. "Nobody? They have to check in; it's a safety measure."

"I'm aware," Stacy said tightly. "Why can't Jewel do it?"

"Jewel doesn't work days."

"You said you'd figure out a way to cover for me. You said—"

"I don't remember saying that."

Ronnie shifted uncertainly from foot to foot. She was there to check in after a job, and it would be wise to stay in her lane, but Stacy looked *awfully* upset. Karla could always check escorts in herself, but Ronnie wasn't dumb enough to suggest that.

"I have to take my midterm," Stacy said, her tone edging into pleading. "It's one afternoon, I know you can do without me for one afternoon. Anybody could sit in for me. The job's not *hard*."

That was the wrong thing to say. Karla straightened, putting her hands on her hips and regarding Stacy coolly. "You're right," she said.

"It's not. Anybody could do it, and I'm sure there are plenty who'd be glad to."

"I'll do it."

Stacy and Karla turned to stare at Ronnie, who'd finally stepped forward. "I don't have anything scheduled on Wednesday." She looked at Stacy. "It's what, a couple hours? What time do you have to be there?"

"Manning the desk is not your job." Karla's voice was almost disturbingly flat.

Ronnie glanced at her and shrugged. "No, but I could do it while she's gone. I don't mind."

Karla sniffed imperiously. "I hope you don't expect to get paid for that time."

It might have been nice, but Ronnie was hardly going to insist. "I don't."

"Fine." Karla swiveled back to Stacy. "You won't be getting paid either, obviously."

From the way Stacy's jaw flexed, Ronnie guessed she was literally biting her tongue. "That's okay."

Without another word, Karla marched back to the door that led into the office's interior rooms, not quite slamming it shut behind her.

Stacy released a breath as Ronnie approached her.

"You okay?" she asked, eyeing the younger woman carefully.

"I'm fine." Stacy's eyes were rimmed with red, but dry. Which was a relief, since Ronnie wouldn't know what to do if Stacy had actually started crying. "Thank you. Will you really cover for me?"

"Sure." Ronnie crossed her arms and half sat on the edge of the desk. The cocktail dress she'd worn for tonight's venture—a flimsy black-lace number with cold shoulders and long sleeves—wasn't super comfortable for sitting on desks, turned out. She slid back off and stood instead. "I've got nothing else going on."

"Oh. Huh." Frowning, Stacy pulled the elastic band from her thick black ponytail before retying it. "I guess I assumed you had all kinds of stuff to do when you're not on a job."

Ronnie snorted. "Such as?"

"Well hell, I don't know," Stacy grumbled, gesturing vaguely at her. "Hanging out with friends, going to clubs, partying. Family? Whatever."

There's a compliment buried in there somewhere. Maybe. Ronnie shrugged. "Not so much. I Skype with my family sometimes, but when I get a day off, I mostly just stay home."

When she put it like that, it sounded a little pathetic.

Stacy's sour expression finally cleared—it became a teasing smirk, but that was better than nothing. "Never would've thought you were a hermit."

"You should see me in my loincloth. So, what time Wednesday?"

"I'll need to be out of here by two." Stacy's expression softened. "Thanks again. I really appreciate it."

Ronnie waved her off. "Don't get all squishy on me. It's fine. You shouldn't have to choose between school and your job."

"This job is the only thing getting me *through* school. Trust me, if—" Stacy glanced toward the back door, then lowered her voice. "If I had a full ride, I'd have walked out of here months ago."

Karla overhearing their conversation was unlikely, but it was probably safer to steer it away from talk like that, just in case. "Don't take this the wrong way," Ronnie said, "but I'm kinda glad you don't have a full ride." Stacy grinned, lifting a brow, and Ronnie rolled her eyes. "Yes, fine, I like you, okay? Mushy friend time is over now."

"You sure?" Stacy asked, grabbing a familiar red folder and waving it playfully.

Ronnie's eyes followed its movement. "Mushy friend time can continue," she decided. "Diana?"

"Diana." Stacy flipped the folder open, pulling out a contract. "Three hours on Saturday night, at a public venue. She'll pick you up here. And she said . . ." She raised an eyebrow. "'Wear the suit'?"

The suit from Ashworth's was hanging in Ronnie's closet, untouched ever since she'd picked it up. It hadn't felt right to wear it for anyone but Diana. Her ears went hot. "I know what she means. Did you say public?"

"Yep. Doesn't say where, but I guess she wants to show you off."

"I love getting shown off." As she signed on the dotted line, Ronnie's mind raced with possibilities. She'd never been out with Diana before. Well, at Ashworth's, but that didn't really count. A pleasant little tremor ran through her at the idea of people *seeing* them together.

She was so preoccupied that she almost missed the dollar amount at the bottom of the contract. She did a double-take. This engagement was going to cost Diana almost as much as their weekend at the lake. "Whoa, why's this so much?"

Stacy's shoulders tensed, her face twisting slightly. "Karla happened to hear me taking the call. When she realized who it was, she told me to bump up the price. She said she knew Princess Charming would pay it."

Ronnie stared at her. "Can she do that? I thought we had standard rates."

"We do. Usually." Stacy gestured helplessly. "I know it was skeevy, but Karla was standing right there and you know how she is. And your girl did agree to pay it, so . . ." She took the contract back and slipped it into its folder. "Next time she calls, I'll put her on hold if Karla's up here."

"Yeah, do that." It was garbage that Karla had taken advantage of Diana, but there was nothing Ronnie could do about it now. She sighed. "Thanks, Stace. Now check me in so I can get outta here and go back to my cave."

CHAPTER 11
The Fun Pair

O n Saturday, Ronnie showed up at the office to check in wearing her Ashworth's suit and buzzing with anticipation. She'd done her best to put the circumstances of tonight's job out of her mind for now; nothing was going to stop her from showing Diana a good time.

As soon as she walked in, she turned around immediately to examine herself in the windows. "Does my hair look stupid like this?"

Stacy's reflection glanced up from the printer. "Is it different?"

"You never pay attention to me." Ronnie sighed. "This marriage is a sham." Stacy chucked a butterscotch at her, and it pegged her right in the back of the head. "Ow."

"Nice suit," Stacy said, flipping through the stack of papers she'd printed.

"Thank you." Ronnie stuck her hands in her nice pockets and started strolling back and forth in front of the door, glancing out every time she passed it.

"Are you getting whisked away in a pumpkin carriage tonight?"

As if on cue, the Aston Martin rolled up to the curb. "Close enough. See you in three hours!" She cast Stacy a distracted wave on the way out.

Outside, Skylar emerged and stood stoically by the car. "Evening, Skylar," Ronnie said. The chauffeur openly frowned as she allowed Ronnie to crawl inside. Ronnie was about to comment on the rudeness, but that thought hurled itself to the back of her mind as soon as she saw Diana.

Diana was wearing a knee-length chiffon dress a few shades lighter than Ronnie's shirt. Her dark hair was swept into an elegant knot at the nape of her neck, and she was smiling like she knew exactly the kind of fireworks she was setting off in Ronnie's brain. "Hello."

"Hi." Ronnie settled in beside her, barely noticing when Skylar shut the door. "You look amazing. We kinda look like we're going to prom together."

Diana gave her a once-over, then quirked an eyebrow. "I'd take you to prom." Her gaze drifted upward. "Did you do something different with your hair?"

"*Thank* you. I thought I'd take a new look for a test drive." When Diana narrowed her eyes, Ronnie frowned. "You don't like it."

"It's not bad," Diana said, shaking her head. "I just like it best when it's a little messy."

"I'm sure you do." Ronnie scooted toward her with a smirk, stretching her arm across the back of the seat. "You wanna fix it?"

Diana leaned in closer with a slow smile, and ran one hand up Ronnie's neck and into her hair, ruffling it out of its structured state. Her other hand joined the first then, finger-combing Ronnie's hair as she rearranged it.

It was a wonderful feeling, and over all too soon. Ronnie opened her eyes—when had she closed them?—to find Diana watching her with a smoky, satisfied smile. "Better?" Ronnie asked, voice rougher than she'd expected.

"Better," Diana murmured, letting her fingertips rest in the space where Ronnie's jaw met her ear and scratching lightly. "You're still missing something, though." Ronnie cocked her head, and Diana leaned forward, speaking to Skylar. "Pull over up here, please."

They eased to a stop in front of a small coffee shop—the one where Ronnie had run into Diana during her jog. Diana reached into the pocket of the seat in front of her and handed Ronnie a slim black box. "Go to the restroom." Diana indicated the café with a tilt of her head. "Put this on."

Ronnie didn't bother asking what *this* was. She had a feeling Diana wouldn't tell her anyway.

She offered the girl behind the counter a nod and a smile on the way to the back, her mind occupied with the box. It didn't weigh much—maybe a collar? Maybe Diana was going to put her on a leash and parade her around like a trophy. Heat shivered up her spine at the thought as she shouldered into the restroom and locked the door.

It wasn't a collar.

The box held a slip of black lace, and when Ronnie lifted it, the fabric sagged with a slight weight at the center.

"Vibrating panties." She shook her head in amusement. "Nice."

She swapped her own underwear for the new pair and smoothed her suit back into order. On her way out, she nodded again at the barista, who looked her up and down with slightly confused interest. The bullet vibe, snug in its lacy pocket, rolled gently against her labia. Its presence was almost unnoticeable for now, but that wouldn't last long.

In the car, she found Diana with her hands folded in her lap, facing forward, looking quietly pleased with herself. Ronnie waited until they were in motion again before she spoke. "So, a public venue and a little friend. What's the occasion?"

"Phoebe's birthday party."

Ronnie's stomach twitched. It wasn't an unpleasant sensation. So she'd finally meet Phoebe. And, presumably, Diana's other friends. She wasn't just being shown off, she was being shown off to people that *mattered*.

A few months ago, if someone had asked her how she'd feel about sliding into a client's social circle, she wasn't sure she'd have had an answer. Now, for reasons she couldn't quite articulate, she was actually looking forward to it.

"Good, I'll get to thank Phoebe," she said, grinning.

Diana gave a puzzled smile. "Thank her?"

"Of course. If it wasn't for her, I'd never have met my favorite client."

A blush spread across Diana's cheeks and downward, disappearing into the neckline of her dress. "I thought you weren't supposed to have favorites," she said, voice barely above a whisper.

Ronnie shrugged. "Yeah, well." She was still holding the box the panties had come in; now she handed it back to Diana, saying lightly, "You sure Phoebe won't mind you playing sex games at her party?"

Diana's blush faded, and she slipped the box back into the seat pocket. "Based on what you've heard about Phoebe, what do you think?"

"Good point," Ronnie agreed. "And you have the—" Diana lifted a small black remote control. "Yep, there it is."

"Anyway," Diana added, "if you do your job right, she'll never even know. How's your poker face?" She pressed the button. Ronnie leaped off the seat with a yelp, and Diana laughed. "Not too good, I guess."

Ronnie glanced toward the front seat, but Skylar drove on like nothing had happened. Diana shook with silent laughter. It was infectious; Ronnie couldn't help grinning as they leaned in toward each other.

When Diana nibbled her lip and the vibrator hummed to life again, Ronnie inhaled sharply, but otherwise kept quiet. After a moment, Diana pulled away and the buzzing stopped. "Good girl," she breathed.

Ronnie just about melted into the seat.

Then Diana's eyes fluttered open, wandering down to Ronnie's mouth. "Oh damn, my lipstick," she groused, sitting back and pulling a compact from her purse. She fixed her face, then offered the mirror to Ronnie.

Ronnie took it, wiping away the evidence of the kiss and hoping Diana didn't notice when she squirmed in her seat.

Skylar came to a stop at the city's museum of fine arts. When Ronnie had unfolded herself from the car, she stared up at the marble staircase and high white columns. "Impressive, isn't it?" Diana said, coming to stand at her side. To Skylar, she said, "I'll text when we're ready." The chauffeur nodded and returned to the car.

"I've driven past this place," Ronnie said, "but I don't think I've ever been inside."

"I was here on a date a few years ago." Diana tucked her arm into Ronnie's, and they started up the stairs. "They have some beautiful pieces."

"If you say so. I don't know much about art."

Diana hummed with laughter. "So uncultured."

"You love it."

The vibrator zapped, but Ronnie only grinned.

"*Very* good," Diana said.

The praise made Ronnie's skin tingle.

They found the party in an atrium on the second floor, the gentle sound of a string ensemble drifting toward them as they entered. An attendant met them at the door and offered to check Diana's purse, but she politely declined. Only Ronnie knew why: with her clutch in hand, Diana could keep the remote both hidden and readily available.

Diana apparently didn't notice the way the attendant stared after her, but Ronnie did. When the attendant saw Ronnie looking over her shoulder, they flinched and turned away.

Diana slipped her free hand into Ronnie's. "Come on," she said, nodding toward a small cluster of people. "There she is."

She led Ronnie to a petite woman in a tawny, floor-length gown, straight black hair wound into an intricate fishtail braid. When they reached her, Diana took her by the shoulders from behind, leaning in to whisper, "Boo."

The woman turned and squealed, pulling Diana into an ecstatic embrace. As soon as she stepped back, her eyes shifted to Ronnie, darting over her. "So," she said, offering her hand, "*you're* Ronnie."

"And you're Phoebe." Ronnie took her hand and, on an impulse, bent to brush her lips against Phoebe's knuckles. "I can definitely see why the guys always get excited when you're on their schedule."

Phoebe laughed. "Okay, no wonder Dee's so into you. You're like a lesbian Disney prince. A bi Disney prince. Pan? Omni?"

"Bi. And thank you." Ronnie shot a look at Diana, who smiled blithely back. The bullet vibe began to rumble again, sending tremors of pleasure down Ronnie's legs.

"I'm gonna need some deets from you," Phoebe informed her. "But *first*—" She turned to Diana. "I have got to get *you* caught up on the latest drama."

"I can't wait." Diana sounded like she meant it. Ronnie never would have pegged her for a gossip, but she had a feeling Phoebe's enthusiasm could be contagious. Diana turned to Ronnie. "Why don't you go get us a drink?"

"Sure," Ronnie said, and headed for one of the bars set up along the walls of the atrium.

Walking while the vibrator was in motion was interesting. The bullet shifted a little with each step, offering a constant—and distracting—change in pressure. The lacy thong was a bit too tight, so the more she moved, the more the bullet nudged against her. By the time she reached the bar, a light sheen of sweat had formed on her upper lip. She brushed it away, hoping Diana hadn't seen.

She ordered two glasses of a red blend and waited, leaning on the bar and watching Diana talk with Phoebe. Diana seemed to be listening intently, nodding as Phoebe spoke but not saying much herself.

When a man in a sharp gray suit paused at Phoebe's elbow and whispered in her ear, Diana glanced toward Ronnie. Her gaze was hot, a low-burning fire that made Ronnie remember Phoebe's words. *"No wonder Dee's so into you."*

Ronnie raised her chin, meeting Diana's eye with a confident grin. In response, Diana smirked and subtly lifted her clutch.

Oh good. The vibrator has speeds.

"Your wine, miss."

Ronnie took the glasses and thanked the bartender, her voice surprisingly steady considering the bullet whirring away at her groin. She headed back toward the conversation, hoping her legs wouldn't commit high treason by giving out.

This wasn't quite how she'd envisioned her first time in public with Diana, but really it was perfect. There was something to be said for knowing they were the only people in the room who knew how wet Ronnie was, something about the shared secret that made the physical stimulation that much more intense. Ronnie's skin felt tight. She wanted to pull Diana away from her conversation. She wanted to drag her someplace dark and quiet and beg until she came.

The vibrations stopped and Ronnie blinked. *Get it together.*

"Besides," Phoebe was saying, "Sam's just mad because Glen stopped talking to him after the whole Paris thing."

Judging from Diana's laugh, the Paris thing must have been priceless. "I wouldn't either, if I were him. Thank you," she said, accepting the wine from Ronnie. To Phoebe, she continued: "Honestly, if Sam's going to act like a child, he shouldn't be surprised when people treat him like one."

"That's what I told him," Phoebe agreed with a gigantic sigh. "But no." She blinked at Diana's glass. "Wine? Seriously?"

Diana glanced in Ronnie's direction. "I've been . . . trying some new things."

Phoebe hooted. "Yeah, I bet." She turned to Ronnie. "So, you gonna help Dee with her political garbage?"

She pronounced it like *garage*.

Ronnie raised her eyebrows. "Her what now?"

Diana gave a soft growl. "Technically, I was supposed to be at a fundraising dinner tonight," she explained. "My mother agreed to me coming here instead on the condition that I do a little campaigning. And no," she went on, addressing Phoebe, "she is not here to help with that. She's here to make it more bearable."

Ronnie thought of the vibrator and fought to keep a shit-eating grin off her face.

"Okie dokie," Phoebe said easily, then caught sight of someone over Diana's shoulder. "Oh, there's Glen. I gotta go talk to him but *you*—" She poked Ronnie in the arm. "You don't get to leave until I hear all about what your buddies say about me."

"Wouldn't dream of it," Ronnie promised.

Apparently satisfied, Phoebe scampered away.

Diana considered her. "Are you allowed to tell her what the others say?"

"Not technically. But I can bluff."

With a thoughtful hum, Diana pressed against her. "Sometimes I forget what an accomplished liar you can be," she murmured. Ronnie couldn't be sure, but a flash of sadness might have crossed her face at the words. "Maybe the campaign could use you after all."

"I'd much rather distract you from it." Ronnie leaned in close enough to feel Diana's breath on her lips and dropped her voice, adding, "And I don't lie to everyone."

Something glittered in Diana's eyes as she smiled. "Well then," she said, stepping back. She twitched her clutch and a familiar buzz began at Ronnie's groin. "Let's do our rounds."

Ronnie swallowed and forced her response to come out steady: "Let's."

They spent the next hour doing exactly that. Ronnie drew stares, and Diana led them from one circle to the next, ruling the remote with an iron fist. Sometimes she switched it on for no longer than a breath, sometimes for agonizing minutes at a time. If Ronnie got too close to finishing, she slid an arm around Diana's waist, thumb pressing careful circles into the small of her back. Diana caught on to the signal quickly and the vibrations would stop until Ronnie released her.

Diana spent as much time chatting about the campaign as she did about anything else. Why she couldn't just tell her mother she'd done what she wanted, Ronnie had no idea. It wasn't like she'd find out one way or another. Then it occurred to her that all Diana's talk about honesty must apply to herself as well.

Even if it meant making her evening a little bit worse.

When she casually asked one partygoer if he'd been following the local debates, he sneered at her and said it was none of her business what he did with his vote. Ronnie momentarily forgot about the state of her underwear and found herself with fist clenched, ready to retaliate.

Diana must have seen it on her face; she laid a hand on her arm as the man stalked away, and muttered, "It's fine. I expected some of that."

The sour taste of indignation lingered in Ronnie's mouth regardless. "I don't know how you stand this," she grumbled. "Do you ever miss your old gig? What was it, event management?"

When Diana didn't answer, Ronnie glanced at her. She was a little wide-eyed, looking stunned but not in a bad way—more like someone had just told her she'd won the Powerball. "Yes," she finally said, voice faint.

Ronnie frowned. "You okay?"

Diana nodded, seeming to snap out of whatever trance she'd been in. "Yes. Sorry." She turned back to the bustle of people. "I do, actually. Miss it. Lawyers really like to celebrate when they win, so there was still a lot to handle, but Mummy generally let me handle it on my own. Her approach to the campaign is significantly less laissez-faire."

"Well that's . . ." Ronnie squinted. "Good?"

Diana laughed, light and unrestrained. "It used to be. Come on." She tugged on Ronnie's sleeve and said, "We can take a break from business." Like Ronnie was the one running into opposition. Then Diana's smile slipped into something a little more devious. "And I haven't buzzed you in a while."

Ronnie grinned. "Better fix that."

So they did. And eventually, the continued introductions and the persistent rumble in her pants made everything else melt from Ronnie's mind.

Finally, between the wine and the remote, she had to excuse herself to the restroom. When she did, Diana pierced her with a look that Ronnie understood as clearly as if she'd spoken aloud. *If you come while you're in there, it's cheating.*

Ronnie ducked into a stall at the back of the ladies' room and jerked her pinstriped pants down, leaning against the wall with a sigh. She'd been edged before, of course, but never for so long. And never in public. The combination was potent. She pulled in several low, slow breaths, trying to steady herself.

It would be so easy. She could touch herself now, as close as she was, and come within seconds. She felt coiled up tight enough to snap, every muscle quaking with the need for release. She could get herself off, pull the bullet from the thong, keep it in her pocket for the rest of the night. Diana would never have to know.

But it wouldn't be honest.

And it wouldn't be near as fun.

So she finished her business and put herself back together. She pressed the vibe—which, thankfully, was still for the moment—into place and sniffed, shaking her head. She could do this.

She was about to leave the stall when the bathroom door opened, the din of the party drifting in on the heels of footsteps.

"And did you *see* Diana Silver's date?"

Ronnie froze.

A second voice answered. "I *know*." It sounded like the women had stopped at the mirror. "Everybody's talking about her, but nobody knows who she is." Ronnie beamed. She felt like Cinderella at the ball.

"What's her name?" the first woman asked.

"Riley, I think?"

Ronnie rolled her eyes. What was the point of being the center of attention if nobody got your name right?

The first woman hummed thoughtfully. "What's her last name?"

"Diana hasn't said, at least that I've heard. So no Facebook stalking."

"Damn."

"I know. Whoever she is, Diana must be getting something good from her. She's looked like the cat with the cream all night."

A warm flush of ego washed over Ronnie at that. Diana Silver, kind and capable and crazy beautiful, was proud of her. She figured as much, or she wouldn't even be here. But hearing other people say it was like icing on the cake.

The women left the restroom after that, their voices melting into the noise beyond the door, and Ronnie emerged from her stall, preening. She smoothed out her suit and fixed her hair in the mirror, smirking at her reflection. The bullet was still quiet, and she was beginning to cool off. Good thing too. There was no way she was going to disappoint Diana now.

She made her way back to the party, scanning the atrium for a glimpse of Diana. A few couples had started dancing in a corner of the room near the string quartet, and Diana was among them, in the arms of a young man with wild brown hair and a slightly dopey face.

Ronnie frowned as a nameless feeling pooled in her stomach at the sight.

Then a presence at her elbow startled her. "Oh my gosh," Phoebe said, "I can't believe she left you *unguarded*. C'mon, let's boogie."

The band struck up a new song, and Ronnie let Phoebe drag her into the middle of the throng, where she adopted a carefully neutral position with her. She lay one hand on Phoebe's waist, the other clasping her palm rather than lacing their fingers together. As they started to move, she asked, "Who's that Diana's dancing with?"

Phoebe peeked over Ronnie's shoulder. "Oh, don't worry about him. That's just Sam."

"The idiot from Paris."

Phoebe threw back her head with a cackle. "Yes, exactly. Good memory."

Ronnie twirled her around, making her squeal. "So, how long have you known Diana?"

"Oh no," Phoebe said, slightly breathless. "You're not getting outta this. I wanna know exactly what the boys say about me."

"Should've known better than to think you'd forget," Ronnie said, grinning.

Phoebe's returning smile made her nose wrinkle. "Yes. Now gimme."

"Well—" Ronnie sighed "—let's see. Who all have you seen? I know you've hired Alex and Vinnie at least twice . . ."

"Way more than twice," Phoebe confirmed. "They're some of my faves."

"I don't blame you." Ronnie spun her again. "I've been out on a few jobs with Alex. He's great. Stacy calls us 'The Twins.'"

Phoebe pulled back, scanning her up and down. "I hadn't really noticed before, but I can see that. Why twins, though?"

"Use your imagination," Ronnie said. Phoebe made a face and Ronnie chuckled. "Hey, don't judge. It's just pretend, and you know he never disappoints."

"That's true." Phoebe's gaze grew a bit distant and dreamy. "He and Vinnie are amazing together."

"I'm surprised you like Vinnie. I always thought he was kinda grumpy."

"That's what he wants you to think," Phoebe agreed. "But Alex can basically turn him into a puddle. I'd almost be okay with nothing but watching them together."

"Almost."

"Get in the middle of that *one time* and tell me I'm wrong."

Ronnie laughed. She liked Phoebe. "Well, they're fans of you too," she said. "Last time you scheduled them, I heard them calling you 'their girl.'"

It wasn't exactly a lie. She'd definitely heard Alex use the term when telling Vinnie who'd they be seeing, and they could just as easily have been referring to Phoebe as anyone else. "You can't tell them I told you, though. Don't wanna embarrass them."

Phoebe snorted. "I don't think they're easily embarrassed, but I won't say anything." She released Ronnie's shoulder to mime locking her lips, then glanced past her. "Uh-oh." Ronnie squinted, confused, then turned.

Diana and Sam had somehow drawn closer to them and were now only a couple's breadth away. Diana held her clutch in one hand, wrist dangling over Sam's shoulder. Her eyes were fixed on Ronnie, her smile almost predatory. Before Ronnie could react, she saw Diana's wrist flex.

The vibrator exploded into motion, whirring at top speed.

Ronnie jerked almost violently and Phoebe squawked. "Sorry!" Ronnie said, releasing the hand she'd squeezed. "Sorry. Guess I got carried away."

Phoebe took a step back, rubbing her hand and grinning. "More like you got spooked." The couple beside them swayed out of the way, and Phoebe added, "I better give you back."

A touch on Ronnie's shoulder made her turn. Diana had detached herself from Sam, who was smirking like an asshead. "Thanks, Phoebe," Diana said, gaze still on Ronnie.

"Yepper." Phoebe grabbed Sam by the wrist and hauled him away. This was not the time for introductions.

The position that Ronnie took with Diana was not neutral. She wrapped one arm around Diana's waist, palm at the base of her spine. Diana draped her occupied hand over Ronnie's shoulder as she had with Sam, leaving her thumb free for the remote. When Ronnie twined their free fingers together, the contact with Diana's skin felt like heaven. The bullet growled at her groin. She never took her eyes from Diana's.

As they danced, the vibrations lanced through Ronnie's limbs like fire. She was soaked and throbbing and so, *so* close.

Diana's gaze drifted down her body like she could read the tension in every line of it. "How are you doing?"

It was like she could hear the way Ronnie's mind was screaming for release. Ronnie swallowed. "I'm great."

The vibe went suddenly silent, and the sinful glint left Diana's face as her smile dissolved. "You will tell me, won't you?" she asked. "If it's too much?" Her voice was quiet now, not with desire, but something that sounded an awful lot like worry.

Arousal made Ronnie brazen. She smirked. "I don't do 'too much.'"

"Ronnie." Diana's mouth hardened, a crease appearing between her brows. She stopped dancing. "I have to know that you'll call red if you need to."

Despite the total lack of movement there, the pulse at Ronnie's center quickened. "If I need to, I will." She reached up to cover Diana's hand with her own, feeling the subtle swell of the button beneath their thumbs. "I promise."

She pressed.

The bullet shuddered, still at full power. Ronnie sucked in a breath and returned her hand to Diana's waist. She concentrated on tracing Diana's curves with her fingers, on the feeling of lace on her skin. The concern had lifted from Diana's face, replaced by a strange sort of admiration. She tightened her grip and moved in closer, nudging her thigh between Ronnie's legs. It wasn't much, the barest of movements, but it was enough to press the vibe home. Ronnie's world shrank.

When she came, her fingertips dug into Diana's back. She closed her eyes and swore, one curse released in a long, low hiss. Otherwise, she was pretty sure she'd been subtle. A clueless observer might only think Diana had stepped on her foot.

But Diana knew. The buzzing stopped and Ronnie opened her eyes to see Diana gaping at her, a smile twitching at the corner of her mouth. "You stubborn little—"

"Take me somewhere," Ronnie said, her voice breaking. "I don't care where." Her bones felt like water.

"All right." Diana stepped back, glancing around, fingers still twined with Ronnie's. "Follow me."

Nobody seemed to notice them going. The atrium split at one end into three dark hallways, leading to other wings of the museum. A white plastic chain hung across the entrance of each; a sign dangling from the center read, *CLOSED FOR EVENT*. Diana ducked under one of the chains, pulling Ronnie along behind her.

The passage led to a room lined with tall glass cases, each filled with suits of armor from around the world. When they reached the last case, Diana finally released her, spinning around to lean heavily against the wall. Ronnie plunged forward, but Diana stopped her with nails digging into her shoulder. Then she flung her clutch to the floor, keeping hold of the remote, and pushed Ronnie to her knees.

Ronnie knelt, groaning. The lingering weight of her orgasm seeped through her body, still echoing in her groin. She wasn't done yet, but her own need could wait. Right now, she existed for exactly one reason: to make Diana come.

Apparently, Diana agreed. She grabbed at her dress, rucking it up around her waist and allowing Ronnie to yank down her underwear and bury her face between her thighs. Diana tugged Ronnie in close by the hair as she rolled her hips, but she didn't need to hold Ronnie in place; Ronnie had a fierce, firm hold on Diana's backside, lapping at her like she was starving.

She groped blindly until she found Diana's fingers and closed them around the remote. Diana gave a breathless laugh and pressed the button.

The shudder of motion made Ronnie moan, the sound lost between Diana's legs. It was almost too much. It almost wasn't enough. Ronnie released her hand and fumbled at the front of her slacks, pressing the bullet closer, its quiet hum audible now that they were alone. The sound mingled with the rising growl at the back of her throat and Diana's distant, rhythmic panting—but all of that was soon swallowed up by the pounding pulse in Ronnie's ears.

Her second orgasm was a force of nature. She was vaguely aware of Diana's body seizing, of Diana's cries and the subtle rush of warmth on her tongue. Suddenly it was too much to take, the overstimulation rattling her to the bone. When she looked up at Diana, a soft black vignette blurred her vision and she choked out, "*Red*."

The vibrations stopped. Diana hurled the remote away like it was on fire and it skittered across the tiles, lost in the darkness as she slid to the floor. Ronnie reached for her and they huddled in the shadows, waiting for their breaths to slow.

"I'm sorry," Diana said after a moment. "I should have realized—"

Ronnie shook her head. "'S fine. You were busy."

"Are you all right?"

"Yeah." Ronnie nodded, drawing a breath and offering her a shaky smile. "I'm great."

"You were *unbelievable*." Diana laid her fingertips on Ronnie's cheek. "You lasted much longer than I thought you would."

Ronnie was basically glowing with pride. Then reality settled in, and she scrubbed at her chin, grimacing at the smudge of lipstick that came away. "Ugh, I think I ruined my makeup."

"You did."

"Great." Ronnie groped around on the floor for Diana's clutch. "Tell me you have something in here."

"Enough to get you presentable."

Ronnie hummed gratefully and pawed through the bag, pulling out the compact and some eyeliner. Diana sat back and watched while she did what she could.

"Actually, it's not as bad as I thought," Ronnie conceded. She dropped the makeup back into the clutch and passed it to Diana, then rose and offered her a hand up.

When she tried to stand, Diana stumbled. "Hold this," she grumbled, thrusting her purse back at Ronnie. "I need to pull up my underwear." Ronnie laughed, and Diana shouldered into her. "Shut up."

Once Diana got herself arranged and straightened, Ronnie smirked at her. "All better?"

"You're being awfully smart for someone who just came in front of fifty people."

Ronnie grinned, but Diana laid a hand on her sleeve, her expression growing serious. "Which . . . wasn't my intention, by the way."

Ronnie frowned. "I know."

Diana shook her head. "You could have stopped it; you didn't have to—"

"I know," Ronnie repeated. Suddenly she felt almost shy. I wanted . . ." She hesitated. *Well, she wants honesty.* "I wanted to impress you."

Diana shook her head, blinking. "You always impress me." She stepped closer, taking Ronnie's chin in her hand. Her grip was gentle, but firm. "But don't you ever do that again, you understand me?" Her eyes glinted. "I don't want to have to worry that you'll let me cross a line."

Ronnie took her by the wrist. "I won't let you." The words came out much softer than she'd expected. "I promise."

Relief painted Diana's features, and she raised her face.

"Your lipstick," Ronnie reminded her. At Diana's exasperated sigh, Ronnie raised the hand she'd taken to her mouth, pressing a kiss to her palm. It was a simple gesture, almost innocent, but it made Ronnie's insides flutter.

Diana must have had a similar reaction; when Ronnie met her eye again, she turned away. "We should get back."

They didn't stay long after that. Diana texted Skylar, letting her know that they were ready to go, and Ronnie was surprised to get a full-body hug from Phoebe when they told her they were leaving. "I'm glad I bought you," she whispered in Ronnie's ear, making her chuckle.

Outside, Skylar waited dutifully by the car. It was like she never did anything but hang around and wait for Diana.

Not that Ronnie could blame her.

Once they'd settled into the Aston Martin and were safely on their way, Ronnie leaned back against the headrest, closing her eyes with a sigh. The leather was cool against her neck, the rumble of the engine soothing. "I am exhausted," she mumbled. "I don't think I'm cut out for fancy parties."

Diana's quiet laughter made Ronnie's skin twitch pleasantly, like it was trying to jump toward her of its own accord. "But you made such a lovely distraction."

Ronnie peeked at her and grinned. "If you ever need to do any more baby-kissing, let me know."

"I'd rather kiss you."

"Yes, miss." Ronnie slid across the seat and let her hands wander Diana's body as their lips moved against each other. Somewhere in the back of her mind, she felt sorry for Skylar, driving in silence while the two of them made out in the back seat like teenagers. Then she ran the tip of her tongue along the underside of Diana's top lip, and the sigh that followed drove all other thoughts from her mind. She didn't have to worry about Diana's makeup anymore.

She dragged her mouth down Diana's neck, pausing to punctuate the journey with tongue and teeth. Diana's hands were in her hair again, ruining it, her nails scraping exquisitely against her scalp. When

Ronnie reached around to find the zipper at the back of her dress, Diana responded with a soft, dazed "Oh." Then she shivered with silent laughter as Ronnie slid the bodice down to expose her flushed chest. "Honestly, I'm amazed you've got another round in you."

Ronnie bit at one of her breasts, making her gasp. "I don't," she purred. "But you do." She turned her mouth to Diana's other nipple, flicking it with her tongue until Diana was panting, then slipped a hand up under Diana's dress and between her legs.

Diana's underwear was still damp from their tryst in the hall of armor. Ronnie paused, offering a few firm presses of her thumb at the center, and Diana groaned. Ronnie lifted her head to murmur, "Too bad you're not wearing the fun pair."

Suddenly, Diana gave a quiet shriek, and Ronnie jolted back in alarm. Diana's eyes were huge and she was biting her lip, a smile jerking at a corner of her mouth.

"What's wrong?" Ronnie asked.

Diana covered her mouth as a snort escaped. Through her fingers, she whispered, "I left the remote at the museum."

Ronnie stared at her for a beat before laughter bubbled up in her chest and spilled out. From the corner of her eye, she caught Skylar glancing at them in the rearview, nose wrinkled in obvious distaste. But Ronnie ignored her as her forehead met Diana's, and they rode off into the night, giggling.

CHAPTER 12
Tired of You

Ronnie was sitting on the couch in her apartment, flipping idly through the apps on her TV without really looking at them. It had been one month, one week, and three days since she'd last seen Diana.

Or something like that. Ronnie wasn't keeping track.

It was just, this was the longest she'd gone without seeing her for . . . well, a while. Since before their weekend at the lake house, definitely. Diana was a busy woman, obviously—that was why Ronnie had been hired in the first place, after all. She had a lot going on and had never been anything but up-front about her packed schedule. So there was no reason to worry. Diana was probably fine.

Ronnie wondered, was all. Wondered whether Diana's schedule was all that was keeping her from calling Night Life and scheduling a meet. It probably was.

But what if it wasn't?

She thought about the night of Phoebe's birthday party—specifically, the way it had taken her a few tries to get out of the car once they'd gotten back to the agency. She'd said good night, been drawn back in for another kiss, tried to say it again but interrupted herself with her teeth on Diana's neck. It had taken Skylar clearing her throat pointedly to finally separate the two of them.

And ever since then, silence.

As Ronnie circled around to Hulu for the fourth time, a new possibility hit her. What if Diana regretted bringing her to the party, regretted introducing Ronnie to Phoebe and the rest of her friends? It was a way more personal thing than her clients usually went for—when others rented her for public events, it was usually in the capacity of mysterious arm candy. She was pretty sure she'd never met anyone who truly meant anything to her other regulars. Maybe Diana had realized what an intimate choice it had been and was intentionally distancing herself from the situation.

Ronnie flung the remote control onto her coffee table and sighed, swiveling around to lie flat on the sofa. She had a job later and needed to get her head in the game. *Can't be thinking about one client while I'm with another.*

Even if it wouldn't be the first time.

Even if she hadn't thought of Diana as nothing but a client for a while now.

She squeezed her eyes shut and shook her head. Time for a nap.

The next time she thought about Diana, it was about a week later and totally not her fault. She was checking in before a job, chatting with Stacy, when the door that led into the office's interior rooms banged open and Karla strode out.

"Ronnie," she said with her typical bite, "glad I caught you. Whatever happened to your little rich bitch?"

Ronnie blinked at her. "My what?"

Karla rolled her eyes, snapping imperiously at Stacy. As Stacy gathered up her stack of contract folders, Karla explained: "That girl who pays stupid prices for you. More money than sense. Diana something?"

Heat rose in Ronnie's cheeks, creeping out to her ears and down her neck. Her jaw tensed. "Diana Silver."

"That's the one." Karla flipped through the folders Stacy had handed her, apparently unconcerned with how awful she was being. "Where's she been? I could use another bonus."

When Ronnie had been about eleven, she'd had an allergic reaction to the peanut butter served in her school cafeteria. She'd gone red all over, her throat closing up and her breath coming in short, labored gasps. Now it looked like she was allergic to Karla's bullshit.

After a moment of silence, Karla finally looked up from the contracts, eyebrows raised. "What's wrong with you?"

At the edge of her vision, Ronnie could see Stacy watching her warily, eyes wide and shoulders tensed. As good as it would feel to tell Karla to watch her mouth when she talked about Diana, Stacy's expression was screaming that it would be a bad idea.

So she swallowed the words she wanted to say and shook her head. "Nothing."

"Never let them get tired of you," Karla warned, like Ronnie needed the reminder. With that, she turned and trooped back to her office, the door clicking shut behind her.

Ronnie took a deep breath, then another, before turning fully to the front desk. Stacy was grimacing, lips pulled back in sympathetic discomfort. "Yikes," she offered.

"Yeah." Ronnie crossed her arms, ignoring the way the beaded sleeves of her wrap dress bit into her shoulders. "So Diana hasn't called recently, huh?"

Stacy shook her head, looking a little pained. "Not that I know of. I guess she could have while Jewel was on duty, but Jewel would've made a note if she had, so . . ."

"Right." Ronnie nodded. Heaving another sigh, she slid the fingertips of one hand across the top of Stacy's desk, staring at the faint lines they made in the thin layer of dust.

When she didn't say anything else, Stacy hedged, "For what it's worth, I don't think she's like, bored with you or whatever."

Halfway through the sentence, Ronnie was nodding again. "Yeah," she repeated, but all she could think about were her words to Diana on the very first night they'd met: *"purely therapeutic."*

Maybe that's really all she'd been to Diana. Maybe introducing Ronnie to her social circle hadn't been too much, and maybe she wasn't swamped with work. Maybe she was just . . . done.

Ronnie had been too hot before, when Karla had been talking. Now she was weirdly cold as the possibility of never seeing Diana again settled over her.

"Hey," Stacy said softly, shaking her out of her head. When Ronnie glanced up, the younger woman was watching her carefully, like she was afraid Ronnie would break. "You okay?"

Her third "Yeah" was bright—maybe too much so, but Stacy seemed pacified. Ronnie rapped her knuckles against the desk and grinned. Her jaw hurt. "I better get going," she added. "Things to see, people to do."

"Gross." But Stacy was smiling, shaking her head good-naturedly. "Get out of here."

Ronnie gave her a limp little salute and did just that, trying to shake the ache from her shoulders and the thoughts of Diana from her mind.

The third time it happened, Ronnie was in the most innocent frame of mind possible—her niece's birthday was coming up, and she was trolling through a line of local shops for something cool enough to impress a four-year-old. It would've been nice to fly out in person, since she hadn't seen her family since Christmas, but there'd been a scheduling slip, and nobody had offered to take the job off Ronnie's hands. So, since she wouldn't be making an appearance, whatever she sent in her stead would have to be extra good.

The last few shops had been disappointing, geared more toward soy candles and embroidered swear words than anything else. Some places boasted a "children's" section, but what kid was out there begging for a hand-illustrated book of affirmations?

Ronnie was starting to get surly. She needed caffeine.

She followed her nose down the sidewalk and found herself nearing the coffee shop where she'd run into Diana months ago. Midmorning light glanced off the windows of nearby high-rises and made her squint, which was a welcome distraction from the odd feeling that curdled inside her.

She wasn't used to missing people. Sure, she sometimes missed her family, but they were only a call away and she went back home every Christmas. This was something else, sharp-edged and acidic, sitting beneath her breastbone. If she could see Diana right now, she'd . . .

Well, she wasn't actually sure what she'd do.

When an Aston Martin slid out of traffic and stopped in front of the café, Ronnie thought at first that she was imagining it. But no, there was Skylar, unfolding herself from the driver's seat and opening the passenger door.

Ronnie jerked her gaze back to the café so quickly she pulled a neck muscle.

Diana stepped outside, eyes on her phone. She looked incredible, of course, in a deep-red mock turtleneck with her hair pulled into a fishtail braid. Ronnie's face lit up and she started forward. *I'll just say hey. No harm in that, done it before.*

Then someone else strode out, a woman in a sweater vest and chinos, and Diana turned to her. Ronnie stopped. It was Evelyn something, the campaign manager.

She and Diana spoke to each other casually, with easy smiles, and when a passing pedestrian strayed too close to them, Evelyn took Diana by the arm and pulled her gently out of his way. Diana barely blinked.

Ronnie stood there and watched. Somebody shouldered into her from behind, muttering about holding up foot traffic. She didn't move. Evelyn's hand was still on Diana's arm.

It's not like that. Diana said she wasn't her type.

Then she blinked, realizing how that sounded. *Stop it. It wouldn't matter if it* was *like that. You don't get to be jealous of the people in your clients' lives. You've never cared about stuff like that before.*

But this wasn't just some client. This was Diana.

This was Diana, being ushered into the back seat by Evelyn like she needed help, even though she was a perfectly capable grown-ass woman.

Before the campaign manager climbed in behind her, she said something to Skylar. And Skylar responded. With several words. And a smile.

"Oh now what the hell is *that*."

A little old man carrying a Pekingese passed her at that moment, casting her an affronted frown. Ronnie barely noticed. She was too busy staring as Skylar closed the back door, shutting Diana in with Evelyn, and returned to the driver's seat. The Aston Martin's blinker clicked to life and the car merged into traffic, gliding away.

By the time Ronnie made herself move again, she was no longer in a mood for buying birthday presents. She'd try again later, when she didn't feel so much like she'd been gut-punched with a block of ice.

CHAPTER 13
A Normal Client

It had been nearly two months since Diana had seen Ronnie. She'd had precisely one gap in her schedule, but when she'd called Night Life, an unfamiliar and very unhelpful voice on the other end of the line had told her Ronnie "probably wouldn't be available," then hung up.

Otherwise, her life had been an endless parade of organizing interviews, meetings, debates, appearances. Privately, she suspected that she was doing more of Evie's job than she ought to be, but Evie was always so thankful for the help and her mother seemed so proud of the work they did. Saying anything about it would make Diana feel ungrateful, so she offered and agreed and generally made herself indispensable.

She'd just finished running errands and coordinating a Q&A with a local online newspaper and, incredibly, had the rest of the day to herself. It wasn't quite six in the evening, but she planned to go straight home once she'd picked up some tea. She was completely out. Not all of Nana Silver's lessons had taken root in her adulthood, but "always have tea in the house" was nonnegotiable.

So she'd had Skylar stop by Short's.

It had become something of a mainstay when it came to Diana's grocery needs. It lay at a midpoint between her parents' office and her own town house. It was on the way.

The fact that she knew Ronnie shopped there too was completely unrelated.

Maybe not completely. Mostly unrelated. To a certain extent.

She'd run into Ronnie there once before. If it happened again, well. Serendipity was funny like that.

She realized she'd been staring at the shelves of tea for five minutes and still had no idea what they actually sold. She blew out a breath and tried to focus.

"Diana."

She whipped around, heartbeat spiking.

Ronnie stood at the end of the aisle, eyes wide, looking very much like she had the last time Diana had seen her here: dressed casually, hair mussed, makeup minimal. They stared at each other for an instant, then Ronnie's lips tipped upward and Diana's breath caught.

"Hi." Ronnie leaned on the handle of her cart, slowly walking it toward her. "Getting stuff for your mom again?"

"What?" Then Diana remembered why she'd come to Short's last time. "Oh no ..." She gestured to the tea. "It's for me this time."

Ronnie nodded, eyes fixed on her face. Then her smile went strange. "Where've you been?"

Before she could check herself, Diana said, "Where do you think?" Guilt dropped on her shoulders instantly. "I mean, I just ..."

But Ronnie laughed. "I should've figured. I hope your mom knows that if you have a stroke before you're forty, it'll be her fault."

Diana's face burned. "I shouldn't have said that. It's not—"

"No, it's okay." Ronnie was watching her with a soft, amused expression. "You can be real with me. I'm not gonna tell on you." Her eyes skated down Diana's body and back up, evidently taking in her spruce appearance. "What've they got you doing tonight?"

"Nothing," Diana said, hoping she hadn't answered too quickly. "I'm all done for the day."

"Me too." Ronnie's gaze, already warm, turned positively scalding. "You wanna come over?"

A bolt of nerves arced through Diana's mind as she stared. When she tried to speak, her tongue felt too large for her mouth. "To ... your place?"

The heat fizzled from Ronnie's eyes, and her ears went pink. "Obviously you don't have to, if—"

"Do you have a car?" Diana was amazed that her voice sounded as steady as it did, considering she could barely breathe. Ronnie's smile returned.

"Yes."

Tea be damned. "Let's go."

If Ronnie minded leaving her half-filled cart in the middle of Short's, she didn't say so. She didn't say anything, in fact, as they stepped outside—just took Diana's hand and led her through the parking lot.

Diana had never been drunk, but she imagined it must feel a lot like this.

The car was small and sensible, a little white sedan that Diana suspected Ronnie had had for years. She ushered Diana into the passenger seat and jogged around the front to slide in behind the wheel. As the engine growled to life, Diana's phone buzzed in her hand, startling her with a message.

Skylar: ?

She had completely forgotten about Skylar, waiting for her out in the Aston Martin. They must have walked right past her. As Ronnie eased out of her parking spot, Diana tapped out a reply.

Diana: *I'm stopping by Ronnie's for a bit. She'll bring me home. Thank you, you can take the rest of the day.*

Hopefully Ronnie wouldn't mind driving her back. Then again, when would she *be* back? Would Ronnie want her gone as soon as they were finished? Was she expecting Diana to stay over?

There was a reason Diana had never really been one for casual flings; the logistics were always a bit of an awkward puzzle.

At a red light, she looked over to find Ronnie stealing a glance at her as well. Ronnie grinned and Diana's heart kicked her in the ribs. "Are you sure this is all right?" she asked, hoping the question would mask her fluster.

"It is with me if it is with you."

It was more than all right with Diana. "I mean with your boss," she clarified.

Ronnie hesitated, and Diana could see the thought tumbling around behind her eyes. After a moment, she shrugged. "I dunno. It's been a long time since I read my employee agreement."

"I don't want you to get in trouble."

Another brief pause, then Ronnie grinned and cut her eyes toward her. "Hey," she said. "Do you really wanna talk about rules and regs right now?"

She laid a hand on Diana's thigh, giving it a squeeze. It was an obvious diversion, and it worked like a charm: the effect of the gesture settled in Diana's chest like sugar in hot coffee. Something fluttered low in her stomach, shoving any other questions aside.

Soon they were easing to a stop by the curb near a modest apartment building. It was old but not ancient, a red-brick affair with only six stories. How much money did Ronnie make on a regular basis? Surely she was popular enough that she didn't need to live somewhere so modest?

That train of thought screeched to a halt when Ronnie took her hand again, tugging her toward the front steps with gentle impatience.

Ronnie didn't make any moves in the elevator, but she also didn't loosen her grip. Diana glanced at her from the corner of her eye, letting herself stare at the line of her jaw, at the curl of hair behind her ear. Taking a chance, she shifted so that their fingers were entwined. Ronnie stayed quiet, but the corners of her mouth twitched up.

At the end of the third-floor hallway, Ronnie reached beneath the collar of her chambray shirt and pulled out a brass key on a shot bead chain. With a yank, she snapped it from her neck and unlocked the door.

Diana barely had enough time to take a brief look around before the door closed behind them and Ronnie swept Diana into her arms, kissing her soundly. She managed to stop herself from squeaking in surprise, opting instead to hum contentedly against Ronnie's lips.

Ronnie released her with a satisfied sigh, like she'd checked something off her to-do list. "You want the grand tour?"

What Diana wanted was to put her mouth on some part of Ronnie that was deemed inappropriate for public viewing. She wasn't picky which.

But she also wasn't about to turn down an opportunity to learn more about her. "Of course."

It was a fairly decent apartment, Diana saw, once they stepped into it properly. They'd entered next to the kitchen, which was smallish but open to the living room. All the walls were white, making the space seem bigger than it was. It was by no means new or terrifically chic, but the building's owners obviously took some pride in its upkeep.

"Kitchen." Ronnie gestured unnecessarily as they passed it on their way further inside.

The sitting room was simple, with only a sofa and a coffee table arranged in front of a sizable flat-screen hung on the opposite wall. Framed photos adorned the wall above the sofa: black-and-white rural landscapes, all wheat fields, barbed wire fences, and broad, clear skies. "I thought you weren't big on art," Diana said as she peered at them.

"Christmas present from my mom." Ronnie shoved her hands into the pockets of her jeans. "She took them herself. Said they were supposed to remind me of home."

"Are you a farm girl?" Diana asked, unable to hide her amusement at the idea.

"Nah. Just a Southwestern girl." Ronnie grinned, regarding the pictures. "Nice place and all, but there was neither jack nor shit to do in my hometown, so."

"So you gave up your bull-riding dream?"

"It was tragic. I can't talk about it." Still smiling, Ronnie made her way out of the sitting room and down the hall. Diana followed. "Bathroom there," Ronnie continued, waving a hand at the door to their right before pushing open the one on the left. "And this is where I sleep."

The bedroom was wonderfully mundane. Double bed with a wrought iron frame, single nightstand, small chest of drawers. It wasn't flashy; it didn't show off—it didn't look as though it had many visitors to impress. Something odd and hopeful leaped in Diana's chest. "For one horrible moment, I thought you were going to say that this is where the magic happens."

Ronnie snorted. "Nah, there hasn't been any magic here since . . ." She blew out a puff of air. "Guess it's been a few years." Wiggling her eyebrows, she added, "Until now."

"If you're going to call it *magic*, I'm going to leave."

"I'll call it whatever you want." Ronnie pushed off the jamb and leaned toward her, one palm on the wood above Diana's head. "As long as it happens pretty soon."

Their lips met, and Ronnie, without preamble, slid her other hand down the back of Diana's skirt. They fit together: Diana pressed against the door, Ronnie pressed against Diana.

"*God*," Ronnie grated, breath hot and damp on Diana's throat. "I have missed this."

Diana, who had unbuttoned Ronnie's shirt and snaked her fingers under the tank top beneath it, couldn't find enough breath to answer. She offered a staccato nod, hoping that would make her feelings plain.

It must have. Ronnie tightened her grip and tugged her away from the door, steering them toward the bed.

Later, Diana lay on her stomach, head pillowed on her folded arms, and heaved a satisfied sigh. Ronnie was stretched out above her, the length of her body pressed against Diana's back. Her lips wandered from the nape of Diana's neck to her shoulder blades, trailing along in slow, shapeless patterns.

The sun had set while they were busy, and now the room was cast in muzzy gray shadows. Diana wriggled out from underneath Ronnie, making her grumble, and reached for the lamp on the nightstand. When the light clicked on, Ronnie whined, but then Diana snuggled back down under her, rolling so they lay face to face. Ronnie hummed happily.

"Use your words," Diana said, running a hand through Ronnie's disheveled hair.

"No." There was a petulant finality in Ronnie's tone as she nudged her nose into the space between Diana's ear and neck. Diana smiled, tipping her head to give her better access.

Just as Ronnie's teeth skated across her throat, they were interrupted by a low, gurgling growl.

Diana burst out laughing, and Ronnie pulled back, her face going red.

"Hungry?" Diana asked.

Ronnie glared down at her with half-hearted superiority. "Normally I'd've had dinner by now. *Somebody* kept me from it."

"Oh yes, you've been a bound captive." Diana's own stomach complained then, but if Ronnie heard, she didn't say anything about it. "Do you want to go out?" Diana asked, hoping the answer was no. She hooked one leg around Ronnie's, toes trailing up the back of her calf. "Or we could have something delivered . . .?"

Ronnie grinned, a confident spark in her eyes. "Nope." She rolled off of Diana and out of bed. Diana watched her, lazily scanning the strips of pink possession her nails had left on Ronnie's back. "I have a better idea." Ronnie slipped back into her briefs as she spoke before pulling on her chambray shirt, leaving it tantalizingly open.

Then she turned to Diana with a frown.

Diana sat up, drawing her knees to her chest and resting her elbows on them. "What?" she asked, suddenly and unaccountably self-conscious. Was Ronnie starting to regret bringing her here?

But Ronnie just glanced around and plucked Diana's clothes from the floor, running the skirt through her fingers. "Is this comfortable?"

Diana shrugged. "It's not *un*comfortable."

Ronnie cast her a dubious look and folded both pieces over one arm before going to the chest of drawers and laying them across the top. She crouched to pull open the bottom drawer, rummaging through it as Diana watched, baffled.

Finally Ronnie stood, now holding a pair of bright-pink sweatshorts and a threadbare T-shirt. "Here," she said, gently pitching them onto the bed.

By the time Diana had gathered the clothes and managed to get up, Ronnie had retrieved her phone from her discarded jeans. With a few taps, she started some music—something drum-heavy that Diana didn't recognize—then, with a swift smile at Diana, swept from the room.

For a moment, Diana stood in the middle of the floor, slightly stunned. Between the anticipation of sex and, well, the sex, she'd been a little distracted. But now that that was over and she was alone with her thoughts, the strangeness of the situation was beginning to settle over her.

Ronnie was an escort. Diana was Ronnie's client. She was supposed to pay to see her. But here she was, in Ronnie's bedroom, about to wear her clothes, having received a very *enthusiastic* freebie.

What on earth was happening here?

She shook her head and got dressed, wondering if Ronnie knew the tee would stretch slightly across her breasts or if that was a happy coincidence.

She found Ronnie in the kitchen, puttering around and singing along quietly with her phone. If the snatches Diana heard were any indication, Ronnie was completely tone-deaf. She still hadn't buttoned her shirt, and every time she moved, Diana caught a glimpse of one of the bite marks she'd left on her breasts. She wasn't sure whether to feel sorry or satisfied.

"Do you eat meat?" Ronnie asked, interrupting her thoughts.

Diana tried to switch mental gears. "Yes." She leaned on her forearms against the kitchen peninsula and watched Ronnie gather ingredients. "Do you cook for clients often?"

"Hell no." Ronnie laughed. "I cook for me." Diana cocked her head and Ronnie explained, "I don't get a whole lot of me-time, doing what I do. But when I cook, it's just me and the ingredients, and . . . I dunno. It's relaxing." She glanced over her shoulder, looking almost uncertain as her eyes searched Diana's face. "And anyway, I don't . . . I don't think you're a normal client anymore, really. Do you?"

Diana's heart performed an embarrassing backflip at the implications. Swallowing, she tried to keep her voice steady. "I wasn't aware there was a hierarchy." Ronnie's eyes narrowed and Diana clarified: "I mean, what's *normal*? I'm either a client or I'm not, right?"

Ronnie slowly said, "I guess so," but offered no further explanation; she pushed away from the counter, reaching for something. When she turned back, the little seed of worry in her expression had dissolved, and she passed Diana a bamboo cutting board, a couple of bell peppers, and an alarmingly big knife. "Here. Can you slice these up?"

Diana absolutely could not slice them up. She'd never helped anyone cook in her life. And she still had no idea where the two of them stood, really. But she knew when to stop pushing, so she accepted the knife gingerly and, once Ronnie was occupied again, started trying her best.

It wasn't long before Ronnie chuckled under her breath. "Don't do this much?"

Diana glared up at her as she strolled around the peninsula, but before she could retaliate, Ronnie slid around behind her, pressed against her back.

"Here," she said, low at Diana's ear as her arms encircled her, "lemme show you what to do."

She laid her hands on Diana's, gently guiding her through the motions of properly slicing the peppers. "Keep the tip of the knife on the board," she advised. "Move your wrist like this. There you go."

Diana was trying to pay attention, she really was, but it was difficult. The close warmth of Ronnie's body, the brush of their legs against each other . . . If Diana didn't distract herself, she might try to start something again, and the two of them would eventually starve to death. She cast around for literally anything that would take her mind off the feeling of Ronnie's bare breasts grazing her shoulder blades.

Her eyes fell on the refrigerator. Rose-shaped magnets held a takeout menu for a hole-in-the-wall Chinese place and a birthday card with a chimpanzee on it. Underneath that, there was a photo . . .

A photo of Ronnie, holding a baby.

Diana blinked.

The Ronnie in the picture was younger, but only by a few years, maybe. Her hair was very short, almost buzzed. It was a close shot, but the setting was obvious: the baby was clearly a newborn, tiny and wrinkled, with a hospital bracelet on one chubby wrist. Ronnie positively glowed, beaming at the camera.

Before Diana could stop herself, she blurted, "Whose baby is that?"

She felt Ronnie lift her face to follow her gaze. "Oh," she said lightly when she realized. "Mine."

Diana turned in Ronnie's arms to gape at her. She wasn't sure what her face looked like, but Ronnie's mouth twitched and she threw back her head, laughing.

Once she'd caught her breath, she said, "That's my niece, Kris. She's my brother's kid." Diana shouldered into her, not nearly hard enough to have any impact, and Ronnie chuckled again. "C'mon, you didn't think she was *mine*, did you?"

Diana pursed her lips. "I don't exactly have extensive insight into your personal life."

"Well, okay, fair." Ronnie grinned as she stepped away and left Diana to finish the peppers. "But still," she said, going back around into the kitchen, "me as a mom, can you even imagine?"

Diana could, but didn't say so.

As Ronnie began to cube chicken breasts, she asked, "Do you *want* insight into my personal life?"

Her tone was light, but she kept her back turned, as though she didn't want Diana to see her expression. It probably wasn't an offer many people got.

"I do, actually. Is your brother in the city?"

"Nah, he went into construction with my dad, back home." Her shoulders shook with a quiet laugh. "Maybe you should've moved out of state too. Then you wouldn't have to deal with your mom."

Even with Ronnie's assurance that she could be real with her, Diana couldn't quite bring herself to agree. Instead, she said, "But then I wouldn't have met you."

Ronnie paused. "That's true," she admitted softly.

"So," Diana went on. "No kids of your own?"

"No kids of my own," Ronnie confirmed. Glancing at her, she added, "Never married either, just to cover all my bases." She scraped the chicken into a bowl and then nudged the faucet to life.

Diana waited until she'd washed and dried her hands and was rifling through the spice cabinet to ask, "Do you want to?"

"Want to what?"

"Get married."

Ronnie stilled, then turned. A smirk had unfurled across her face, and Diana instantly regretted her choice of words. "Well, gosh, Diana, this is so *sudden* . . ."

Diana chucked a slice of pepper at her. "Not to *me*," she said, ignoring Ronnie's indignant squawk. "To anyone. Ever."

Scooping the slice up from the floor, Ronnie waved it at her. "Wasteful," she chided before tossing it into the garbage. Diana stared at her expectantly as she went back to her spices. "I guess I've never really thought about it," she said, picking out a few small jars. "Like I said, it's hard enough just to date somebody, let alone anything more serious." She started to shake seasoning into the bowl of chicken. "And I mean, I get it. I wouldn't wanna share me either."

"So modest."

"Always." Ronnie's brow furrowed as she added a few more shakes of something to the bowl, leaned in to smell the chicken, then reached for another jar. "Anyway, I guess basically it boils down between that and my job, and . . ."

"And you like what you do," Diana finished. "I remember."

After another sniff, Ronnie nodded in satisfaction and put the spices away. "What about you?"

"I like what you do too."

Ronnie shot a sideways grin at her. "Smartass. I mean kids and everything."

"I know what you mean." Diana brought the cutting board of peppers around to set it by the oven. "I'd like to get married," she replied. "Eventually. Both of my parents are on their second marriage, and I've seen how much trouble paperwork exes can be, so I don't plan on rushing into anything." She glanced up to see Ronnie watching her thoughtfully. "What?"

"I'm having a hard time picturing the kind of girl you'd settle down with."

"Why's that?"

Ronnie bent down to pull a baking sheet from a lower cabinet. "I dunno, just . . ." She chuckled almost nervously, sliding the peppers onto the sheet. "She'd have to be pretty amazing."

Something in Diana's brain shorted out.

With a little difficulty, she said, "Thank you," then took the cutting board back when Ronnie passed it to her, along with an onion.

"Now what I *can* picture," Ronnie continued in a much lighter tone, "is the ceremony." Diana raised an eyebrow at her as she moved back to her cutting station.

"Stay with me here." Ronnie started tossing the chicken, coating it with whatever mixture she'd concocted. "Big church wedding. The whole place is covered in red roses. No—" Ronnie eyed her. "*White* roses. Very tasteful. You're in a lacy ivory princess dress with a ten-foot train." Diana snorted at the mental image, but Ronnie charged on, undeterred. "Organ music, something involving doves. Phoebe could wear something pink and hideous, with big poufy sleeves."

"Do I really seem like the type to torture my bridesmaids?"

"Torture? She'd love it."

Diana laughed. "She probably would." She sliced the onion in half and peeled it all by herself, thank you. "Anything else?"

"Nah," Ronnie sighed. "I think I'm done." She spread the chicken out in the middle of the cooking sheet and washed her hands again, then turned to lean on the peninsula and watch Diana's progress with the onion. "Look at you," she drawled. "A regular Martin Yan over here."

Diana didn't know who Martin Yan was, but she knew when she was being teased. She lifted her eyes to glare, but Ronnie's expression was so soft and her mouth was so temptingly close that Diana found herself leaning in to kiss her instead. When she did, a growl rumbled in the back of Ronnie's throat, sending shivers of satisfaction down Diana's spine.

When they parted, Diana went back to her onion. "Well, I'm sorry to say that I don't think I'll be hiring you as my wedding planner."

"*Damn*." But Ronnie was chuckling as she pushed away from the cabinet. Under her breath, she added, "All that research wasted."

"What?"

"Nothing. Done with that?"

"Don't change the subject," Diana said, pushing the cutting board across the counter toward her. "Here. Tell me."

Ronnie sighed good-naturedly and took the board. "There's this show," she began, her tone creeping around on tiptoe. As she arranged the onion slices on the baking sheet, she went on: "It's stupid. They take people who want to get married at the beach and try to throw these huge weddings on a budget—"

"Oh my God."

"I know, it's—"

"Are you talking about *Island Bride*?"

Ronnie turned. "You watch *Island Bride*?"

"I *love Island Bride*." An almost giddy feeling bubbled in Diana's chest. It was like Christmas had come early, even if Ronnie was looking at her like she'd grown a particularly amusing second head.

"But it's garbage."

"I know!" Diana managed to stop herself from giggling. "I can't help it."

"It's just—"

"Mindless."

"Exactly!" Ronnie was smiling now too, wide and unabashed. Diana wanted to kiss her for a month.

"I don't know anyone else who likes it," she said. "Not even *Phoebe*. Nobody will watch it with me."

"Well, now somebody will." Ronnie slid the baking sheet into the oven and set the timer, adding, "And hey, maybe we can get that wedding planned after all."

When Ronnie woke up later, the two of them were still sprawled in the living room. She was tucked up against a pillow shoved against the arm of the couch. Diana was asleep, head in Ronnie's lap, her breath coming in warm, steady puffs.

Netflix wanted to know if they were still watching *Island Bride*.

Ronnie blinked down at Diana with a drowsy smile. This evening had been about as close to perfect as an evening could get. She ran her fingers through the dark hair spilled across her legs, trying to remember the dream she'd been roused from. The details were long gone, though—all she knew was that Diana had been in it.

"Hey," she whispered, not wanting to startle her. Diana's brow crinkled, but she didn't wake, so Ronnie brushed a thumb lightly across her lips. "Rise and shine, pretty lady," she murmured. "Let's go to bed."

Blue eyes made black by the darkness fluttered open, focusing on Ronnie before widening. "What time is it?"

"Stupid late."

"Oh God," Diana groaned, sitting up and rolling a shoulder. "I have a 7 a.m. meeting, I have to go."

"Shit." Ronnie straightened and shook her head. "I'm sorry, I shouldn't have kept you so late—"

But Diana shushed her with a soft kiss. "It's fine. I wanted to stay."

It would be bad for the couch if Ronnie literally melted, so she made herself maintain a solid state and smiled. The smile was probably dopey as hell, but she couldn't help it. "Lemme get my keys," she said, standing and holding out a hand.

Diana took it, but frowned as Ronnie pulled her to her feet. "I can get a Lyft. You don't have to drive me home."

Oh no. No, that's not happening. Ronnie kept a hold on her hand and lowered her voice. "Can I, though?"

The living room was dim, lit only by the glow of the TV and a streetlamp on the other side of the curtains. But she could clearly see the blush that settled on Diana's cheeks and the smile that made her, incredibly, even more beautiful. She nodded, and Ronnie squeezed her hand before letting go and striding down the hall.

In the safety of her bedroom, she buttoned her shirt and pulled on her previously discarded jeans before digging in them for her keys. After grabbing Diana's clothes from where they still lay on the chest of drawers, she glanced around to make sure she hadn't missed anything. Then she did a quick little victory dance and headed out.

CHAPTER 14
Pull Yourself Together

I f Diana had to list events where an aspiring politician should make appearances, "the grand opening of a casino" wouldn't have made the cut. And yet here her mother was, playing to the elderly crowd who'd shown up looking for a way to blow their pensions. She wasn't sure how Evie had pulled it off, but somehow her mother had wound up cutting the literal ribbon on the place—after a short speech, of course, about the way Sapphire Bay would boost the city's economy and morale.

Diana couldn't care less about the surroundings, and the hard part of the night seemed to be over, so she'd been allowing her mind to wander a bit, thinking back to her time at Ronnie's the week before. She was replaying a particularly delicious moment, remembering the sting of Ronnie's teeth on her inner thigh, when Evie's voice yanked her unceremoniously back to the present.

"That went well."

Diana nodded vaguely. The two of them were standing near one of the cash-out counters, watching as Diana's mother socialized like a shark in a sea of seniors. They'd been tailing her surreptitiously as she made her rounds, staying nearby in case they were needed.

It had taken a little over a half hour, but her mother finally realized they were there and, excusing herself from the group of little blue-haired ladies, swept over.

"I don't need a babysitter, girls," she said, grabbing them each by a shoulder and grinning slyly. "We've gotten all the business out of the way—go have a look around, go have fun!" She leveled a fixed gaze on Diana. "Unless you have somewhere to be?"

Diana barely kept herself from blanching. *Did I space out again?* When she shook her head, her mother simpered and pulled a money clip from her pocket. "Good," she said, pressing a bill into Diana's reluctant hand.

Calm down, Diana told herself. *She can't suspect anything about Ronnie. She was just being snide.*

"Maggie," Evie was saying, sounding half-cautious and half-amused, "you haven't been giving cash to the old folks, have you?"

Diana's mother cast her a politician's smile. "Just a bit here and there, to play on for a while. Don't worry," she said when Evie's brow furrowed in warning, "I haven't said a word about their votes."

"All right." Evie gently grasped Diana's elbow. "Come on, let's take a break. Ever played one of these?" she asked as they walked down a line of jangling slot machines. Diana shook her head. "They're pretty fun, actually. I guess something about them appeals to our monkey brains. Bright colors, loud sounds . . ."

They paused in front of a machine. The bright title card above its screen featured a mustached man in a beret and a line of improbably bosomed can-can girls.

"Colossal breasts?" Diana suggested.

Evie laughed. "Those probably don't hurt." She pulled a slim wallet from the pocket of her sage-green chinos. It was the most casual Diana had ever seen her: no jacket, just an open vest and a button-up left loose at the collar. She looked nice, even if the relaxed aesthetic felt a bit too familiar. "I figured you wouldn't want to spend your mom's cash," she said, taking out a few bills.

Diana glanced dubiously down at the fifty in her hand. "You're not wrong."

When Evie slid her money into the machine, a box at the bottom of the screen illuminated with an accordion-like chime, indicating twenty dollars. She bumped the bet down to ten and said, "Here we go," before pressing the Spin button.

"Ooh la la!" the machine giggled. "*Bon chance, mon ami!*" Diana and Evie shared an incredulous glance as the spinners on the screen whirred into motion.

Before they clattered into place, Diana heard a familiar voice. "Dee!"

She turned to see Phoebe, of all people, scampering their way. Phoebe launched herself at Diana, hitting her with a hug that all but knocked the breath from her. When Phoebe pulled away, Diana wheezed, "What are you doing here?"

Phoebe brandished her pocketbook. "I've been waiting for this place to open for months. I can never go to Vegas 'cause my skin would dry up and fall off, so this is the closest I'm ever gonna get."

Before Diana could reply—and honestly, she wasn't sure how she would—Evie quietly cleared her throat. "Oh!" Diana said, turning to gesture at Evie. "Evie, this is Phoebe Truong. Phoebe, Evie Richards."

"So *you're* Evie," Phoebe said, accepting Evie's polite handshake. "I've heard about you."

"All good things, I hope," Evie replied, smiling.

"Eeeh, I dunno . . ."

Evie laughed, and Diana fought the urge to grimace. Would it be possible to kick Phoebe in the shins without anyone noticing?

Fortunately, Phoebe's gaze seemed drawn to the slot machine. "Are you guys playing? Did you win anything?"

Diana glanced back at the screen as Evie shook her head. "Played ten dollars, lost five," Evie said. "Not a great start."

"Ooh, let me try." Phoebe, with her classic subtlety, elbowed past them to the next machine over. "Wow," she said, blinking at the title card. "Now *those* are some boobs." Evie laughed again and pressed Cash Out on their machine as Phoebe shoved a bill into hers.

Diana's head was swimming. Phoebe and Evie occupied two entirely different hemispheres of her life, and having them together was a bit overwhelming. Not that she was worried they might not get along. Evie was always pleasant and everyone liked Phoebe—well, except Diana's mother. But seeing them in the same place was like watching a conversation between a hawk and a hummingbird.

And she hoped to God the hummingbird wouldn't say anything about Ronnie.

"*Sacre bleu!*" Phoebe's machine exclaimed in its ridiculous accent, yanking Diana away from her thoughts. "Zat's a beeg win!"

"Look!" Phoebe squealed as Evie stared in disbelief. "I got a jackpot!"

"I'm proud of you," Diana said.

Phoebe mashed Cash Out and ripped her ticket from the machine, examining it. "Welp, dinner's on me." Then she glanced up, dark brown eyes darting back and forth between them. "Unless you two had other plans . . . ?"

"No, I think we're free after this," Diana cut in before Evie could reply. She passed Phoebe a bill. "Here, this can be for dessert."

Phoebe raised an eyebrow. "Where'd this come from?"

"Mummy."

"You don't want it?"

"Not particularly."

Phoebe shrugged and chirped, "Okay!" Then she shoved the bill and the ticket into her pocketbook and nudged her way in between them, looping one arm through each of theirs. Diana blew out a quiet breath, grateful for the buffer. "Let's go watch people throw dice," Phoebe decided, striding away with the two of them in tow.

The craps tables were on the second floor, which unfortunately meant that Phoebe had to release Diana and Evie so that they could mount the ostentatious, gold-trimmed escalator. Somehow Diana found herself in the middle, Phoebe two treads above her, Evie one below.

"What are you guys even doing here?" Phoebe asked, surveying the breadth of the casino as they ascended.

"Campaign work. Mummy's wooing the septuagenarian set."

When Phoebe swiveled and looked down at them, baffled, Evie took the next step up, leaning around Diana. "Older people," she explained.

"*Oh*, okay. That makes sense."

Phoebe turned her gaze to the bustling lobby. Evie stayed where she was. She wasn't quite touching Diana, but their proximity made Diana think abruptly of standing in the kitchen with Ronnie, wearing Ronnie's clothes, in Ronnie's arms. There had been something like electricity in the air then, the same crackling energy she felt any time they were together.

Right now, there was nothing.

At the top of the escalator, they saw a small crowd of chattering people gathered around one of the tables. As they approached, a great cheer went up, the spectators hooting and clapping. "What's going on there?" Phoebe wondered as the three of them approached the back of the throng.

A tall, bearded man with a red nose and a shock of white hair stood at the head of the table, muttering to the man on his left. On his right, a breathtaking blonde in a sparkling gold dress blew on the dice in his hand, gazing up at him with lidded eyes and a suggestive smile.

Ronnie.

Phoebe made a weird little noise in the back of her throat. Luckily, Diana was close enough to gently tread on her foot, making her cough and stay quiet.

Diana couldn't stop staring. Ronnie obviously hadn't noticed her; she was too busy leaning on the man's shoulder, speaking into his ear as he juggled the dice. He grinned at her, whispering something in response, and let the dice fly. When they settled, the crowd gave another whoop and Ronnie applauded, beaming at the man as he raised his fists in victory.

"Looks like he's having a good night," Evie commented.

Diana had nearly forgotten about her. "Looks like," she agreed, suddenly wishing more than anything that she was anywhere but here.

She wasn't sure what made Ronnie tear her eyes away from her client. But she finally did, scanning the faces of the people gathered around the table. Diana waited, breathless with anticipation, as Ronnie's gaze made its way to her.

She saw Phoebe first. A half second of recognition flashed across her face, and then her eyes met Diana's. She smiled.

Diana wanted to smile back, but her thoughts were racing. *Don't stare at me,* she silently implored. *Don't stare or Evie might notice, might say something, might start asking questions—*

But it seemed Evie's attention had already wandered. "They've got poker over there," she said, apparently addressing both Diana and Phoebe. "It's a lot less crowded."

"Yeah!" Phoebe said, a little too brightly. "Yeah, let's go over there!"

It was probably a good idea. The best thing Diana could do right now would be to get away from Ronnie. If being with both Phoebe and Evie felt like the meeting of two hemispheres, throwing Ronnie into the mix felt like planets colliding. At this point, the night couldn't possibly get any weirder.

As they backed out of the pack of onlookers, Diana felt Evie's hand on the small of her back, warm and solicitous. She fought to keep herself from tensing up, didn't want to be too obvious, but she needed some space.

"You two go on ahead," she said, stepping away from Evie as subtly as possible. "I'm going to find a restroom." *If nothing else, that'll give me a second to collect myself.*

Evie seemed concerned, but Phoebe, bless her, said, "We'll be at the blackjack table." She grabbed Evie by the sleeve and tugged her along, leaving Diana to make her way toward the opposite far wall.

She charged into the ladies' room, keeping an ear open toward the long row of beige stalls. Mercifully, they seemed to be unoccupied. Diana leaned against the sink, gripping the cold marble. She took a deep breath, then another, and raised her head. Her flushed reflection stared at her from the mirror.

"Pull yourself together," she hissed at it. She straightened, rolling her shoulders and closing her eyes. When she opened them, she relaxed. She at least looked a bit less flustered.

A memory stirred and she glanced back at the door. Months ago, the last time she'd seen Ronnie with a client, she'd given in to temptation and followed her into the restroom. She'd told herself it was nothing, harmless flirtation, an attempt to convince herself that her tryst with the escort was a one-off bit of fun, never to be repeated. But the draw between them had been almost palpable, a current running through their words like a live wire. She hadn't touched Ronnie then, even though she'd wanted to. The intensity of her own desire had surprised her. And far from quelling that desire, their continued meetings had only made it worse. Touching Ronnie was kindling, feeding a fire Diana probably should have put out long ago.

She chewed on her lip, staring at the door. *Please,* she thought despite herself. *Please, please . . .*

The door cracked open.

Ronnie was heartbreakingly beautiful. Between her hair and the way her dress sparkled in the light, she reminded Diana of a bolt of afternoon sunshine. All she said was, "I shouldn't be in here."

All Diana said was, "I know."

They stared at each other, then turned in tandem to look down the aisle.

They slammed into the last stall. As soon as Diana got the door locked, she found herself wrapped in Ronnie's arms, tight enough to take her breath away. "Please," she gasped before pulling Ronnie closer, kissing her like she was starving. There were no more words for a long while after that, only the soft sounds of them devouring each other.

Finally they parted, panting, and Diana had to take Ronnie's face in her hands to keep them from shaking. Ronnie didn't seem to notice—she was busy rucking up Diana's skirt.

Diana choked away a moan when Ronnie reached into her underwear, arching away from the hard metal wall and closing her eyes. *This has got to be a new low,* the voice in her mind sighed. *You're getting fingered in a bathroom. A casino bathroom.*

Yes, growled a voice farther down, *and it feels incredible.*

She knew she ought to keep quiet, but couldn't stop the full-throated groan that erupted when Ronnie circled her thumb in a particularly clever way. Ronnie pulled away from her neck, hushing her with a staccato hiss. "I've got you, beautiful," she breathed into Diana's skin, voice tight. "I've got you."

Diana broke apart, coming with a desperate whine muffled against Ronnie's temple. "Oh my God, oh my *God*," she whimpered, hips jerking as another wave crashed over her. She sagged into the metal divider, drawing a shaky breath before offering a faint, final, "Oh my God," and lifting her head.

Ronnie reclaimed her fingers, now glistening, and slid them into her mouth with a satisfied hum. The visual set off another distant pulse between Diana's thighs, and she drifted forward, eager to return the favor.

But Ronnie raised her other hand before Diana could get too close. "I can't," she rasped. "He never wants sex, but still."

Her client. Of course. Diana stepped back, smoothing down her skirt. "Are you going to get in trouble?"

"For what, going to the restroom?"

She said it with a smirk, but there was no sign of the confident spark that had dazzled Diana so much the last time they'd been alone together. "Are you all right?" Diana asked.

"I'm great. How's my hair?"

Her hair was fine. Diana smoothed it anyway.

"Thanks." Ronnie's fingers whispered along Diana's jaw, the pad of her thumb tracing her lower lip. "I guess I better get back out there."

"I guess so," Diana agreed.

Ronnie nodded, and when she leaned in for a kiss, the taste of herself on Ronnie's lips made Diana shiver.

Then she was alone in the stall. She heard Ronnie wash her hands, followed by a short stretch of silence as she presumably checked herself for any signs of their rendezvous. The din of the casino amplified, then quieted again as the restroom door eased shut, and Diana finally made her own way up to the mirror.

She tried to pay attention to her appearance, to make double and triple sure that she wouldn't give herself away, but it was difficult. Ronnie had seemed so strange, quiet and almost withdrawn, so unlike how she'd been at her apartment. Diana hated to see her like that, hated even more that she didn't know what was wrong.

But she had to push all that aside if she didn't want to explain herself once she found Phoebe and Evie. *Especially* Evie. She ran her fingers through her hair and wiped at the places where her lip gloss had smudged.

Then she took a few deep breaths, squared her shoulders, and stepped back out into the lights.

CHAPTER 15
Enough

Ronnie drummed her thumbs on the steering wheel as she drove back to the office, distractedly humming along to the song thumping through the Bluetooth. Her high-roller was always a pretty good time and an easy job—all she had to do was show up, look pretty, blow on some dice—but tonight had come with an unexpected bonus. Any evening that included her body on Diana's was time well spent.

Still . . . she'd been a little surprised at herself. In all her years with Night Life, she'd never abandoned a paying customer, not even the most boring ones. A few months ago, if anyone had told her she'd sneak off from a job to play around in the bathroom, she'd have laughed in their face.

She hadn't been able to help it though, not when she'd seen that Evelyn woman touching Diana again. If Diana had been on her own, or even just with Phoebe, the sight wouldn't have been enough to make Ronnie abandon her professionalism.

Probably. Maybe.

Yeah, she'd asked Diana over to her apartment, but that didn't count. She hadn't been on a job then, hadn't been ignoring a client. What she did on her personal time was nobody's business.

And anyway what happened tonight was *fine*, she hadn't been gone for longer than a normal trip to the toilet would take and hadn't given herself away. Her gambler had won big, like always, and slipped her a few hundred in cash—he wouldn't have tipped her if he suspected anything or been unsatisfied.

She pulled up in front of the office and killed the engine, sliding out of the car with a sigh. It was fine.

Once she got inside, the first thing she noticed was Stacy's empty desk. The second was Stacy herself, huddled at the door at the back of the foyer, one ear pressed to the wood.

She saw Ronnie and held a finger to her lips, then waved her over. Ronnie, taller by a head, had to hunch even further to mutter, "What's going on?"

"Karla's got Sabrina in there," Stacy answered, squashing her face closer to the door as though that would help.

Ronnie ran through her mental list of the other escorts, finally settling on a short, sprightly woman with straight brown hair. Ronnie knew her but barely; they'd never been on a job together, and worked different enough hours to rarely cross paths at the office. "Why?"

A shrug. "No idea. Neither of them looked happy, so I'm guessing it's not a raise."

Sabrina had never seemed like a troublemaker, and it didn't sound like anybody was yelling. Ronnie hadn't seen many serious incidents in her time at Night Life—but what she *had* seen made her hope, for Sabrina's sake, that this wasn't one. They stood at the door for another moment. It seemed a little silly to do this in a floor-length gold dress, but curiosity was stronger than dignity.

Wait, it's past midnight. Jewel should've come in hours ago. She leaned toward Stacy. "What are you still doing here?"

Stacy rolled her eyes. "Jewel called in sick."

"Nice of you to cover for her."

Something about Stacy's answering hum gave the impression she hadn't had much choice in the matter. "Somebody's gotta be here."

"Don't see why it always has to be you."

With a wry smile, Stacy said, "See, why can't *you* be the boss?" Then her eyes went wide and she raised a finger with a shush.

"I didn't say—"

Stacy hissed and then went still, holding her breath.

Somewhere in the hall beyond, hinges squeaked and Karla's voice grew audible. "You understand, I'm sure."

Ronnie and Stacy scrambled back to Stacy's desk and tried to strike halfway natural poses. By the time the door opened, Stacy was in her chair, staring at a contract, and Ronnie was tapping at nothing on her phone.

As subtly as she knew how, she glanced up from the screen.

Sabrina wasn't crying as she walked past, but she obviously had been: her face was streaked with mascara, her eyes and nose red. Still, she walked upright, back straight, jaw tight. There was something resolute about her, something that seemed at odds with her recent tears.

Karla marched behind her like a prison guard, wordlessly pulling the front door open. Sabrina, equally silent, stepped out into the street. Only once she'd disappeared from sight did Karla release the handle, letting the door sink back into its frame. Then she crossed her arms beneath her breasts and sighed.

"Ronnie."

Night Life's proprietress was a smoker, but years of tar and nicotine had only slightly roughened her whip-crack of a voice. Ronnie stood a little straighter. "Yeah?"

Without looking back, Karla said, "You know that outside relationships are . . . *discouraged*, don't you?"

Ronnie's stomach dropped. "Of course," she lied.

"Good. At least *somebody* does." With that, Karla spun on her heel and strode past them, slamming the door behind her.

Silence hung in the air, and dread began to slide down Ronnie's spine like cold oil.

She'd been having such a nice night.

"You okay over there?" Stacy asked.

Ronnie turned to her slowly. "I know it's been forever since I read the manual, but I don't remember the rules saying we can't date."

Stacy shook her head. "They don't. There's nothing about outside relationships in the employee agreement." She tossed the contract she'd been holding aside, sending it spinning across the desk. "Karla just doesn't like it. Last time this happened, I heard her telling the guy that escorts can't give clients their money's worth if they've got someone waiting for them at home."

Guess I've never been serious enough about someone for it to matter, Ronnie thought. Then she registered what Stacy had said. "Last time? This has happened before?"

Stacy screwed her face up thoughtfully. "I've seen it . . . three times, I think, since I've been here? So not a lot, but . . ."

"But enough," Ronnie finished.

She couldn't banish the memory of Diana in her apartment, her own words clanging around in her skull. *"I don't think you're a normal client anymore."* She'd taken Diana into her home, made her dinner, spent the evening watching awful television. Fallen asleep with Diana's head in her lap, for God's sake.

She and Diana had never talked about this . . . *thing* between them. But it probably counted as an outside relationship.

An outside relationship with a client.

Which was so, *so* much worse.

Stacy's voice lanced through her thoughts. "Weren't you here to check back in?"

"Oh, right." Ronnie shook her head, trying to clear out the fuzz as Stacy pulled up the log on her laptop.

"You sure you're all right?" Stacy had paused in her typing and was peering up at her, dark eyes intent.

Ronnie hesitated. She *wasn't* sure, and she almost wanted to say so. She almost wanted to tell Stacy everything that had happened with Diana recently, maybe even what had happened tonight at the casino, maybe—

But that would be a bad idea, with Stacy obviously drained from a long day and Karla within spitting distance.

So she forced what she hoped was a reassuring smile. "I'm good. Just tired. How much longer do you have to stay?"

Stacy glanced at the log. "Not long. Vinnie's back at one and he's the last one out."

"Good." On autopilot, Ronnie grabbed a butterscotch from the bowl. "See you later."

It was almost one in the morning when Ronnie got home. She locked the door behind her, chucked her purse onto the kitchen counter, and walked straight into the living room to collapse on the sofa.

For the longest time, she did nothing but stare at the ceiling.

She'd been sucking on the butterscotch candy since she left the office, but it didn't taste right, kept brushing bitterly across her tongue. Finally she bit it, shattering it between her teeth and swallowing the pieces.

She thought back to her first night with Diana, to Diana asking if she liked what she did. Ronnie had been honest about that. She loved her job. It sated any need she might have for human contact, without the risk of emotional exhaustion or baggage. Her professional life in the city before Karla found her had been dull and draining; she'd never even considered escorting before, but once she'd started, it was like a switch had been flipped inside her. It was something she enjoyed, something she was *good* at. Something she could do forever.

Unless she did something stupid enough to get fired over. Which had never seemed like a possibility until recently.

It would be bad enough—apparently—if she'd gotten herself tangled up with some rando. But she'd managed to get involved (*involved*, the word burned at her insides) with a regular client. Someone who'd made Karla a lot of money. Someone who, if Ronnie made the right move, would never contribute another cent to Night Life.

She scrubbed her hands over her face, smearing her makeup. If she kept this up with Diana, getting fired might be the least of her worries. Karla had connections all over the city, the state, probably the country. She'd see to it that Ronnie never escorted again. Her savings wouldn't last forever, and then she'd be right back where she was before—maybe even all the way back home, where she'd be a clock-watching cube monkey for the rest of her life.

On the other hand, she'd known Diana for all of what, eight months? Was that it? Not long at all, no matter how it might feel. And even if they were . . . together, what would happen if it went south? If Diana's mother won her stupid election, she'd hoard all Diana's time and Ronnie would probably never see her again anyway. Then she'd be left with nothing to show for it. If she was going to wind up brokenhearted either way, she might as well hold on to the only job she'd ever loved.

She sat up and heaved a sigh, then reached around to unzip her dress.

In the shower, she pressed her forehead to the cool, smooth tile, letting water spill down her back. It was physically soothing, but did nothing to calm her mind. Sounds and images ricocheted around her brain: Diana smiling at her across the kitchen, Sabrina's tear-streaked face, Diana's gasps of pleasure, Karla's unrelenting voice saying *discouraged*.

It should be an easy decision, really.

Her phone read 2:10 when she crawled into bed, nauseated and with a migraine threatening at the edge of her brain. She lay there for a while, staring into the darkness and trying not to remember being there with Diana, trying not to think of Diana in her home, in her bed, surrounded by all her things like she belonged here.

Finally, she forced her eyes shut. She'd fall asleep eventually.

CHAPTER 16
We're Together

Diana's phone rang just as she and Evie were finishing their meeting with the manager of the Old Town Theatre. "I'm sorry," Diana said as she stood, "I need to take this." She didn't even know who it was, but the odds of a call being campaign-related were always good these days.

"I can finish up here," Evie said. The manager, a bohemian-chic type in her fifties, gave Diana a polite nod.

As soon as Diana stepped out to the lobby, she answered, not really looking at the screen. "This is Diana Silver."

"Hi, Ms. Silver." The voice on the other end of the line was familiar, but was tinged with a shadow of formality that Diana wasn't used to. "This is Stacy, with Night Life. Is this a good time?"

Glancing over her shoulder to make sure Evie wasn't on her way out of the manager's office, she said, "Give me a second."

Excitement shot through her veins as she hurried across the foyer. She'd contacted Night Life a few days ago, asking to schedule Ronnie the day after the city council vote would take place. She was rather hoping this appointment might be a sort of last hurrah—one final fling before she casually suggested they cut out the middle man and make things official. The possibility of Ronnie being her girlfriend made Diana a little light-headed.

She shouldered out one of the theater's sets of double doors, getting halfway down the front steps before she raised her phone back to her ear. "All right, here I am."

"It's about your request to see Ronnie."

Stacy's voice still seemed oddly formal, but Diana ignored that. Her heartbeat was thundering in her ears. "Yes?"

"I'm sorry, but she's, um. Declined."

The words took a moment to sink in. ". . . Excuse me?"

"She declined the contract."

Diana reached for the nearest handrail, steadying herself. *What on earth . . .* "Did she say why?"

A pause. "Escorts are not required to provide grounds for refusing a contract."

It was a phrase almost certainly plucked straight from the company handbook. "Oh." Diana's pulse kept racing, but now it seemed to skip every other beat. She looked up at the sky, which had the audacity to still be clear and blue. So many thoughts had crowded into her mind at once that it had somehow managed to go blank.

"Ms. Silver?"

"I'm here," Diana muttered, snapping back to the moment. "I'm sorry. This just seems . . . unlike her."

She heard Stacy suck in a breath, and when she spoke again, all the formality was wiped from her voice. "*Yes*, yes, it does. She's never done this before, and I damn sure never thought she'd do it with you. I *know* she likes you." Diana's face heated and Stacy went on: "Did something happen?"

Diana thought back to Sapphire Bay. Ronnie's strange aloofness, the remote look in her eyes. "I'm not sure."

"Well, I'm sorry." This time, the scheduling manager actually seemed sincere. "Technically, I'm supposed to ask if you want to try a different escort, but . . ."

The laugh that forced its way from Diana's throat sounded sour. "No, thank you."

"I didn't think so. Have a good day."

"You too," Diana replied absently. She lowered the phone, her other hand still gripping the rail, and gazed out into the street, seeing nothing.

Had she done something wrong? Pushed too far by going to Ronnie's apartment? But no, that had been Ronnie's idea. Maybe she'd broken some sort of rule by acknowledging Ronnie at the casino. Maybe she should have ignored her and continued with her night. But she hadn't approached Ronnie in the open, hadn't spoken to her where anyone could see or hear.

How had she managed to ruin this?

"Everything good?"

Diana nearly leaped off the stairs at Evie's voice. She hadn't even heard the front doors open. "I'm fine," she said, turning and forcing her face into a normal shape. Her eyes stung. "Appointment stuff."

"Gotcha." Evie bounded down the steps, beaming. "Debate's set for Saturday after next, so that's that handled," she said once she'd reached Diana. They took the rest of the stairs side by side. "I'm sure you'll be busy helping out when your mother wins," Evie hedged as they made their way to her BMW, "but I hope we'll still be able to see each other."

"I'm sure we will," Diana said as she slid into the passenger seat. When Evie smiled, Diana mirrored the gesture, wondering if it looked as much like a rictus as it felt. *I just wish I could see Ronnie instead.*

Two days later, Diana found herself at Baba's, where a dinner reservation had been made for three. So of course only Diana and Evie had wound up there. Normally, Diana would have been beating back irritation at her mother for standing them up—again—but tonight she just felt muzzy and gray.

"What'd the naan do to deserve that?"

Diana blinked back to the warm light and jewel tones of the restaurant, looking down at her plate. She'd been steadily tearing a piece of flatbread to shreds, dropping the remnants into her untouched korma. Cringing, she glanced back up at Evie, who was watching her with a hesitant grin.

"Sorry." Diana sighed, laying the naan aside and picking up her fork instead. She wasn't hungry, but poked around in the sauce for a smallish piece of chicken anyway.

"Listen," Evie said, her voice going gentle. "I don't want to pry, but ever since the other day, you've seemed a little . . ." She tilted her head from side to side. "Absent? I don't think you heard a word of your mom's interview with that podcast."

Diana bullied her mouth into a half smile. "Did I miss anything?"

"Nothing crucial." Evie chuckled. "But still." Her dark, warm eyes searched Diana's face. "You can talk to me, you know."

It was kind of her, and Diana truly appreciated the gesture. But she couldn't imagine a more excruciating conversation than trying to discuss her current situation with Evie. What could she possibly say? *I fell head over heels for a call girl and I thought she liked me too, but now she won't let me pay her for sex.*

Just thinking it was enough to make her consider drowning herself in the korma.

So she shook her head and did the mental gymnastics needed for an explanation that was technically true. "It's fine. I thought I'd be seeing a friend soon, but she canceled. Abruptly."

Evie frowned. "That sucks. Can you reschedule?"

"That's . . . up to her, I guess."

"Well, she's missing out." Evie took a sip of nimbu pani and cleared her throat. "I know I'm probably not as cool as she is," she hedged with a small smile, "but I'm pretty much always available for hanging out. If you want."

I've had worse company. A leaden lump still sat in Diana's chest, but she managed to push enough air out around it to say, "I'd like that."

Evie proved just as reliably available as promised.

It wasn't bad. Diana got along with her well enough outside of their campaign responsibilities, and Evie knew a great little tea place in midtown. And Diana's mother was certainly happy to hear that they had plans. True, being alone with Evie was a bit like walking a tightrope, a careful balancing act between friendship and leading her on. But the challenge was enough to occupy Diana's mind, sometimes even enough to push Ronnie from her thoughts entirely.

Not often. But sometimes.

In the meantime, she and Evie became regulars at RoyalTea and the election loomed ever closer. Then, before Diana knew it, the night of the debate was on them.

The foyer of the Old Town Theatre was lit from top to bottom with original stained-glass sconces, the crimson carpet painstakingly restored over the years. It was a lovely and very popular venue, and securing it for the debate had been an impressive feat, especially on short notice.

Even if the other candidates weren't intimidated by Maggie Silver's policies, they had to be impressed with her connections.

"Not a bad turnout," Diana commented when Evie joined her near one of the old ticket counters, where she'd been watching people mill about before things got started.

"Not bad at all." Evie scanned the crowd, eyes narrowed. "I see a lot of Oliver buttons, though."

Diana inclined her head in concession. "Oliver's good. But Mummy can talk circles around her, so I think we'll be all right."

The foyer lights blinked, and Diana and Evie exchanged glances. "Here we go," Evie said. They slipped through a side door leading backstage, where they'd planned to watch the whole circus. The schedule for the night was simple: each candidate had the opportunity to give a short speech, after which all three would respond to questions posed by the audience and regulated by a moderator.

Things went smoothly, all told. Evie had a copy of the speech they'd worked on together, and pored over it while Diana's mother had the podium. Diana had begged her to stick to the script, and for the most part, she complied. The debates were mainly civil and, as Diana had predicted, even Katherine Oliver couldn't stand up against thirty years of law and motherhood.

An hour and a half later, it was over. Diana released a relieved breath and returned Evie's smile.

The moment of serenity was shattered almost instantly by Diana's mother sailing backstage and enveloping the pair of them in a hug. She smelled of light sweat and heavy Dior.

"Well, girls, what do you think?" she said. "I knocked that speech out of the park, huh?"

Diana was actually glad for their current position; it meant her mother couldn't see when she rolled her eyes. Evie had written the speech, Diana had edited it, and her mother had barely looked at it until the night before.

But Evie said, "It was great, Maggie," and Diana said nothing.

Out in the foyer, there were plenty of people who wanted a one-on-one with the candidates. Diana and Evie hung back and let it happen, much as they had at Sapphire Bay. Only this time, there were no flashing lights to distract, no diversions from what needed doing.

And, Diana thought dismally, *no Ronnie.*

Evie's hand closed gently around her elbow. When Diana cut her eyes sidelong at her, Evie's gaze was still on the crowd. And she kept it there even as her fingers made their way, light and tentative, down Diana's forearm to carefully twine with hers.

It was sweet. Cautious.

Diana let her do it. She didn't expect to feel sparks, and she wasn't disappointed, but it wasn't uncomfortable.

Evie leaned toward her slightly, their shoulders pressed together, to murmur, "Gershwin's already left, did you see? She knows she doesn't have a chance."

Before Diana could reply, Evie glanced across the room, her eyebrows perking up. Diana followed her gaze and saw her mother waving Evie over, clearly intent on introducing her to someone.

Evie squeezed her hand and cast her a bright smile. "Be right back."

Diana watched her sweep across the room to shake hands with the man currently in her mother's thrall. Evie spoke to him with an earnest expression and casual charm, the easy manner of someone who was comfortable with themselves and sure of their place in the world.

That sort of confidence could be very attractive. Diana had fallen for it before.

And Evie is so nice, she thought with a sigh. *Nice and smart and respectable and my mother would be* ecstatic . . . Her hand was still warm from where Evie had held it. She waited for the warmth to spread through her whole body, for it to pool in her chest and stay for a while.

Her hand cooled.

The World's Ocean Aquarium was one of the largest in the area, famous for its shark tunnels and collection of aquatic mammals. Diana had been there several times—once or twice on school field trips, but mostly with her sister. On the rare occasions when Esther came home to visit, she always wanted Diana to come with her to see the latest additions.

Diana had never been there on a date before. Until now, apparently.

The votes for city council were being tallied that night. Evie had assured Diana's mother that there was nothing else to be done at this point; anyone who hadn't already made up their mind would decide at the polls. All they could do now was wait.

Then she'd asked Diana if, while they were waiting, she wanted to visit the aquarium.

They'd gone to a lovely dinner at a new spot called Café Sforzando, where Evie had insisted on footing the bill, and now they were strolling through the Southeast Asia exhibit.

"Blue-spotted Mudskipper," Evie read, peering at a plaque. "Weird-looking little guy, huh?"

Diana stepped up beside her, peering into the tank. "That's actually a female," she said, pointing. "Males have a smaller dorsal fin." When Evie shot her a bewildered glance, Diana shrugged. "My sister's two great loves are billiards and brackish water life."

Evie laughed. "Everybody's got to have a hobby, I guess."

They moved on, departing Southeast Asia and finding the North American river otters. The aquarium had three—Moe, Larry, and Curly—and they were all performing, diving and splashing and spinning for the delighted crowd of onlookers. Diana focused on their slippery antics, rather than on the fact that Evie was holding her hand.

She wasn't having a bad time. Dinner had been delicious and she liked the aquarium well enough. Evie was as easy to talk to as ever. Diana *was* enjoying herself. She was. Maybe she could even get used to this. Functional relationships had been built on less than the rapport they shared. And it would mean Diana finally doing something right in her mother's eyes.

It could be worse, Diana thought as they left the otters to their showboating. *It could be so much worse.*

The giant Pacific octopus hadn't attracted much of a crowd; Diana and Evie were the only ones in the darkened alcove where it was housed. They watched it drift eerily from one side of its tank to the other, only stopping occasionally to rest one thick tentacle against the glass.

After a stretch of silence, Evie said, "Your mom asked me to stay on after the election. Lead adviser to her team."

Diana followed the octopus's progress. "What did you say?"

"I agreed. Tentatively."

From the corner of her eye, Diana could see that Evie was still watching the tank too. "Tentatively?"

"I wanted to talk to you about it first."

Now Diana looked at her. "Why?"

Evie shrugged. "I thought you'd be all right with the idea, but I wanted to make sure." She still hadn't moved, but Diana could tell she wasn't really seeing the octopus anymore. "I'd like to stay on. Help your mom with her run, if I can. Especially since she's new." A grin hovered at a corner of her mouth. "Maybe actually meet your sister someday."

She finally turned, Diana's hand still in hers. "But I won't lie. Probably the biggest factor in my wanting to stay is you." Her dark eyes searched Diana's face, and she quietly added, "Is that all right?"

The lining of Diana's throat throbbed; for one horrible moment, she was afraid she might cry. But she pushed the feeling away—she pushed all her feelings away.

Evie would make a wonderful adviser, and Diana suspected her mother would need all the advice she could get. She wanted her mother to do well in her position if she won. And, since she'd likely be working for her parents no matter what, it would be nice to know that it would be with someone reliable.

So when she said, "I would like it if you stayed," it wasn't a lie.

Evie's grin settled into place, and her grip on Diana's hand tightened. Then she leaned in carefully, giving Diana plenty of time to step back.

And she did.

It was instinctive, some sort of antimagnetic reaction over which Diana had no control. All she could think about was the last time she'd been kissed, Ronnie's lips in the darkness of the casino, the way Ronnie's mouth seemed to fit perfectly against hers.

Seeing the hurt and confusion on Evie's face, she felt like a heel. "I'm sorry," she stammered. "I just . . ." She took a deep breath. "If this is going to happen, I need to move slowly."

"Okay." Evie nodded. "All right, yeah, that's fine." She watched Diana cautiously. "Have I ruined the whole afternoon?"

Diana smiled. It made her jaw hurt. "No, not at all." She glanced toward the octopus. It seemed to be staring right at her, baleful and judgmental. She turned away and linked arms with Evie, leading her out of the alcove. "Come on. We can go visit the manatees."

But before they got too far, there was a soft buzz and Evie started, pulling her phone from her pocket. Diana released her arm as she checked the screen, then glanced up. "It's your mom." She swiped and brought the phone to her ear, keeping her eyes on Diana's. "Hello?"

Diana's mother's voice skewered down the line like a migraine, and Evie's face lit up. "Maggie, that's great!"

Oh no.

"Of course, we knew you'd do it." Evie nodded, positively glowing. "Congratulations, that's great news. We're so happy for you."

Maybe Diana ought to have been surprised that her mother had called Evie first. But she wasn't.

Evie paused as Diana's mother's tone changed, slipped into something more wheedling. "Yeah, we're together. I mean—" She actually went a bit pink, her grin growing sheepish. "She's with me. We're in the same place. I'll tell her." She shot Diana a thumbs-up. "Sure thing. We'll get it handled. Be there first thing in the morning." A pause, and her cheeks darkened further. "Oh, yeah. Okay. See you—"

She stopped there, presumably hung up on.

"Oliver's supporters had made a good show." Evie cleared her throat as she tucked her phone away. "But Maggie's leading by a good thirty percent. Won't be official until tomorrow, but it's in the bag."

She was all smiles, so Diana arranged her face appropriately before getting swept up into a hug.

As if realizing what she'd done, Evie pulled back almost instantly. "Sorry! Sorry, I got caught up—"

"It's fine." Diana waved her off. "You're fine. I suppose we'll be drafting a statement tonight?"

But Evie shook her head, taking her by the hand again. "I already took care of that," she said as she got them back on track toward the Everglades exhibit. "You can look it over if you want, obviously, but I had that ready halfway into the campaign."

"That was optimistic."

"Not really." Evie glanced at her, eyes soft. She didn't elaborate, but she didn't have to. "Anyway," she continued, tone considerably lighter, "we'll get with her to release it in the morning, then it's time to celebrate. She wants us to throw together something for the backers."

"'Us'?"

"Well," Evie half shrugged. "She said you, but I assumed I'd help. And . . . I have no idea how she knew, but she wants us to be there together. Going public, kinda." She gently squeezed Diana's hand. "You know."

Diana knew.

When she stayed silent, Evie cleared her throat again. "Only if you're comfortable. Obviously. You've got some time to think about it—she wants something ready out at the lake by Friday."

Memories of Diana's last visit to the lake house blasted everything else from her mind, almost physically staggering her. *I can't go back there,* she thought desperately. *Not after being there with Ronnie.*

But another voice, one that sounded an awful lot like Council District 7's new representative, muscled into her thoughts.

Oh, but you can. And you will.

CHAPTER 17
You Had a Thing for Her

Stacy looked surprised when Ronnie shouldered heavily into the office at six thirty. "You're early," she observed, glancing at her phone. "Thought he had you until seven."

"He did." Ronnie sighed. She leaned on the desk, running her hands through her hair and instantly ruining the meticulously sleek style. "He finished up early."

When Stacy grimaced with a quiet, "Yikes," Ronnie just shrugged. The client's performance hadn't been the problem, but Stacy could think whatever she wanted. It was probably better than having to explain that the client had suggested she head on out, saying she seemed distracted. Ronnie honestly hadn't been able to tell whether he'd been angry. She wasn't super sure she cared.

"I'm actually glad you're here," Stacy was saying. She produced a couple of folders. "You've got some contracts to sign, and I do not trust Jewel to let you know about them."

Ronnie limply took up the nearest pen and held out her other hand for the paperwork.

But Stacy didn't pass them over, narrowing her eyes instead. "Okay, what is up with you?"

"What do you mean?"

"You're all . . ." Stacy fluttered a hand at her. "Mopey. Again."

"Again?"

"You've been like this for a couple of weeks."

Maybe the accusation should have stung, but it didn't. Ronnie just shrugged again.

"Ronnie." Stacy's voice was soft. "What's going on?"

Even if Ronnie had wanted to answer, she didn't have time: the door to the back offices swung open, revealing Karla. "I thought

I heard your voice," she snapped. She whipped a finger around to indicate the hall behind her, wielding the red lacquered nail like a sword. "Get in here."

It had been a very long time since Ronnie had gotten called to the principal's office. Back in school it happened at least once a year, and was always accompanied by a sick, sinking worry about what was coming next.

Now she mostly just felt muzzy and gray.

The back rooms were small and few, mostly relics from when the space was used for some other business. A conference room with five or six chairs, a restroom, a nook for the coffee machine, and one dark, polished door with a nameplate: KARLA SHIRES.

Karla led her inside and settled at her desk, a sleek and modern curve of glass that took up most of the space in the room. She didn't speak. She grabbed a gold fountain pen and started scratching something into a notebook. On the wall behind her were rows of slots, each labeled with an escort's name and color-coded according to specialties and preferences. The slots held papers, in singles and stacks: upcoming and active contracts.

One slot was empty, residue from a ripped-off sticker the only clue that it had once been labeled. *Must have been Sabrina's.* Ronnie stared at it, eyes drifting in and out of focus.

The scrape of pen on paper had stopped, but it took Ronnie a second to realize it. When she did, her gaze swiveled to Karla, whose sharp green eyes were fixed on Ronnie's face like a crosshair. "Sit," she said, voice perilously level. Ronnie did.

She sat and she waited for another minute or so while Karla went back to her notes. It was a power move—obviously—and it was working like a damn charm. Ronnie was actually starting to get a little nervous.

Finally, Karla plunked her pen into the spine of her notebook and flipped it closed, then folded her hands on top of it and stared at Ronnie. "How long have you been with us?"

"Six years next . . . May, I think."

"Next June. You've stuck around longer than almost anyone else, you've got a ton of experience under your belt—so to speak—and you're one of the most popular escorts in my catalog. To be perfectly blunt, losing you would be a major blow to my business."

Ronnie swallowed. She wasn't sure whether she should say thank you, so she kept quiet.

Karla leaned forward. "I've gotten a complaint."

A what? "A what?"

"You're not an idiot, Ronnie," Karla said. Then she narrowed her eyes. "I think." Ronnie frowned but she went on: "Does your last job with the Campbells ring a bell?"

Sort of. Greg and Carrie Campbell were regulars, a married couple who liked Ronnie sandwiched between them once a month or so. Ronnie racked her brain, but couldn't remember a single detail about her most recent night with them. "What about it?"

"I'll tell you what about it. I was at brunch with Carrie today, and she happened to mention being disappointed. Said they may as well have been by themselves."

"What were you doing out with a client?" Ronnie blurted before she could think better of it.

All Karla did was raise her eyebrows, and not even very much.

"Sorry," Ronnie muttered.

"Explain."

Ronnie forced out a noise that sounded like a laugh played backward. "Just an off night, I guess."

"An off night?" Karla's tone was cold and brittle, the thin ice Ronnie was currently on. "My escorts don't *have* off nights. And they don't get two strikes." She leaned back, elbows on the armrests of her chair. "I mean it: I don't want to lose you. But you either get your shit together or you get going. Is that clear?"

Throat tight, Ronnie nodded.

"Good." With that, Karla flipped open her notebook once more, snatching up her pen and getting back to work.

Ronnie took it for the dismissal it was and rose.

She had her hand on the doorknob when Karla said, "Oh, and Ronnie." She turned to find Karla watching her with an almost detached expression. "If you do decide to walk, just remember that I know people."

There it is, Ronnie thought grimly. She nodded again.

Out in the foyer, Stacy stood as soon as Ronnie opened the door. "Are you fired?" she asked shakily.

"No." Ronnie sighed. "I'm not fired." She glanced at the clock—just past seven. "You heading out?"

Stacy made an expansive gesture at the otherwise empty room. "Do you see Jewel?"

Good point. "*You'd* be fired if you were late all the time," Ronnie observed, frowning and indicating the back offices with a jerk of her chin. "How does she not know about Jewel?"

Stacy scoffed. "Oh, she knows. She just doesn't do anything about it. Being the boss's cousin has its perks."

One more layer in this bullshit tiramisu.

"So," Stacy said as she settled back into her chair, "are you gonna tell me what that was all about?"

She waved a hand at the back door, like Ronnie would think she meant anything but the meeting with Karla. "Yeah," she decided with another sigh. "But not here. D'you have dinner plans?"

Stacy immediately whipped out her phone, thumbs flying over the screen. "Nothing concrete. Lemme just . . ."

When she brought the phone to her ear, Ronnie stepped away from the desk and wandered in a slow circle, hoping to give her a little privacy. Turns out it was harder than she thought—she wasn't *trying* to eavesdrop, but the office wasn't huge and she couldn't help overhearing Stacy's half of the conversation.

"No, I'll still come over, just a little later than I thought." A pause. "Yeah, I'll text when I'm on my way. Good luck, love you too." She lowered the phone and huffed. "Okay! Now as soon as Jewel decides to show up—"

Like some kind of bargain-bin Bloody Mary, Jewel chose that moment to fling open the door and stride into the office. "Hi, ladies!" she greeted them with a waggle of her fingers.

Ronnie waved limply back. Stacy did not. As Jewel settled in behind the desk and kicked her feet up onto it, Stacy mutely lifted her purse onto her shoulder and marched out, Ronnie close behind.

Out on the street, Stacy finally spoke. "Did you have someplace in mind?" When Ronnie shook her head, she said, "Good, then I get to pick."

They walked in silence for a minute or two. Then, just for something to say, Ronnie asked, "Who'd you call?"

"My girlfriend."

Ronnie glanced at her. "I didn't know somebody had snatched you up. How'd you meet?"

She was putting off her own issue and she knew it, but Stacy didn't seem to care. In fact, she looked downright pleased.

"We had a few classes together before," she began. "I'd noticed her, but we never really talked until we got paired up for a project in Issues in Psychotherapy."

Ronnie had never asked what Stacy was going to school for. She nodded like she understood.

"We met up at her place to work on it a couple of times," Stacy continued, smiling. "One minute we were doing research, the next we were making out all over our notes. I'm not sure how it happened, but I'm glad it did."

There was nothing particularly special or romantic about the story. But it still made Ronnie's chest constrict. "That sounds nice."

"It is. Here we go," Stacy said, nodding toward an ancient little café called Bean There, Bun That. Ronnie opened the door, letting Stacy in and a powerful cloud of coffee smell out.

While Stacy settled at a table near the window, Ronnie paid for her combo meal and a small cappuccino for herself, loitering at the counter and taking in her surroundings.

At the moment, her surroundings mostly seemed to be shades of yellow and rusty orange. *Good thing tonight's client didn't want me looking fancy,* Ronnie mused. She'd be way overdressed in anything but her button-up and jeans: the café and everything in it looked like it hadn't been updated or cleaned since about 1976. But Stacy apparently liked the place, and Ronnie trusted her judgment. And she finally felt far enough away from the office to safely talk about what had happened.

"Here ya go, babe."

The girl behind the counter was offering Ronnie a tray laden with two paper cups and a thick lump of sandwich wrapped in greasy white paper. *You trust Stacy's judgment,* Ronnie reminded herself, gingerly taking the tray.

"Okay," Stacy said, once Ronnie had settled and she'd unwrapped whatever the hell it was she was about to eat. "What's up?"

Ronnie sighed, trying to gather her thoughts. She opened her mouth, shut it again, took a sip of coffee. "Karla got a complaint about me."

Stacy's eyes went round and she stopped midchew. Swallowing, she said, "And you're *not* fired?"

"I'm not fired," Ronnie promised. She took another drink. The cappuccino was too hot and too sweet, but it gave her something to do. "Not yet, anyway. But I don't get another shot."

"What did you *do*?"

With a shrug, Ronnie popped the lid off her cup and swirled the coffee into a frothy brown whirlpool. "Didn't have my head in the game, apparently."

Stacy snorted and Ronnie glanced at her, brow furrowed. "Sorry," Stacy said, thumbing sauce from the corner of her mouth. "But like, yeah. Like tonight, you've been all . . ." She bobbed her head and gave an exaggerated hangdog pout.

There was no point in denying it. Ronnie twitched her shoulders in a shrug.

"You haven't really had your head in the game since Sabrina left," Stacy went on. "I thought maybe you had a thing for her, but that didn't seem right." She pulled an onion off her sandwich and tossed it onto the wrapper, where it landed with a wet slap, and looked up. "That's not it, is it?"

"No, no." Ronnie pressed her thumbnail into the side of her cup, etching a series of short lines into the paper. "I barely knew Sabrina." She started to take a drink.

"Right. Which means it's about Diana Silver."

Ronnie choked. Stacy watched, expression neutral, as she hacked unattractively.

"How—"

"I'm not stupid."

"Could you at least pretend to be, just for a minute?"

"No." Stacy took another bite, talking around it. "Sabrina gets fired for fooling around outside work, and not even a week later you turn down a contract with your favorite client? I put it together eventually. Were you dating her?"

"No!" Stacy gave her a flat stare and Ronnie flinched. "I mean, not really? I only saw her one time for free."

Stacy nodded, only looking a little bit smug, and laid her sandwich on the tray. "Here's what I don't get. Why stop taking her contracts? Wouldn't her hiring you work out for everybody?"

Ronnie's face went warm, and she dropped her gaze. "I . . . didn't want her to be a client anymore."

"So your solution was to *ghost* her?"

Well, when she put it like that, it made Ronnie sound like a jerk. The heat in her face tripled. "I can't lose my job. It's all I'm good at, it's all I know, it's—"

"I get it, I get it." Stacy gave a long exhale through her nose and went back to her sandwich, removing another onion. "Look," she said after a silent moment. "You want my opinion?" Ronnie nodded and Stacy mirrored the gesture. "If you want Diana, go get her. Just do it. Now, it's fine if you wanna pick Night Life, but if you *do*, then you have to tell her. It's not fair not to. Suck it up and face her, get some closure, and maybe you can get back to doing your job."

It sounded so easy when she said it like that. But it wasn't easy. Ronnie took another drink as Stacy tucked in to what was left of her sandwich.

"And when you do find a new job," Stacy said after a bit, popping the last bite into her mouth, "keep an eye out for a spot for me."

Ronnie flinched. "Why would I need a new job?"

Stacy rolled her eyes and stood, grabbing her tray. "Just saying," she said, heading for the nearest trash bin. As she got back to the table, a muffled *ping* issued from her purse; she reached in and retrieved her phone. "I should go study. I haaate Friday morning classes." When Ronnie didn't respond, Stacy laid a hand on her shoulder. "You gonna be okay?"

Ronnie looked up at her. "Probably." Her voice echoed in her ears. She patted Stacy's hand. "Thanks for listening. Say hi to . . ."

"Lizzie."

"Right. Say hi to Lizzie for me."

A smile tugged at the corners of Stacy's mouth. "Will do. I'll see you later."

With a chime, she was gone, leaving Ronnie to stare out the window as her cappuccino slowly grew cold.

CHAPTER 18
Let's Go

Things were shaping up for the party. Between the two of them, Diana and Evie had managed to get everything pinned down—caterers, a pianist, buffet tables, and a rent-a-bar. Evie had even sweet-talked the people at AlphaGraph into fast-tracking a job on a banner that read, *CONGRATULATIONS DISTRICT 7*, as though it was the public at large who'd won some victory.

Diana watched it all come together as though from a distance, engaging when she had to and checking out as soon as her input was no longer needed. She felt like she passed most of her time like that, these days. She kept waiting for the pain to go away, for the dull red ache in her chest to disappear. Or at least for it to lessen.

But it persisted, sitting on her sternum like a stone, and being back at the lake house was only making things worse. She kept catching phantom glimpses of Ronnie, looking the way she'd been when they were here together. Laughing, watching Diana from across the dining table, lifting an eyebrow in clear invitation . . .

"The piano man's on his way, baby doll," Lena said, pulling Diana from her memories. The housekeeper stood in the foyer, holding Diana's phone. She was the only person Diana trusted to handle incoming calls so she could focus on anything else that needed her attention. "I told him to— What's wrong?"

Get a grip, Diana told herself. "Nothing."

Unfortunately, Lena knew her better than that. The older woman's face was drawn with worry, her eyes warm. "I think that Richards gal mostly has things under control," she offered slowly. "You could probably take a quick break."

Diana couldn't stop a wry chuckle before it scraped out of her throat. "Maybe. But I'd rather keep busy." It was technically true: the more she focused on work, the less brainpower she had left over for anything else.

Curiosity mingled with the concern in Lena's expression, and it was clear she was about to tread dangerous waters. "Is Miss Ronnie gonna be here tonight?"

Hearing someone else say Ronnie's name was like a blow to the base of Diana's spine. To her horror, she felt her throat closing up, the backs of her eyes stinging. "Oh, Lena," she said, sounding pathetic even to her own ears, "she's not . . . It wasn't . . ."

Lena drew her into her arms, rubbing her free hand up and down her back. Diana buried her face in Lena's shoulder and used every trick she knew not to actually cry. The last thing she needed was Evie seeing tears—or worse, being seen by her mother.

"It's all right, baby doll," Lena said soothingly. "I know she was special."

"She was. I miss her so much—I don't know what I did, but . . ."

Stop this. It won't change anything. Diana drew in a deep breath and pulled away, the pinpricks in her eyes now mostly gone. Lena's mouth was twisted, and she looked like she might refute Diana's fault, but Diana kept going. "And Mummy wants to tell everyone tonight about how Evie and I are together, but—"

Lena blinked, starting. "About how you and . . . I didn't even know you *were*."

We weren't. But that doesn't matter. "She's nice," Diana said with a shrug. "Mummy likes her."

"Do *you* like her?"

"She's nice," Diana said again. The argument brewed like a storm on Lena's face, so Diana shook her head, trying to close a window against it. "It's fine. I'll be fine. You told the pianist to pull around back?"

"I did."

"Thank you." She squeezed Lena's arm. "And thank you again for being on phone duty."

Lena flapped her hands dismissively. "Least I could do. D'you mind if I make a call of my own when I get a minute?" She brandished the cell. "Mine's up in my room."

"Of course not." The smile Diana cast her was small, but the first one she'd really felt in a while. "I'd better go see how the caterers are getting on."

She'd checked on the caterers not ten minutes earlier. But it was something to do.

Ronnie stared dully into her closet, trying to pick an outfit for the night's job. The client wasn't picky, unfortunately—it would've been nice not to have to put any thought into the decision. Since her little chat with Stacy the night before, her thoughts had been spinning around like fruit in a blender. It'd feel pretty good to turn them off.

Her phone, lying on the nightstand, buzzed loudly enough to make her jump. Eyes still on her closet, Ronnie drifted across the bedroom to answer without looking. "This is Ronnie."

"Hey."

Ronnie blinked. "Stacy? I thought I wasn't due in till eight."

"You're not." Stacy sounded oddly cautious, like she was peeking around a corner. "Just, something weird. You got a call."

"Me personally?"

"Yeah, the lady asked for you by name. Do you know somebody named Lena?"

Ronnie's stomach lurched and she settled onto the edge of her bed. "Yes."

"Do you want the message?"

It was as if Ronnie's heart hadn't beat in a month—it kicked into gear almost painfully, thudding like a freight train. She swallowed. "Yeah."

"She said . . ." A quiet rustle of paper, and Stacy switched to the universal *I'm reading this word-for-word* tone. "'There's a victory party at the lake house tonight, and you're a fool if you let her mama give her away.'" Back to a normal voice. "What the hell does that mean? Is this about Diana?"

Blood rushed in Ronnie's ears like high tide.

"Ronnie?" Stacy sounded very far away. "You still there?"

Ronnie cleared her throat. "Yeah, yeah, I'm still . . . I gotta go, though."

"But—"

"Thanks, Stace."

She hung up and looked back at her closet. In the far-right corner, crammed between a red cocktail dress and a corset, was the suit Diana had picked for her at Ashworth's. Ronnie stared at it for a long moment, then strode forward and snatched the hanger from the rack.

It took Ronnie twenty minutes to get to the front door of the lake house after she parked. Not so much because she'd parked far away—although, with the assembled BMWs, Jaguars, and Audis, she certainly didn't get a spot on the front drive—but because she spent a while just sitting in her car, forearms braced against the steering wheel, staring up at the house and steadying her breath. It was hard to know for sure what Lena had meant about Diana being given away. But knowing her mother, it couldn't be good. She wasn't going to let Diana get away. She *couldn't*.

And if it meant losing her job . . . Something squeezed in Ronnie's gut. *Well. One thing at a time.*

By the time she reached the open front door, her heart was slamming so hard against her chest that she was genuinely afraid it might break through. She took several deep breaths, listening to the dull buzz of conversation, and stepped inside.

The parlor was packed with guests, all the furniture moved out to transform the space into a paddock for the upper class. Light piano music drifted through the room and underscored the constant hum of conversation between people who probably weren't actually *saying* much.

It was a good thing she'd worn her suit; it meant she could blend in easily with the partygoers and move around without really being noticed. Every now and then she'd get a smile or a nod from those who assumed they'd met her somewhere, but nobody approached her.

Which was fine. Most of them were wearing *MAGGIE SILVER FOR COUNCIL* buttons, and if they were friends of Diana's mother, Ronnie wanted as little to do with them as possible.

After a stop at the open bar, she wound up standing with her back to the wide bay windows, sipping wine and scanning the room for any sign of Diana. She had no idea what she was going to say when she found her, but she could improvise. Probably.

"Hello."

Spinning around, Ronnie was met with a sharp-faced woman wearing a pale-pink bolero and a practiced smile. Her eyes were like two metal shavings, almost stinging as they flicked over Ronnie's face. "Are you here with the Dicksons?"

Ronnie shook her head. "No, I'm, uh, a friend of Diana's."

The woman's eyes twitched, like they wanted to narrow but she was keeping them reined. "Really." She held out her hand, a little limp-wristed. "I'm her mother."

Everything below Ronnie's neck went cold, but she somehow forced herself to accept the handshake. Turned out the limp wrist was deceptive; Maggie Silver's grip almost made the delicate bones in the back of Ronnie's hand squeak together.

"Oh," Ronnie managed. "Congratulations."

"On being Diana's mother?"

With a tight grin, Ronnie said, "I meant the election, but that too."

The other woman's laugh was so unlike her daughter's that it was hard to believe they were related. "Thank you. Now why don't you show yourself out?"

Ronnie blinked. "Excuse me?"

Maggie tugged her in close, her voice soaked in sugared gasoline. "I know exactly who you are," she said. "You think my daughter goes anywhere without me knowing about it? I was prepared to tolerate Diana playing around with you, up to a point. We all have our little indiscretions. But she's finished with you now, and you do not belong here. So finish your drink, make a graceful exit, and that can be the end of it."

Her smile never faltered.

Ronnie couldn't find the breath to form a response. Not that it mattered. They were interrupted by a pair of guests with buttons, who simpered and cooed at Maggie with disgusting admiration. Accepting their praise was clearly more interesting than threatening Ronnie, because Maggie didn't even look back at her; she only offered a vaguely sanguine, "So nice to finally meet you," before sweeping away, leaving Ronnie alone again.

How could she possibly know who Ronnie was? Surely no one at Phoebe's party would have mentioned her, and the people at the suit place wouldn't care. Everyone at Night Life was impeccably careful, even Karla, and nobody else knew about their arrangement. Right?

Doesn't matter, Ronnie thought fiercely. *That little warning was eloquent as hell, but it's not gonna stop me.*

She set her glass aside and scanned the room. As she did, a few people by the far wall stepped aside, and there was Diana.

Her back was to Ronnie. She was speaking to a tall, thin man with a moustache and an unimpressed frown. Ronnie moved forward almost mechanically, drawing near and unsure how to make her presence known without startling Diana.

Fortunately, the tall, grumpy man did it for her—he glanced over Diana's shoulder at Ronnie, his frown growing more pronounced, and then he walked away from Diana without another word. Before Ronnie could really reflect on what a bastard move that was, Diana was turning.

Seeing her again, after what felt like ages, was enough to steal the breath from Ronnie's lungs. It was like she'd forgotten how dazzling Diana was, how blue her eyes were, the way her dark curls gently framed her face. She wore a creamy A-line dress under a gray chiffon shrug, and she looked soft and beautiful and—

And she was staring like she was just as stunned as Ronnie was.

Ronnie opened her mouth, and it all spilled out like change from a pocket.

"I'm sorry," she said, voice scraping the sides of her throat. "I'm so sorry. I thought if I stayed away, maybe I'd get over you but it didn't work, and I've been such a huge idiot—"

"Ronnie—" Diana's eyes had been growing steadily wider. "What are you . . . I can't, my mother—"

"Excuse me." Evelyn appeared at Diana's side, casting Ronnie a politely confused smile. Turning to Diana, she said, "Your mom's about to give her speech, and she wants us all up there." Then her voice dropped and she added, "Are you ready?"

Ready for what?

Diana's gaze flicked back and forth between them, brow drawn, face flushed. Evelyn laid a hand on her elbow, offering Ronnie an apologetic nod, and steered them away.

Ronnie watched them go, her heart sinking into her stomach. So that was it.

The pianist played a delicate fanfare, and the crowd applauded. Maggie had taken her place at the front of the room, smiling serenely at her supporters. Once Evelyn and Diana reached her, she started speaking.

Ronnie didn't hear a word. She only saw Diana, standing between Evelyn and her mother, her head bowed. There was an awful neutrality to her expression, a sort of hollow resignation that made Ronnie's chest constrict. She was so used to seeing that face lit up with laughter, relaxed and content, eyes sparkling with mischief and amusement. This wasn't her Diana. This was someone who had given up, someone resigned to their choices being made by others. Ronnie had been that person before, and she couldn't let it happen to anyone else.

By the time her brain caught up with her body, she was halfway across the room, shouldering past strangers and ignoring their grunts of annoyance. Maggie was still talking. "And I can never thank you all enough for your generosity, your support . . ." She hesitated and frowned, seeming to finally notice the disturbance. "And your faith in me—"

A few months ago, Ronnie wouldn't have been caught dead making this kind of scene. If word got out that one of Night Life's escorts had interrupted a political event, she'd be out on her ass so fast her head would spin. But that didn't matter now. It didn't matter that the partygoers were muttering in undisguised interest, that Maggie was glaring like she wanted to throw Ronnie out a window. All that mattered was the light that soaked into the edges of Diana's eyes as Ronnie reached her.

"I love you."

It wasn't loud. She wasn't even sure whether she'd said it or just mouthed the words, but it was enough. A smile blossomed on Diana's breathtaking face. "Ronnie."

Ronnie swept forward, taking Diana's face in both hands, and kissed her like she'd never kiss anyone else again.

And hell, maybe she wouldn't. That would be fine.

The muttering became something short of an uproar, and Ronnie pulled away in time to swipe her thumbs over Diana's cheeks, banishing the tears that were trying to fall. "I'm sorry." She'd say it as many times as she had to.

But Diana shook her head. "I know. It's okay." She nudged Ronnie's nose with her own. "Let's get out of here."

Ronnie was nodding before she'd even finished.

They pushed through the commotion hand in hand, and had made it all the way out to the circle drive before Maggie caught up with them.

"Diana Rose Silver, *stop*."

Diana stopped. She looked up at Ronnie fiercely and squeezed her hand. "I've got this," she whispered. Then she turned. "Mummy."

Maggie stormed forward. "How could you be so selfish?" she snarled. "Did you even *once* think about how this would affect me? My reputation, my image, they're more important now than they've ever been, especially if I'm going to get further than the city council. I never imagined I'd have to tell you unequivocally to be with Evie, but apparently that's the case. People *expect* things from their leaders, they expect things from their families. I've worked too hard to get where I am for it to be ruined just because you've found some little tramp you want to f—"

A slap rang out, stopping Maggie's tirade cold.

"Don't." Diana's back was ramrod straight, her voice pure iron. It was incredible. "I've put up with a lot from you," she said. "To be honest, I'd resigned myself to putting up with whatever you threw at me. But you will *not* talk about the woman I love like that."

"How *dare* you—I've given you everything you have, you ungrateful—"

"Maggie."

They all turned to see Evelyn standing at the front door, staring at Maggie like she'd never seen her before.

Maggie laughed like a ruined record. "Evie, this is— It's not—"

"Yes, it is." The campaign manager stepped forward, face screwed up in disgust. "Don't talk to her like that."

Maybe she's not so bad.

Maggie gestured sharply at Diana. "She doesn't even *want* you!"

"She's still my *friend*," Evelyn said icily, striding past Maggie to where Diana stood. "Are you okay?" she murmured. At Diana's tight nod, Evelyn gave a more measured one. "Good." She looked back at Maggie. "It probably goes without saying, but consider this my resignation."

"You *cannot* be serious," Maggie scoffed.

"I am. I'll handle that—" Evie tilted her head toward the house, indicating the mess inside. "—but after that, I'm done."

She turned a steely gaze on Ronnie. "I hope you know what you're getting."

"Trust me," Ronnie assured her, "I do."

"Good." Evelyn started back toward the house, but Diana shot out a hand to grab her arm, stopping her.

"Evie," she said, "I'm so sorry—"

But Evelyn was shaking her head. "Hey, don't be." She smiled sadly. "I like you a lot, but I wouldn't want you to be with me if you weren't happy."

With one last glare at Maggie, she disappeared inside.

Maggie immediately whirled on Diana. "I hope you know you're not getting another *penny* from me. There's no severance package in this family."

"Keep your money," Diana said with a shrug. "I don't need it. I don't need *you*."

Then she turned, snatched up Ronnie's hand in a vise grip, and pulled her away, leading her down the hill.

They made it to the bottom of the hill before Diana began to cry.

She crumpled into Ronnie's embrace, clinging to her and sobbing on her shoulder. Ronnie held her, pressing kisses to her temple and murmuring, "I'm sorry. I'm so sorry."

Eventually Diana's tears gave way to sniffles and the occasional head shake. When she seemed able to move again, Ronnie led them to her car and leaned on the trunk, letting Diana sag against her.

After a stretch of silence, Diana took a shaky breath and looked up. "What just happened?"

Ronnie couldn't fight back a smile. "Well," she said, squinting out at the lake, "I realized I'm stupid in love with you and you mean more to me than anything, so I drove up here to crash your mom's party and ruin your relationship with her forever."

Diana gave a watery laugh. "I think she's the one who ruined our relationship." Then she slipped a hand into Ronnie's hair, scratching at her scalp. "Did you say 'stupid in love'?"

"Yeah. Yeah, I did." Ronnie took her other hand, brushing lips against her knuckles. "Is that okay?"

Finally, Diana graced her with the smile she'd been missing. "Better than okay."

She was leaning up for a kiss when Ronnie's pocket jangled, making them both jump. Frowning, Ronnie pulled out her phone and checked the screen. *Night Life.*

The hell?

"This is Ronnie."

"I would *love it*," Karla seethed, "if you'd tell me why you didn't show up for your job tonight and if you'd tell me why I just got an anonymous tip that you gave a client *gonorrhea*."

A bark of laughter forced its way from Ronnie's throat. "What!"

"Is there a bad connection? Did I stutter? Explain yourself!"

Ronnie sighed, tightening her hold on Diana's waist and smiling down at her. "Y'know what, Karla?" she said. "I have no idea why you got that call. Couldn't tell you." She stroked at Diana's side with her thumb. "But I'm in the middle of something you're not gonna like, so I'm gonna go. Okay? Okay, good night."

She hung up, practically glowing at the sound of Diana's laugh.

"What on earth?"

"I dunno who's been ratting on us to your mom, but she just tried to torpedo my career by saying I had the clap."

"Ratting on us?" Diana asked, squinting.

"Yeah, your mom said something really gross about knowing everywhere you go?" Ronnie shrugged and tucked her phone back into her pocket.

Diana sucked in a breath. "Skylar."

Everything settled into place. "Oh my God, you're right." Ronnie shook her head. "She always brought you to see me."

"And we picked you up for Phoebe's party," Diana added. "So she knew which agency you work for."

"Yeah, well, I was gonna quit anyway," Ronnie said with a grin. "Joke's on her."

She thought that might get another laugh, but Diana frowned. "Why?"

"It's either that or wait to get fired once Karla finds out about us." Ronnie shrugged. "No outside relationships. *Especially* with former clients."

Diana looked a little dazed, but her lips twitched. "I don't know whether to focus on how disgustingly unfair that is or on the fact that you called this a relationship."

Ronnie rested her forehead against Diana's. "Do you love me?"

"Yes."

"And I love you. Sounds like a relationship to me." She pressed their lips together, head spinning when she felt Diana smiling into the kiss.

When they parted, Diana said, "What will we do now?"

Ronnie wiggled her eyebrows. "Right now?"

Diana laughed, nudging her. "You know what I mean. Long-term."

"Hm, that's less fun." But her mind was already racing, combing through the last few months for ideas. "We'll figure something out."

EPILOGUE

I t took some time, but they figured it out.

Ronnie had never been gladder for her habit of squirreling money away. It wasn't enough to fund everything, but it was enough to live on while things got rolling.

They made calls. They signed papers. They told Phoebe about their plans and she was more than happy to spread the word—for the promise of a discount, of course. Their lives were a whirlwind of plans and documentation and each other.

When Stacy found out what had happened, she quit too. But not before passing the news along to Sabrina and a few of Ronnie's old coworkers who'd had their fair share of quiet complaints about Night Life over the years. Alex and Vinnie made the move together, much to Phoebe's delight. Ronnie was looking forward to being able to give all of them a fair shake.

After all, Karla might have had the means to blacklist Ronnie as an escort. But nothing had stopped Ronnie and Diana from opening their own agency.

"Listen," Ronnie said to Diana. "It's perfect. What's your degree actually in?"

"Hospitality management, but why—"

"See? Escorting is the best kind of hospitality!" Diana snorted but Ronnie went on: "You know how to schedule things and do books and all that boring business stuff, and I know how things work in the field, so to speak. Won't be out there myself anymore, but still."

Diana ran her fingers thoughtfully along Ronnie's shoulder. "Won't you miss it?"

"Maybe? Probably not though, if I get to be in the office with you all day."

"You should take jobs, now and then," Diana said, her touch sliding from shoulder to neck. "If you want to."

Ronnie blinked, then offered a hesitant grin. "You sure?"

"I told you I don't get jealous, and I meant it. As long as you come home to me, nothing else matters."

Ronnie hummed. "You're good like that." She brushed her lips against Diana's. "I'm having a hard time imagining kissing anybody but you, but I might make an appearance or two. Especially if anybody's in the market for a hot blonde." She shrugged. "So. You and me, storming the escort market. What do you think?"

Diana smiled and quirked an eyebrow at her. "It would be nice to be my own boss for a change."

"Absolutely. What you say goes." Ronnie's hands began to wander. "Especially once we get home."

Diana laughed and kissed her.

Two months later, everything was ready.

Ronnie and Diana stood in the lobby, looking things over. It was tiny, with just enough room for the reception area and a couple of chairs. The only real office space was right next to the restroom, behind a door marked *MANAGEMENT*. Ronnie and Diana shared the desk inside.

"Here we are," Diana said, looking around with a satisfied sigh.

"Here we are," Ronnie agreed. She slipped an arm around Diana's waist and pulled her in to her side, kissing her cheek.

"Get a room," Stacy griped half-heartedly, flipping through the textbook on her knee.

"Good idea." Ronnie led Diana toward their office. "You got things handled here?"

As if on cue, the phone on Stacy's desk rang. Ronnie and Diana shared an excited smile.

The last thing they heard before closing the door behind them was, "Purely Therapeutic, how can I help you?"

Dear Reader,

Thank you for reading S.J. Hartsfield's *Night Life*!

We know your time is precious and you have many, many entertainment options, so it means a lot that you've chosen to spend your time reading. We really hope you enjoyed it.

We'd be honored if you'd consider posting a review—good or bad—on sites like **Amazon, Barnes & Noble, Kobo, Goodreads, Twitter, Facebook, Tumblr,** and your blog or website. We'd also be honored if you told your friends and family about this book. Word of mouth is a book's lifeblood!

For more information on upcoming releases, author interviews, blog tours, contests, giveaways, and more, please sign up for our weekly, spam-free newsletter and visit us around the web:

Newsletter: riptidepublishing.com/newsletter
Twitter: twitter.com/RiptideBooks
Facebook: facebook.com/RiptidePublishing
Goodreads: tinyurl.com/RiptideOnGoodreads
Tumblr: riptidepublishing.tumblr.com

Thank you so much for Reading the Rainbow!

RiptidePublishing.com

ACKNOWLEDGMENTS

Thank you a billion times to my wife (who was very gracious about sharing me with my first novel), my parents (who let me use the old Smith-Corona typewriter when I was seven), and James (who loves Phoebe with his whole heart).

ACKNOWLEDGMENTS

About
THE AUTHOR

S.J. Hartsfield is definitely a human being. You can usually find her watching *MST3K*, being a horror movie snob, or making vague attempts at calligraphy. Oh, and banging her face against the keyboard until a story comes out.

She lives in Oklahoma with her wife and three cats. They're little monsters (the cats, not S.J. and her wife).

Find her on Instagram: @sjhartsfieldwrites

Enjoy more stories like
Night Life
at RiptidePublishing.com!

The Persephone Star	*Love Under Glasse*
Love looks different from a thousand feet up.	This runaway might want to get caught.
ISBN: 978-1-62649-931-7	ISBN: 978-1-62649-876-1